Mr

a MISTER
STANDALONE

CORPORATE

New York Times Bestselling Author

JA HUSS

MrCORPORATE

New York Times Bestselling Author

HUSS

DEDICATION

For everyone who loved the Goonies.

PROLOGUE

WESTON

"Say it." Victoria Arias looms over me, her feet planted on either side of my hips, seething. "I want to hear you *say it*."

She looks like the storm that just passed. That poor lavender shirt is rippling in the remnants of the wind. It's ruined. And out of nowhere, like God was playing a trick on us earlier, it starts to rain. Hard, pouring-down rain.

"What's your fucking problem?" I ask. "Just what the fuck, Tori?"

She drops, her ass sitting on my dick, but nothing about this moment says seductive. She slaps me six times in the face. Both hands, one after the other. Six times. *Bam, bam, bam, bam, bam, bam.*

"Say it!" She yells it this time.

I taste blood in my mouth and reach up to wipe it away as I look her in the eyes.

Those beautiful violet eyes. That wild dark hair is sticking to her face as she rages. And her breasts are practically bursting out of her shirt—those last two buttons have no hope of containing them.

Another slap, and this time it stings.

"Stop it," I say, grabbing both her wrists and pulling her down onto my chest. "Just fucking stop it."

"I hate you more, Weston Conrad." Her voice is low. Even. Controlled. "I hate you more than you will ever know and I want to hear you say it."

"Why should I give in to you? Why the fuck should I? Do you really think this badass attitude you have is cute, Miss Arias? Well, it isn't. It's fucking old, OK? I'm sick of it. I'm sick of you. And I'm not giving you what you want. Ever."

I push her off me and get up. I'm wet, I'm covered in sand, I'm hungry, I'm thirsty, and my dick has been hard for three days.

"You're a coward," Victoria says, her South American accent appearing. "You're a coward and a cheat."

"That makes no sense. And I'm not a cheat. You're the fucking cheat. How the hell did you get here, huh, Victoria? You *cheated*!"

She's on her knees now, that goddamned lavender shirt blowing open. "Well, just give me what I want, Weston Conrad. And then we can part ways and never see each other again."

"I'm not giving you this contract. Fuck that. I earned it. You're the one who tried to steal it from me."

"I don't just want the contract, you idiot. I never wanted the contract. I wanted *you*."

I just blink at her. "What?"

"Did," she clarifies. "I don't want you anymore. I wouldn't want you if you were the last man on Earth!"

"Or a deserted island?" I say, laughing.

She throws a handful of sand at me, but the wind catches it and it goes in her eyes. Her hands fly up to her face as she doubles over in pain.

Fuck.

"Victoria," I say, dropping down to see if she's OK.

She's not. She's crying.

"Victoria," I say again as I try to pry her hands off her face. "Let me see."

2

She shakes her head and starts to sniffle. "Just tell me what I want to hear."

"What?" I ask. "What the fuck are you after? I can't ever make you happy for more than a few hours. I don't fucking know what you want!"

She drops her hands and looks me in the face. "I hate you more, Weston Conrad. I hate you more than you hate me. And I want to hear you admit it."

"Fine." I shrug. "Whatever. You hate me more. What the fuck do I care?"

"What the fuck *do* you care?" Her makeup was washed off in the rain days ago. There's no leftover mascara to stain her perfect cheekbones. And her lips are naturally pink and plump. I can't stop looking at them.

Her.

I can't stop looking at *her*.

"Why are you doing this?" I ask.

"I want that contract."

"No. I told you no. How many times do I have to explain this to you? It was my contract to begin with. You fucking cheated!"

"But I need it more!" she yells.

"I said I'd help you, Tori. I already said I'd help you, for fuck's sake!"

"Don't call me that *ever again*!"

Jesus Christ. Why does she have to be so wild?

"If you give me that contract, I will give you something in return."

"What?" I ask. "What do you possibly have that I want?"

"Me."

Her eyes search mine. Back and forth. Back and forth. I do want her. I want her so fucking bad. But I can't give her that contract. That contract isn't even enough to fix her problems. But it's mine. It's *mine*, dammit. If it's still available, I cannot let her have it. I just can't. If she ends up with this contract, my world shifts. And not in a good way. She can't have it and I'm tired of talking about it. Thinking about it. So I change the subject. "I thought *you* wanted *me*?"

"Not anymore," she says, tipping her head up to regain some of her dignity. And even though most of the people on this planet wouldn't be able to conjure up some dignity while sitting half-naked, half-starved, and half-satisfied at the tail end of a hurricane, Victoria Arias manages. "I mean nothing to you, West. You used me last night. You used me just like you use everyone else." She pokes me in the chest to emphasize her words. "And you know what? I'm tired of you, too. You checked out ten years ago and never came back. Turned into Mr. Corporate and said, 'Fuck you, Rhode Island. I'm going to LA.'"

I'm just about to open my mouth and tell her off when it hits me. She's been mad at me this whole time. Not because we broke up. Not because we couldn't make the long-distance relationship work. But because she thinks I left her behind.

But I don't get the chance to say any of that. Because the sound of a helicopter comes into range.

"Here!" Victoria yells, jumping to her feet and waving her arms. "Here! Here! Here! We are here!"

She bolts down the beach, her perfect legs stretching out into a full run, her dark hair flying out behind her like a banner that dares me to follow her into war.

I want to follow her. I want to think so anyway. I want to believe that I can fight her battles, and take no prisoners, and come out on the other end a winner.

But I don't believe it.

Because she doesn't need anyone to fight her battles. She's made that perfectly clear.

And I don't believe I could match her passion and commitment anyway. I don't believe I could keep up with her, to be honest. Or hold on to her, or even make her the slightest bit happy. I don't believe I can do anything right when it comes to Victoria Arias.

And it's not because I feel like sulking against the wall at my own pity party.

It's because I've hurt her so many times in the past, it's become a habit.

It's because we're in this endless pattern of destruction. We're a trainwreck. A plane crash. A hurricane of nothing-will-ever-come-of-this.

Ever.

CHAPTER ONE

VICTORIA

FIVE DAYS AGO

"AriasCorp, best headhunters in the business, this is…" I hesitate and make up a name on the fly as I search through the drawers of the empty reception area. "Cynthia. How may I direct your call?"

"Victoria Arias, please."

Hmmm. I don't recognize the voice. "Who may I say is calling?"

"That information is private and confidential. But I have information about a contract coming up for bid and I wish to discuss it with her."

"One moment," I say. "I'll see if she's available."

I push the hold button and place the phone back in the cradle, then continue my search. Whoever that is can just wait until I'm good and ready to answer this call.

"Victoria?" my father calls from my office down the hallway.

"One second, Pops. I have it here, I know I do."

He appears just as I finish talking, a scowl on his face. "Why are you looking for receipts at the reception desk?"

"It's just where I'm keeping them these days. Hold on, I have it." I pull the bottom drawer out and pray. *Please, please, please let this receipt be in here.* "Ah-ha!" I beam my father a smile as I pull out the papers and stand up. "I

7

knew it was here."

"We wouldn't have this problem if you weren't paying cash for everything."

"Look, Pop, I don't need a lecture today, OK? I found the receipt. Here."

He takes it from my hand, then shakes his head. "You know what we need."

Oh, I know what he *thinks* we need. "I'm not even discussing what you're proposing. And I'm hurt and furious that you'd even bring it up."

My Pops looks properly admonished. But there's a desperation inside of him these days. It's dangerous, that desperation. He's seeing everything we've done over the past few years slip away and he's got that look on his face. A look I'm very familiar with. And now I just feel sad that it's come to this.

"We don't just need money, Victoria. We need *direction*."

"What?" How could he say that? I am not taking money from a criminal. I don't care how desperate I get, he's out of my life for good. I am never looking back again. I am forward-thinking now. "I'm the direction, OK? *Me*. I know where we're going and I know exactly what it will take to get there. Just trust me, I've got a plan."

"I hope your plan is a quick one. The mortgage is due in two weeks. We're going to lose everything and be out on the street."

Why is he so mean these days? Why does he say things like this? I know we're at the end there. What does he think? I woke up today and forgot I'm in debt up to my ears? I take a deep breath and smile. I don't want to fight with him. Not now. I can't. "We're not going to lose anything. OK?" I kiss him on the cheek and try to walk away, but he grabs my hand. I close my eyes and sigh before turning back. "*What?*"

"You need to call him. At least listen to the offer."

"No. And how can you even ask me to do this? After everything I did to put it behind me?" My Pops has a brain tumor. I know he's not thinking straight, so I try not to let it bug me. But... of all the ways to go out, he has to go out thinking that asshole is... what? Some kind of Prince Charming?

I feel ill.

"I will figure it out, OK? Now go. I've got an important client on hold. I have to take this call."

"I'm going to call him, Victoria," my father says.

"No," I say, laughing it off. "You're not. You're going to go rest up and meet me for dinner in an hour. That's what you're going to do. Understand?" I love my Pops, but I might kill him over this.

"I know how proud you are. How you refuse all help and won't accept his offers. But we need it, Tori. We need it."

"Not yet we don't," I say. "Not yet. I have two weeks to figure this shit out and I will, Pops. I promise. I will. Just trust me. And don't talk to that asshole again! I mean it!"

I don't give him time to reply, just walk back to my office and close my door. I wait there, just looking out the window. It's not a great view. Street-level urban. Mixture

9

of commercial and residential apartment buildings. If I go outside and stand in the middle of the street I can see the Empire State Building. But I didn't get this office for the view. I can't afford a view in New York City, so why torture myself wanting one?

I don't want one. I just want to keep what I have, that's all.

My father thinks we didn't need this six-story, twelve-thousand-square-foot building. At least not yet. But it's Manhattan. Midtown East, but still. Manhattan. I bought it in the middle of the real-estate crash for two million under asking price. And it's worth fifteen million today. Too bad I've used up all my equity in loans. Too bad all my credit cards are maxed out and I can't even fix the plumbing on the fourth floor. Too bad all my ideas and good intentions are about to blow up in my face. Too bad, too bad, too bad.

Still, we are in Manhattan. And even though Brooklyn is not that far away distance-wise, it feels like the other side of the world.

That's where it needs to stay. On the other side of the world.

Manhattan was a dream of mine. God, how badly I wanted to be across the river when I was growing up. And I'm there. I'm so there.

We're on the verge of something big. I can just feel it. A breakthrough. I just need a lucky break, that's all.

But my father is right about the mortgage. I'm broke. And all the progress I've made has been slowly receding. It's slipping away. We are going backwards fast.

Everything I've worked for these last ten years is slipping away. Why is everything so expensive? Why is everything so complicated? I feel like I'm close, too. That's the part that sucks so bad. I feel like I'm three-quarters of the way there and I just need one lucky break.

Get it together, Victoria.

I walk to my desk and sit down, take in a deep breath and answer the phone, letting the Argentinian accent I picked up from my father slip through a little so this guy won't put two and two together and know I'm really the receptionist. "This is Miss Arias, how can I help you?"

"I think," the deep voice says on the other end of the call, "the better question is... how I can help you, Miss Arias. And that phony accent isn't hiding anything."

"I beg your pardon?" Just who the fuck does this guy think he is?

"Let's skip the small talk, since you felt it necessary to let me wait on hold while you brushed your hair or put your lipstick on—"

"Excuse me? Look, I don't know who you are, but I'm a busy woman. And—"

"Quiet, Miss Arias. I'm only going to say this once, so please listen carefully. I need you to headhunt someone for me. Someone you know. Someone I want. But this isn't just any ordinary job, Miss Arias. It's a lot more than that. And your money problems—"

"I don't have money problems," I finally say, catching up with the conversation. He stunned me for a moment. Men. They are so full of themselves. They think I'll just cower and listen quietly while—

11

"Don't waste my time. Do you want my information? Or can you afford to lose out on placing someone in a job that pays seven figures?"

Jesus. Seven figures. I couldn't pay everything off with that commission, but it would keep things afloat for a little while longer.

"Seven. Figures. Miss Arias. Are you interested?"

"Um…" What choice do I have? Maybe this is a sign that I'm just about there. Just about to get to the top of the mountain and then going down the other side will be fast and quick. "Yes."

"Are you sure?"

"Who is this?"

"It's not important. What is important is the information I have. And what I need from you."

"What do you need?" I'm kind of nervous. This sounds… weird.

"First let's talk about what I can give you."

"The placement retainer?"

"Not a retainer. It's a contingency."

I huff out some air. "Well, way to waste my time. I don't have the resources to recruit someone for a seven-figure salary right now. Not unless they're already in Manhattan. I'd have trouble paying my toll across the Midtown Tunnel."

"It's not Manhattan."

"Then I can't compete." A retainer means you get a contract and fill the position. No other headhunter is trying to fill them at the same time. A contingency means you're competing with other firms to fill the same position. I hate admitting it, but I really don't have the resources. My car might be repossessed if I don't get the back payments in soon. I can't even afford to park that thing at this point. I'm fucked. Good and fucked.

"Miss Arias," the man says on the other end of the phone. How old is he? Not very old. Maybe not even as old as me. But he sure is cocky.

"What?"

"A retainer is a sure thing."

"I know that, thanks." I should just hang up now. I don't have time for this.

"Usually."

"What do you mean?"

"I have it on good authority that SeaGlobal is interested in hiring a woman to headhunt a very specific person for their open board seat."

"And they wanted me?"

"No." The man laughs. Why is that funny? "I found out about their hesitation and thought of you."

"But you won't tell me who you are?"

"It's not important. What is important is that you are in SeaGlobal's main office in Miami tomorrow afternoon."

"Who do they want?"

"Wallace Arlington the Third."

"Oh, you've got to be kidding me. How the hell am I going—"

"Miss Arias," the stranger says sharply. "I've booked you on a flight this afternoon and a five-star hotel to hold you over until tomorrow afternoon. The details have been sent to your phone."

Just as he says this, my phone buzzes on my desk. "What the hell is going on? I'm not even going to get in the same building with Wallace Arlington, let alone slip him a contract and ask if he'd like me to place him in a job. And I know that little asshole. I went to school with him."

"Exactly. He had a thing for you."

"Who is this? Do I know you?"

"You might. But I'm not going to tell you who I am and you will never guess. Now, do you want a chance to fill that position or not? Because if so, I need something from you in return."

Here it comes. "What?" I ask.

"I want you to headhunt someone for me as well."

"Who?" I ask, thoroughly intrigued at this point.

"It's confidential. So get your ass on that plane, settle into that hotel that you could never afford, and get your contract. I'll be in touch later tonight."

CHAPTER TWO

WESTON

The view of Biscayne Bay from the thirty-third floor of this Miami office building is almost enough to make me move from LA.

Almost.

The dark mahogany hardwood floors are in perfect contrast with everything else in the office, which is stark white. The offices are all glass-enclosed, and the conference room, where I'm standing, has an elaborate white table with chairs that look like glass.

My office in LA is nice. I have a view of the ocean as well, but I don't go all out on the décor. I don't do much business in the office. That's what sets me apart from my competitors. I come to the client. Every contract is signed in person, not online. I like to scope out each and every one of them.

SeaGlobal doesn't need my critical eye. They are at the pinnacle of their industry. They buy oceanfront land all over the world and develop some of the most innovative communities imaginable. This office is their showroom.

The tapping of dress shoes on the floor pulls me away from the view and then Liam Henry is there, all smiles, his old gray eyes as bright as his casual Miami suit, his hand reaching for mine.

"Weston," he says, clapping me on the back as we shake.

"Hey, Liam. How's everything?"

"Good," he says, in that subtle Southern drawl you only hear in Florida. "Cannot complain, my boy. How's your father these days? I haven't talked to him in a long time."

"Oh, great," I say. "My mother says to tell you hi and that you and Jennie better be up at the Cape for Labor Day."

"Can't wait." Liam chuckles. "We look forward to it every year."

"OK, well, I got your message and did some research. Wallace Arlington won't be easy to get, that's for sure. He's filthy rich and he's retired."

"That is so ridiculous," Liam says. "He's thirty-four years old. He'll be bored by next weekend. I know he's the right man for this job, Weston. We want him. The board has already voted and they are adamant that we get him on the team."

"Which is why I'm here." I smile as I wait for Liam to offer me a seat at the conference table. But he doesn't. And he hesitates. "Is something wrong?" I ask.

"No," he says, still chuckling. "Not wrong, exactly. It's just… the board is adamant that we *get him*, Weston."

"Understood. I've got my feelers out and I have it on good authority he'll be somewhere specific tomorrow morning. I plan on meeting there and wrapping this up over the weekend."

Liam sighs. And shakes his head.

"What?" I ask, getting a bad feeling.

Then people are talking in the lobby. The conference room door is open, so this bit of bustle knocks us out of the conversation and refocuses our attention to the new arrival.

"What the fuck?" I say, as Victoria Arias starts walking towards the conference room, her smile so big she might have a canary in there. "What's she doing here?"

Liam shrugs. And when Tori comes in, greeting him loudly as she reaches for his hand, I think that old bastard actually blushes.

Not that I blame him. Victoria Arias is strikingly beautiful. Tall, and curvy, and… and… the definition of sexual with her low-cut imperial purple power blouse that accents her incredible violet eyes and contrasts them with her raven-dark hair.

"Liam," she reaches out for him with both hands, then waits for him to come to her so she can lean in and give him fake European kisses on the cheek. And that fucking accent comes through. One word. She's uttered one word and everything about it is exotic and dangerous. My eyes drop to her legs. Which are fucking long. And bare, since she's wearing this tiny black skirt that says, *Lift me up and see what's waiting for you.*

Jesus Christ. *Get it together, Weston.*

"Oh, Weston," Tori says, her attention on me. "I had no idea you would be here."

She's using that accent on purpose. That bitch comes from Brooklyn. I know. I know everything about her. Including just exactly how long those legs are and how she can bend like a pretzel during sex.

I know because I dated her on and off for six years after all that shit went down with the cops.

But I've made a point to stay far, far away from her for a long time now. Long time.

She's fucking wild. And not in a cute way, either. She's wild in a dangerous way. She took me down using one of her fancy jujitsu moves when I didn't remember our third anniversary.

Bitch. That's what she is.

But I smile and say, "Tori. How nice to see you again."

"Victoria," she corrects me. "No one calls me Tori, West."

"Weston," I say. "People do call me West, but you're not one of them."

"Ah," Liam says, smiling and waving for us to take a seat at the conference table. We both do, Victoria angling herself in her chair as she crosses those damn legs, rubbing her calves together, like she's getting herself off. "You two go back a long way, right?"

"Yes," Victoria says.

"Yup," I reply. "But what's this about, Liam? We have a deal. It's a retainer. It's *always* a retainer."

"Look, Weston," Liam says. "We're in a pickle here, OK? The board has spoken. And they're not sure you can pull this off. It's not easy to get Wallace Arlington's attention."

We both look over at Tori, who has no trouble getting anyone's attention. "Won't be a problem for me," she says, unbuttoning the top button of her silk blouse and tossing her hair.

Liam blushes like a teenager.

What the fuck is happening? "Are you giving this contract to *her*?"

"No, no, no," Liam says. "It's a contingency. You remember those, right, Weston? Headhunters go after the same position and the best one wins."

"I remember them, *barely*," I add. "Since it's been eight years since I took one on. And you know damn well," I say, squinting my eyes at him, "that we've *never* had that kind of arrangement."

"I don't normally do them either," Tori says, distracting Liam from the hidden meaning of my words. That fucking Argentinian accent. She's doing it on purpose. She knows it drives me crazy. "But..." She stops to give Liam a long seductive gaze. "I was asked to come and compete. Isn't that right, Liam?"

What the fuck is happening. My mind spins. Like actually spins as I run every possible reason why this could be happening. "Liam." I sigh, trying to sound unaffected and bored. "Look. I know Wallace is a difficult target. But we go way back. We were in boarding school together. We even went to Brown together. He's gonna listen to me."

"We also went to Brown together, Liam. And you might not know this, but—" Tori cups her hand to her mouth, like she's about to whisper a secret in Liam's ear, and says, "He has a thing for me. Has had one for years. In fact, Wallace and West used to fight over me all the time."

I roll my eyes. "That's not true. You had no interest in him."

"But I have interest in him now, Mr. Conrad."

"Mr. *Conrad*? Really?"

"Anyway," Tori says, shaking her hair again, "I can have him in my little pocket and wrap this up by Monday.

I assure you, Liam. I promise, I can deliver the goods on this job."

Liam claps his hands together and gives them a rub for good measure. "OK, I'm sold. The first one back with a signed offer gets the deal. Have fun, kids."

Victoria gets to her feet and kisses him on the cheek again.

I get up as well, a little flustered at how this retainer was just stolen from me by my traitorous ex-girlfriend, and shake his hand. "I'll be back with the contract on *Sunday*."

"Good! Good!" Liam says. "Pick up your packets at the front desk and we'll see you next week."

Victoria smiles as he walks away. She's smiling the whole time... until he disappears into another part of the office. And then she turns her venom to me.

"Stay out of my way, Mr. Corporate. I will take you down, boy. *Down*."

I grab her by the arm before she can finish her dramatic escape and lean down into her ear. "Miss Arias. It's spectacular to see you again. I've missed you. So much."

She slaps me in the face before the last word is out of my mouth. "No funny business, Weston. I'm not that innocent girl you knew in college."

"Innocent," I bark, then laugh. "Innocent? Shit, Tori. You came out of the womb armed and dangerous. You've never been innocent."

"I won't fall for you again. Ever. Do you understand me?" She's pointing her periwinkle-blue nail up into my face as she says this, and I have an urge to slap her hand away.

Control, Weston. Control. She's pushing all your buttons.

"I was just being friendly," I say. "I can handle a little competition. Especially from you."

"What's that mean? Don't think I won't do everything in my power to get this retainer, West. I will. I'm hungry." She licks her lips seductively and blows me a kiss. "Very, very hungry for this job. And hunger will win over complacence every time. You're complacent, Weston. You think you own the world. You've always thought you've owned the world. Well, now it's my turn. Stay out of my way."

And then she spins on the most ridiculously high stiletto heel I've ever seen and walks off.

Fuck. Fuck. Fuck.

I'm pissed off and turned on at the same time. That fucking slap, man. She knows it drives me crazy when she's wild. Crazy.

And the whole time she's chatting with the receptionist as she gathers her packet up, I stare at her perfectly round ass and those long, long legs.

Stay focused, Weston.

I pretend to take a call while Tori finishes up, then make my way to the reception desk to pick up my packet.

I know she won't win this little contest. I have inside information. I have a friend in the spying business and by the end of the day I'll know exactly where to find Wallace Arlington tomorrow—the perfect opportunity to get him alone and get this shit finished before the weekend even starts.

I picture the phone call to Tori once that's done. I rehearse my lines in my mind as I take the elevator back down to the valet and get in my car.

I'm not going down. She is.

Victoria Arias will regret fucking up this job for me.

I'm going to make sure of it.

CHAPTER THREE

VICTORIA

Weston Conrad. Such an amateur.

I have to smile as I track his car through downtown Miami. What does he take me for? And how stupid can he be? That tip yesterday might be the reason I'm here right now, but my intuition and tenacity are what will get me across the finish line first.

He weaves his way through traffic and crosses the Port Miami Causeway. What is he doing? Where is he going? I have a hunch he knows exactly where to find Wallace Arlington. He had that cocky scowl on his face up in the office. I am very familiar with that look. He used it on me often back when we were dating and we were fighting for control.

"Tori," he'd say. Or if he was really pissed he'd call me Victoria. "Victoria," he'd say. "Don't play me, honey. I know all your tricks and more."

But he never counted on me taking notes of all his tricks.

I did. I know them all. Hell, I helped come up with most of them. And I know that look he gave me was confidence.

He pulls into a parking garage next to a cruise ship terminal and I follow. If he's checking the rearview mirror, I didn't notice. So he hasn't made me yet. Probably too wrapped up in his own ego to even consider me a threat.

I'm a threat, baby. Just watch out.

We wind our way up the garage levels until there are plenty of open parking spots, and then he goes left and I continue up one more level and park in the first space I find.

I jump out and take off at a jog, even though my heels are high enough to break an ankle. He's just disappearing into the connecting building when I catch sight of him again.

It's an entrance to a Cuban cafe.

I stop at the door, catch my breath, and shake my hair. *Can you feel me, West? Because here I come.*

I pull the door open and walk into a hazy restaurant filled with men in suits.

This must be the good ol' boys club. I should've figured. Weston has good ol' boy written all over him. Old money with even older attitudes about women. He was always trying to protect me. Tell me to do things for my own good. It was patronizing and borderline sexist. I hated it.

But when every head near the front bar turns to look at me, I let it go. I'm used to the attention of men. It's not my fault I was born looking this way. I tried my best to be a tomboy all growing up. I just don't have the body for it. So when I hit puberty and my aunt told me to play up my best assets instead of hiding them behind big shorts and loose pants, I took her advice.

Maybe it's cheating, maybe it's not. But here I am, fifteen years later, still in the game, still scoring points, and still letting everyone think I'm a stupid bimbo.

A beautiful woman couldn't possibly be ruthless.

That's what I like them to think.

But I am ruthless. In every way that counts. And I know Weston Conrad is in this restaurant somewhere with the answer to every problem I have.

All I need to do to get those answers is show up.

I smile at a table of gentlemen wearing casual suits as they stop their business and stare, but keep my eye on the prize.

Which is missing at the moment.

Where did he go?

Ah. There's the bastard now.

West slips behind a scarlet curtain on the side of the restaurant that faces the water and I follow.

A few other people go through as well and they are all greeted by name.

Hmmm. What is going on behind that curtain?

"Excuse me?" I say to the host standing guard. He's wearing a different kind of uniform from the rest of the servers. They are all in black pants and white shirts. But this man wears a suit with a red tie and matching red pocket square. "May I go through and look for my husband?"

I realize too late that I have no wedding band on my finger to shore up the lie, and even as I'm thinking about being turned away, my heart has a little ache in it.

"Are you on the guest list?" he asks, smiling, even though he knows perfectly well I am not or I wouldn't be asking for permission.

"No, but my husband is." I have my left hand behind my back so he can't notice I have no ring.

"I'm sorry, ma'am," the host says. "It's invitation only. What's his name? I'll see if I can find him."

My eyes dart to another part of the restaurant and I say, "Oh, there he is! Never mind, thank you." And I slip away, hoping I didn't draw too much attention to myself.

Shit. I know West is in there getting info. Hell, Wallace might even be there. If he is, I've lost.

Think, Victoria. Think.

I go outside onto the patio where people are eating and drinking underneath large canvas umbrellas, and walk along until I reach the end. There's a kitchen door propped open, so I look over my shoulder to see if anyone is watching, then open it up and go inside.

There's commotion and bustle as cooks and servers do their thing, but I raise up my head and walk through like I own the place. Everyone glances twice, but that's because I'm a beautiful woman. Not because they feel like stopping me.

Where was that back room? I bet they have an entrance from the kitchen.

I spy a server with the same red pocket square as the host, and follow them down a hallway and through a swinging door. On one side of the hallway are restrooms, the open kind that have a curvy wall made out of stone and not the kind with a door. On the other side is another door.

"Please don't let this lead to the front," I mutter, ducking into the women's restroom when the door starts

26

to swing open again. I turn around as soon as I get around the corner of the marble wall and head right back into the hallway, smiling at the server carrying a tray as I let him pass towards the kitchen. I push open the door he came through and smile.

OK. I'm in. Everyone in here has that same uniform on. So this is the private area where Weston is surely meeting some contact.

I scan the room, which is partitioned off with hand-painted folding screens depicting scenes of Cuba, but come up with no Weston Conrad.

Dammit. Where is he?

I'm just about to give up when I hear his familiar laugh.

He's on the other side of a screen. And even though there are at least fifty diners in here, now that I know he's here, I can't miss him. That arrogant voice carries through the screen and across the room. I find myself leaning in to try to hear what he's saying. And in another moment, my feet are traveling that direction.

His voice grows louder as I approach, unseen because of the screen, and I take a seat at a table that has been recently vacated.

I look around for a server, but they are all busy.

I look down at the table setting and realize this is some kind of event. A party or some luncheon for a club. So I relax and concentrate on Weston's words.

CHAPTER FOUR

WESTON

"OK," I say, barely managing to contain my bad mood through the whole Mr. Mysterious act Paxton puts on. "What do you have for me?" I don't know why Pax always has to fill me in on his life these days. But he does. It's always something with this guy. These jobs he takes. I can't stand it. I liked him so much better when he ignored me. But ever since that whole thing with Mr. Romantic went down he's been over-sharing like a motherfucker. It's way too much TMI for me.

"You didn't answer my question," Pax says.

"What was the question again?"

"Where do you see yourself in five years?"

"What?" I know my expression says, *Come the fuck on*, but I hold it together. Pax has info I need. And I need it now. Before Victoria gets it first. She has something up her sleeve. Or down her bra, more likely. "Shouldn't I be asking *you* that question, Mysterious? I'm the headhunter here. Besides, I'm on track. I got it all planned. You, on the other hand, I have no idea what you're doing."

"I got a track. I've got many tracks, in fact."

"Name one," I say, the annoyance leaking through.

"You name one. I'm the one who asked."

"Is this what you need to fill me in? Fine. In five years I've gone global. I've got offices in LA, New York, London, Paris, Moscow, Berlin, Hong Kong, and Tokyo."

"Is that where you're headed? Global?" Pax takes a sip of his drink, which is a fucking mint julep of all things, and I suddenly feel like I'm being played.

"Yeah," I say. "Global. I've got the London office set up. Hong Kong is next. And after that, it's on to Russia. I'll be in Tokyo and Paris in three years. Hell, in five years, I might retire."

"You ever think about doing something else?"

I don't have a word for the look on my face or the depth of confusion in my mind. "What? What the fuck else would I do? This is my job. I fucking rock this job. I'm heading out and moving up. Why the hell would I do something else?"

"Hey," Pax says. "I'm not knocking it, man. I'm just asking."

"Why, are you? Gonna do something different?" I ask him.

"Sure. Why the fuck would I be a fixer for the rest of my life? People get old, Weston. Shit gets old. My shit is getting old. I'm ready to do something else."

"Like what?"

"I dunno," Pax says, sipping that ridiculous drink.

Is he playing me?

"Well, you can do something else after you give me my info. I need to know where Wallace Arlington is *today*." I knock my knuckles on the wooden table to emphasize my point.

"Do you like the party?" Pax asks, changing the subject.

"What?" I look around as he pans his hand, like he's showing off this event. "Whose party is it, anyway?"

30

"Some charity thing. Do-gooder awards. You win any of those things, Weston? Do-gooder awards?

"I'll let Mr. Perfect corner that market, thanks. And yeah," I say, one hundred percent bored and well on my way to irritated. "It's a great party. Now where is Wallace?"

"Well," Pax says, lowering his voice and leaning in, "I hear he's going to be on some island tomorrow for a corporate event."

"What kind of event?"

"What do I look like, fucking Google? I don't know."

"What island? I need to make arrangements."

"Well, you can't take the jet, it's float plane or boat access only. And the water is gonna be rough, so I doubt you'll get a charter boat to take you."

"Who fucking cares? Fuck the boat ride. I can get a float plane. Just tell me where I need to be." Why is he dragging this shit out?

"Sandcastle Cay. The northern part of the Exuma Cays. It's about fifty miles southeast of Nassau. He's gonna be there tomorrow, but after that I have no clue where he's going. I only got this tip after I threatened to expose a secret I'm holding for a friend of his."

"Shit. How the fuck am I gonna get a private flight out there with half a day's notice?"

"I got a guy if you need a reference."

I almost don't stop my eye roll. A reference. Jesus Christ. "Yes, Pax. I'd like a reference. Just get me to this guy tomorrow and I'll knock off half a mil from that debt you owe me."

"I pay my debts, Corporate. I don't need your charity."

He laughs hard as he tries to take a sip of his girly drink, and doesn't quite succeed without dribbling it down his chin.

I can't even with this guy.

"Here," he says, pulling a business card out of his wallet. "Give my friend a call this afternoon and tell him Mysterious gave you his number. He'll take care of you."

I take it and stand up, ready to get the fuck away from him. "OK, well, thanks. And hey, if you'd like to pay that debt off, it's seven point five million now. With the interest."

Mysterious sends me a wide grin and shoots me with his finger. Something that reminds me a little too much of the equally cocky Mr. Match. They have been spending far too much time together if he's picking up his mannerisms.

"See ya around," Pax calls, after I'm already walking away. "And don't fuck this up. We can't afford any more mistakes."

I'm not the fuckup. What kind of drugs is he on? *He's* the fuckup. But I don't stop. He's crazy. We all know he's crazy. I got what I needed and I'm gonna nail down Wallace Arlington tomorrow. This whole deal will be one and done and then I can get back to building my global empire.

CHAPTER FIVE
VICTORIA

I met Weston Conrad the night before the night before the big night. You'd think that it might get lost in the hustle and bustle of what happened over the next two days, but it didn't. Because the night before the night before the big night was the best one of my life.

Even up to this very moment.

No other night, before or since, will ever be able to compare.

He wasn't Mr. Corporate when we met. He was just Mr. Conrad.

He wasn't sweet, he wasn't particularly smart—I mean, everyone at Brown was smart, so I'm just saying he didn't stand out—and he wasn't particularly motivated.

But he was very drunk.

I found him sitting under a tree in front of the administration building holding a bottle of whiskey wrapped up in a paper bag. He was wearing a suit, was covered in leaves, and he was singing *Swing Low, Sweet Chariot*. His voice was deep, mimicking the Johnny Cash version perfectly.

He was a cliché of desperation and defeat.

I joined in from a tree nearby and we sang that song together.

That's how I met Weston Conrad. The night his world *really* fell apart, although I still don't really understand what all that melancholy was about. That was forty-eight hours before he was accused of a crime that would test my limits and my faith.

I always knew he was innocent. It was not me who questioned his morality and virtues. It was him.

We talked all night long. I never once joined him under his tree, just kept my distance about twenty feet away from under mine. And I didn't even know who he was until daylight broke and he was almost sober.

"Let me walk you home," he said. "It's an ugly, fucked-up world out there and I'd kill myself if anything happened to you on your way home." He said it like it was fact. And looking back, it sounds a little bit like a premonition.

I said yes, of course. By this time, I knew he was handsome. I knew something had gone terribly wrong with his life, and I knew that he was planning something and my appearance several hours before had interrupted those plans.

But I still don't quite comprehend his desperate situation that night. Why he was sitting under the tree in front of administration. And why his world was falling apart even before that girl accused him of that crime.

He said he was broke, now that I think back. Hmmm. Funny how I never thought about that little detail ever again. Or maybe not so funny. Life got weird, and complicated, and messy.

Well, he isn't broke now, so I guess prosperity begets prosperity. Isn't that what they say? Money makes money? Power gains power? It's a never-ending cycle of predetermination.

When we got to the house I shared with my roommates he leaned against the porch railing and looked at me.

I was waiting for him to try something. Kiss me or grope me like most men did at the end of a first date.

But he didn't. He just looked. Not leered, which again was atypical.

And I told myself that he was hungover and it really wasn't a date. Because it made me feel... a little... insecure, I guess.

I have been beautiful all my life. I expect men to treat me a certain way. So when Weston Conrad didn't meet those expectations I was thrown.

Instead, he said, "Thank you."

And I said, my heart beating faster than it should, "For what?"

"Saving me." Then he turned away and walked off.

"What's your name?" I called after him.

"It doesn't matter," he said, never looking back. "I know yours."

He was waiting for me after my four o'clock class that afternoon, looking more handsome and more put-together.

"Miss Arias," he said, when I noticed him leaning against the wall as the people poured out of the auditorium. "Can I interest you in a coffee?"

I was more put-together as well. The night before was one for the books in my little world too. I had just had a fight with an ex and I was questioning everything about my life when I stumbled upon Weston Conrad. I was angry that a man would make me question things that should be certain. I was angry that I had let myself be controlled and manipulated into being someone I wasn't.

But West smoothed all those wrinkles over. He was like a balm on a burn or a soothing tea before bed.

We talked over coffee. I got his name, of course. He already knew mine. Coffee turned into dinner, turned into drinks.

And even though I should've felt dirty for moving on to another man so quickly, I didn't. The whole thing felt like fate.

And then... everything fell apart. Again, and again, and again.

I pull myself out of the past with a shake of my head. Weston is walking down the beach of Virginia Key and I'm relaxing under an umbrella, a big straw hat giving me cover. He's dressed for a business trip and I'm immediately grateful I didn't opt for casual wear either. I can't see his eyes because he's wearing dark streamlined sunglasses.

His tan slacks are pressed and crisp, accentuated with a brown belt. The dress shirt is white, sleeves rolled up like he's about to get his hands dirty, and the tie...

Well, my heart skips a beat when I see the tie. It's a light purple. Lavender, actually. Which is my color and that tells me something.

He's been thinking about me.

This morning. When he got dressed, he was thinking

about me.

Get it together, Victoria.

I almost laugh. If Weston Conrad was thinking about me, it was not in a flattering way. It's far more likely that he spent the night cursing my name and he reached for that tie unconsciously.

I'm going to steal this contract from him and he knows it.

CHAPTER SIX

WESTON

"Vlad?" I ask the pilot as I make my way onto the beach and towards the sea plane. What kind of guy is called Vlad in Miami? Well, if he's Pax's friend, you never know. The guy is probably some international criminal. "Are you Vlad?" I call again when the guy ignores me.

He looks up from whatever he's doing to his seaplane and squints his eyes. "That's me," he says, in a perfect American accent. He looks a little bit familiar.

Well, at least he's not some displaced Romanian.

"I'm Weston Conrad. We spoke last night." I pause to look him over. Why does he look so familiar? "Have I met you before?"

Vlad wipes his hand on his jeans and extends it. We shake as he says, "Nope, never seen you before in my life. Nice to meet you. We'll get started as soon as the other guest arrives."

"Other guest? This is a private charter, Mr.... *Vlad*."

"I told Pax I'd take other clients since this was a favor. And I have one. Here she comes now."

"She?" But I know who it is the moment before I turn and look in the direction he's pointing.

Victoria Arias' long dark hair is billowing out behind her, her heels clasped in her fingertips, swinging as she walks across the sand to meet us. She's wearing a silk lavender shirt that ripples in the ocean breeze, giving me… and *Vlad*… a nice peek at her matching bra between the buttons.

"What the fuck are you doing here?" I ask.

"This was the only Sandcastle Cay charter available, Weston. Do you really think I didn't know where Wallace Arlington would be today?"

"You two know each other?" Vlad asks.

"Yes," we say together, sneering the word with equal amounts of contempt.

God, just what the fuck?

"Back off, Victoria. This is my contract and you know it."

"It's not," she says, flipping her hair in that way that drives me crazy. "We're vying for it, Weston. The sooner you get that through your thick skull, the sooner you come to terms with the fact that I will be the one who gets this contract when this is all over."

"Like hell." Goddammit.

"Is there going to be a problem?" Vlad asks. "Because if so, one of you has to stay behind. Since this is a favor for your friend, Conrad, that would be you. Miss Arias paid me in cash last night."

That bitch. "No," I say, the word rumbling out like a growl. "Everything is fine."

"Good," he says. "Stow your… oh, you don't have any gear." Vlad turns to look at Victoria and notices she has no gear either. "You're not staying overnight?"

"No," we say together.

"Day trip only, I told you that last night," I say. "It's a one-day corporate event on Sandcastle Cay. I'll only be an hour. You can just wait."

"I'm not waiting," Vlad says. "I have clients on another cay who need a ride back this afternoon. I'm gonna head over there, get lunch and a drink with them, then fly them back to Miami."

"Pick me up on the way home," Victoria says. "I'll be ready."

"I won't have room, Miss Arias. This is a four-passenger plane and there are three of them plus luggage."

"So we're just going to be stuck out there?"

"I can come back. But it won't be until late afternoon."

"Fine, that will work," I say.

"Good," Vlad says. Then he winks at Victoria and points to the co-pilot seat. "You can sit next to me if this guy creeps you out. We're gonna land during low tide today, so the beaches will be nice for whatever you have going on out there. Perfect, actually."

Victoria smiles that beautiful smile and says, "Why, thank you, Vlad. I think I'll take you up on that. And thanks for the tip about the tides." She slips those high heels back on and makes a big show of getting in the plane and crossing her legs.

I get in the back and pretend that the blatant flirting going on up front isn't pissing me off. She's doing it on purpose. In fact, I think he's doing it on purpose too.

It's one day, Conrad. One day and then you'll get the contract signed and never have to see Victoria Arias again.

"Are we stopping at customs?" I yell once we are taxiing on the water.

Vlad shoots me a grin over his shoulder as he pulls back

41

on the control wheel and we take flight. "What do you think, Mr. Corporate?"

I'm going to kill Mr. Mysterious for this. Kill that crazy motherfucker. Why does he have to live on the edge all the time? Why does he have to court disaster and jail time? Does he regret that we were never found guilty for the rape accusation back in college? Does he want to go to prison? Sometimes I wonder. Sometimes I think that guy has 'suicide mission' listed as his main goal in life. That's his five-year plan. Get arrested for the stupid fucked-up shit he does to earn money in the world.

I should never call him again. I should forget I ever met the guy. I should cut ties with all of the Misters, now that I think about it.

Weird shit is happening. Weird shit that makes me think way too much of the past.

And the fact that Victoria Arias has suddenly appeared back in my life isn't making things look any better.

In fact, it looks a lot like a setup. It looks a lot like someone really is fucking with us again. It looks a lot like a mistake.

And if I get arrested because Paxton Vance's pilot is some kind of international criminal, I'm definitely taking him down with me.

Victoria and Vlad chat back and forth on headsets after that. I stew in the back wondering just exactly what brought her back in my life. It's suspicious. I know what's going on with the rest of the Misters. Match filled me in about Nolan's whole trainwreck of a night a few weeks ago and that alone is enough to make me suspicious.

42

walk up to the beach where Vlad and Victoria seem to be having regrets about parting.

"So," I say, bringing Vlad's attention back to me. "I think I'll be done here in an hour. Can't you just wait?"

"Wait?" Vlad laughs. "No. I already told you. If you want a ride back, I'll be here late afternoon."

"That's no problem, Vlad," Victoria says, blinking her eyes at him. "I'm sure I'll have this contract wrapped up in no time and then I'll just work on my tan for the rest of the day."

"Sounds good, sweetheart. Then we can get that drink when we get back to Miami."

"Sounds like a great time," Victoria purrs. I wait for her to grab his shirt collar and pull him in for a dramatic goodbye kiss. But she doesn't, just turns away, looking back over her shoulder with a smile.

Vlad and I both watch her make her way towards a track in the sand that leads up a dune and then he turns to me.

"So you don't have a problem with that, do you? Us having drinks later? I mean, she said you two were never serious and you broke up years ago."

"Did she?" Bitch. "Well, don't worry about me. I'm immune to her charms. But you, buddy, I worry about. She's got you wrapped around her pinky finger."

"Hey." Vlad smiles as he walks off into the water, ignoring the fact that his pants are soaking wet up to the knees. "Don't you worry about me, man. I can handle anything."

He gives me a little salute and slams his door closed as

he starts the engine.

I don't bother watching him take off. I head up the beach by way of the path to catch up with Victoria. I'm not letting her get the jump on Wallace. And if she thinks she's going to play dirty by using her female assets on him, well, I'll just have to use my male assets on her.

CHAPTER SEVEN

VICTORIA

I know he's jealous. Weston Conrad might be a lot of things, but he is not subtle. And I know he's jealous because flirting with other men has always been my fallback with him when he's difficult. There is no way he's going to give up this contract to me, but it doesn't matter. By the end of this day, Mr. Corporate will only have one thing on his mind. Me. And how I won.

I smile into the wind as I walk up the sand dune and come to higher ground. We landed on the deserted side of the cay, but that's not uncommon here. Most of these little islands are small and uninhabited. Even the inhabited ones, like this one, have little to nothing in the way of buildings and amenities.

If you want a resort experience you don't come to a place like Sandcastle Cay. You go to the main islands and stay in a real hotel.

Still, when I shade my eyes with my hand to block out the sun, I can't see any structures at all.

"Hey," Weston calls from behind me. "Look, Victoria. I know you think you're going to play hardball with me today, but—"

"Wait," I say, putting up my hand to shut him up. "Where are we?"

"What do you mean?"

"I mean, look, Weston. There's no buildings over

there. That's the other side of the island and there's no buildings."

"What?" he says, looking around. "There have to be buildings. Look," he says, pointing to the ridge off to the left. "There's a roof. It's this way."

We start walking, both of us holding our shoes in our hands, and Weston continues to talk. "Whatever you need, Victoria, I'll help you. But you're not taking this contract."

"I don't want your charity. I can get this contract all on my own. I don't need you, West."

"No," he says with a sigh. "No, you've never needed anyone."

"Don't get all broody with me, Mr. Conrad. I'm not playing your games again. Let's just agree that we both get a shot. We're both here, right? So we both get a shot to make our case and then Wallace can decide."

"Whatever. But you know he'll never sign with you. You have no contacts. He's got no reason to think you'll be able to pull this off."

"It's guaranteed, Weston."

"Is it? How do you know Liam hasn't hired other headhunters, hmm? Why would he hire the two of us? When he knows I can deliver?"

"Maybe you can't deliver?" I snap. "Obviously he doesn't have complete faith in you, Weston. If he did, I wouldn't be here."

"How did you get here?" he asks. "I know you have no connections in Miami. Not like I do."

"I'm resourceful, West. You, of all people, should know that." We reach the top of another ridge and both of us go silent for a moment.

"Where the fuck is everyone?" he asks.

I turn and look around. There is a building. It's not big and it's not extravagant—they never are out here. But there's no people. "Are we on the right cay?"

"We better be on the right fucking cay," West says. "I'll kill that motherfucker if he dropped us off on the wrong goddamned island."

"OK, well, if we are on the right island, then where is everyone? They can't be inside. And there's no boats? No planes? Just what the hell is going on?"

"You know what?" West asks.

"What?" I say, starting to feel a little creeped out. We are in the middle of the Caribbean Sea, on a deserted island, and might be in the wrong place.

"I'm starting to think you set this up. Did you tell that pilot to drop us at the wrong island? Are you sending someone else in to talk to Wallace five islands over?" West whirls around, looking at all the nearby cays. There's plenty of them. We could probably swim to four, at least, that's how close they are. But for what purpose? They all appear to be deserted too.

"Weston," I say. "I'm sure you know by now that my headhunting business is on the verge of insolvency. So cut your shit and don't make me angry. I don't have the manpower to send someone else to do my job."

"Your father is still involved. I keep track, Victoria. I keep track of every one of my competitors."

"Well, then you'd know that my father is not doing well and the last thing I'd ask him to do is to come all the way out here and risk his health so I can play games with you." I whirl around and point my finger in his face. "So don't fuck with me. Why are we the only people on the island?"

He slaps my hand away and drops his shoes. "Don't point at me. I don't like it. You know I don't like it because we've fought about that little move hundreds of times. So don't fucking point at me."

I rifle through my purse and get out my phone. Of course, there is no service out here. "That's great. Now we're stuck here all day and Wallace Arlington is somewhere else. Who the hell gave you this information?"

"What do you mean 'who gave me?' Where did you get *your* information?"

Shit.

"Victoria?"

Fuck.

"Victoria?" He's getting mad now. "Who told you to be at that plane this morning?"

"Who told *you?*" I say. It's not clever and it's not much of a deflection. But I have nothing but the truth. And the truth will piss him off.

"A very good friend. A very reliable friend."

"I guess he's not so reliable, is he?"

"Who said it was a he?" West growls.

"Um…" *Dammit. Think, Victoria. You can handle this overgrown child. You did it for years.* "Of course it's a *he*, Weston. You'd never take the word of a woman."

"Oh, you're going with that? Really?"

"You've always been a caveman. So don't even deny it. How many women do you do business with, Mr.

Corporate?"

"Don't call me that."

"I've earned the right," I snap back. "If anyone can call you that, it's me."

"I do business with whomever is required. And hundreds of them are women. So don't push your little feminist agenda on me, honey."

"Honey?" I laugh. "OK, you're on your own, Corporate. I'm going down to that building to see if they have a radio."

"Well, if you looked at the roof," he says, keeping pace with me as we walk down the overgrown path, "there's an antenna, so they do."

"Are you going to pull the big, strong man routine on me again? If so, save your breath. I'm not in the business of playing damsel in distress. And the antenna could be obsolete. I won't know until I see for myself. Unlike you," I say, looking over at him, "I don't jump to conclusions."

"I didn't need to jump, Victoria. I saw it all with my own eyes."

"Oh, fuck you. I won that Fullerton contract, too. Fair and square."

"Fair? Square? Hardly." He laughs. "You slept with me and then cheated me out of a contract. I can forgive you for a lot of things, Victoria, but stealing from me isn't one of them. I gave you anything you wanted, everything you needed and you shit all over me."

"I told you back then, it was delivered to your apartment with my name on it. It was for *me*, Weston. Not you!"

"Liar," he mumbles. "We weren't living together at that time. It was a very convenient one-night stand for old times' sake. And you just happened to be there when the courier came and you signed for my package and took it. Seven million dollars, Tori. That's what I lost on that deal."

Fuck him. Just fuck him. He wants to bring up the past? I'm happy to bring up all the little things he seems to have conveniently forgotten.

"You will not win, Mr. Corporate. You will not. Because I'm the one who *always* wins when it comes to *us*."

He stops walking and I keep going. But before I step off the path to make my way down the hill, I look back. He's about twenty yards behind me, standing still. His hair is tousled and messy. His hands are fists, like he's really angry. And his face. That handsome face, impassive. Because that's how he rolls. He shuts down the minute he feels challenged.

"You win because I let you, Tori. And do you know why I always let you win?"

"Let me?" I snort. "Please."

"Because I loved you. I loved you, but all you ever saw was a ticket. A ticket out of the prison you locked yourself in. And I'm telling you right now, Victoria Arias, for the hundredth fucking time, I'm nobody's ticket but mine."

CHAPTER EIGHT

WESTON

The most ironic thing about Victoria Arias is her refusal to need anyone. Because she's always been needy. And I'm kinda lying about the whole ticket thing. I like being needed. Most men do. But the thing I hate is the fact that she refuses to *admit* she needs me. She's always been that way. Always.

She doesn't wait for me to catch up, just runs down the hill, that long dark hair flying in the wind again.

I sigh and pick up my shoes, then follow her down to the little building. How the hell did things get so fucked up? Last night this was a sure thing. Twenty-four hours ago I thought this contract was a retainer.

Now I'm even farther away from nailing this down than I was when Liam said I had to compete. Wallace Arlington is probably hundreds of miles away. Hell, maybe Mysterious set me up? He's always been weird. Maybe he's working for someone else these days? How would I know? He barely gives us Misters the time of day. And despite helping out with Nolan's little predicament, he hasn't been around much as far as I can tell.

Maybe he and Match have some kind of business going, but who really trusts Match, either? He doesn't even have a girlfriend. And the fucker runs a dating site. What kind of dating site mogul has no significant other?

That little fact has been eating away at me for a while

now. I just don't know what to make of it. Add in all the hush-hush shit that went down back when we were arrested, and that guy, Five, whoever he was. I don't know, but I do know he was dangerous. Like Mysterious kind of dangerous. He just walked in like he was some kind of king and took over.

Do this, do that.

No one knows how to work the legal system like that unless they have experience doing it. And the guy was probably not much older than I am now. So what kind of shit was he into? What kind of life was he part of that he knew so much?

Granted, his advice was all solid. But it still bothers me. *Match* still bothers me. Where did he pick up a friend like that? I mean, Match was only eighteen years old when we were charged.

And I've looked into his family. I have the family histories of all the Misters memorized, even Mysterious'. And that was not easy to come by, considering he's the illegitimate son of a big-time Hollywood movie star on one side and the blue-blood heir of a one-hundred-fifty-year-old Kentucky breeding farm on the other.

But Match's family history comes off as very blue-collar. Custom motorcycles. And a reality show a while back. Hell, he still lives in Colorado where he grew up. Perfect lives in Colorado now too, but that wasn't by design. It just happens to be where the headquarters to his family company is.

And that Five guy was anything *but* blue-collar. He reeked of money and breeding. So where did that connection come from?

I don't know. And I don't need to care about it right now. My only concern is radioing for that pilot to get his ass back here and pick us up. Get us somewhere with service so I can call Mysterious up and ask him just what the fuck.

This Wallace Arlington contract is the pinnacle of everything I've been doing for the past fifteen years. I'm there. I am so close I can practically taste it.

And it's slipping away. Everything feels like it's slipping away.

When I get to the building I realize it's more of a house. There's a lot of windows and I can see inside as I walk to the door and pull it open.

Victoria is sitting at a kitchen island, her head in her hands.

"What's up?" I ask. Because I know that means she's frustrated.

"It doesn't work."

"The radio?" I say, dropping my shoes at the front door. "Let me look at it. I'm good with electronics. Maybe I can—"

"You can't, Weston. It's smashed."

"Smashed?"

Victoria is pointing to the counter across from where she's sitting, and when I step a few paces to the side I see that, yes, there is a radio, and yes, it is smashed to bits on the counter. "Who the fuck would do that?"

"Someone who doesn't want us to be anywhere but here today, West."

West. She almost never calls me West. It's like me calling her Tori. Reserved for intimate moments.

"Something is wrong," she says.

Or vulnerable ones.

"Why do you say that?" I ask, walking up to the island and taking a seat next to her. She smells good. She always smells good. Always something flowery, too. Jasmine or honeysuckle. Gardenias or roses.

Today she smells like something else, though. The one I always preferred. It's fitting. Her eyes are violet, her shirt is lavender, and her scent is lilac. She is purple.

And right now those eyes… they are stuck. On me. The past. The present.

Why is she here?

"Because we are in the wrong place."

I get up and go into the kitchen, pulling open cupboards. Empty. I open the fridge. Empty. "Fucking great."

"Look," Victoria says, leaning over the island and lifting up the tap. "Water. At least we have water. That Vlad guy will be back tonight. So as long as we stay inside and hydrated, we'll be fine."

"Assuming he comes back."

"Why wouldn't he come back?"

I'm sorry I said it because Victoria's eyes get wide with concern. "Never mind. He will."

She goes silent and I know she won't forget those words. It's going to haunt her all day. She will dwell, and fret, and work herself up into a blind obsession.

Because that's the kind of girl Victoria Arias is.

Wild. It's her default setting.

Victoria taps her nails on the countertop and I can't help but look at them. Yesterday they were periwinkle, but today they are the lightest shade of purple imaginable. So light, they are almost white.

"So…" she says.

"So…" I say.

"Are you doing well?" she asks.

"I am, thanks. And you?" I roll my eyes. Are we so far apart this is all we have to talk about? Are we so far apart that polite conversation is all we have left between us? "Your dad," I say. "What's wrong with him?"

"Oh." Victoria sighs. "Too many things to list."

"I'm sorry," I say. And I am. I always liked him.

"He was talking about you the other day."

"He was?"

"Yes. He asks about you a lot. And before you ask, it's always good."

"Well, when you see him tell him I said hi. And ask him if I can come by and say it in person."

"He'd like that."

"Me too."

The silence takes over again. I'm actually stuck in it, I think. I want to say something. Anything to make the distance between us go away. But… I get caught up imagining all the things I could say. All the ways they could come out wrong. All the misinterpretations they might come with. And then one second has turned into thirty. And then thirty has turned into two minutes. And… Victoria gets up and goes into the bathroom.

She closes the door, then immediately opens it. "Do you think it works?"

I shrug. "The water works."

She disappears again and I'm left here alone, my mind still trying to catch up with the fact that I'm on a tropical island with Victoria Arias. Alone. After not seeing her for more than three years.

She still looks good. Better than ever, actually.

But she's still the same in other ways as well. That mean streak she has, that will never fade. I don't doubt that Victoria Arias' grandchildren will be whispering the words 'crazy,' and 'wild,' and 'stubborn' thirty or forty years from now.

When she comes out the bathroom I feel more stuck than ever.

I have so much to say to her and none of it should be said out loud. I want to scream at her. I want to yell insults and make threats to walk out of her life forever. This time, on *my* terms. Better than the way she walked out on me. I want to be meaner than she was. I want to throw more insults than she did. I want to make accusations that she knows to be true, just like that last night. I want to make her hate me and miss me in the same moment.

I want to…

I sigh.

Because I don't really want to do any of that. I want to say I'm sorry. I want to say I've missed her. I want to say there has never been another woman in my life like her and there never will be.

I want to say… I love her.

Because I do. I have never loved a woman whose name was not Victoria Arias. And I will never love another woman. I am destined to walk this life alone because she's it for me. The beginning and the end when it comes to love.

I had her and I lost.

I had her and I chose to leave her behind.

I had love and I chose blind obsession instead.

So there's no use feeling sorry for myself. I made this chasm between us. I am the empty space. I am the long drop to the bottom. I am the only one I can blame.

CHAPTER NINE

VICTORIA

"It's not even noon," I say, after using the bathroom. West is eerily silent and contemplative as he stares out the window. It's like he doesn't even notice me. I dressed in these clothes to taunt him, wore this low-cut shirt to pique his interest. And all I've gotten so far is indifference.

He's always been that way, right?

Big, strong, powerful Weston Conrad. Untouchable, I used to call him. And not because of his wealth or status. But because Weston doesn't deal in emotions. He is impossible to rattle. Insults wash off him like water off a duck. He fields accusations like a major leaguer, throwing them back to home base, always preventing a score.

He is indifferent. Always uninterested.

"I know," Weston says.

"What should we do all day?"

He's not talking. He's just staring out the kitchen window like there's something magical out there.

But then he gets up and walks towards the window, leaning his hands on the countertop as he tries to see something, but can't quite make it out. "What's that?" he says, stepping back and walking out of the kitchen to the main living area where he stops in front of the big picture window.

"What's what?" I ask, lost in thought. God, he looks... fantastic. I've seen him in magazines a few times over the past three years, and he always looked more like a *GQ* model than a businessman. But Jesus. I talked myself into believing that was all Photoshop and none of it was real.

It's real. *He's* real.

"Is that a storm?" Weston says, pointing out the window.

I walk over to him, trying my best not to get lost in his cologne. Weston never liked to wear cologne when we first met. He was so different back then. But then I bought him some for Christmas that first year and he's worn it ever since.

That's what he's wearing now. Same brand I got him all those years ago. I'd recognize it anywhere.

"Look, Victoria. Did you catch a weather report before you left this morning?"

"It's going to be hot in New York, if that's what you're asking."

"No, that's not what I'm asking," he says, irritated. "Is there a big storm coming *out here?*"

"How would I know?" I snap. I'm letting that indifference get to me again. I always let it get to me. It makes me ragey. "I'm not from here," I say, trying to ravel all the parts of me that are coming unraveled by being here alone with him. "So I wouldn't know. Sorry," I add, to try to defuse my anger.

Weston sighs, like I'm grating on his last nerve. "Well, I'm not from here either. But that purple mess of clouds looks like a giant fucking storm to me."

I'm about to toss him another ball of insults to field when it hits me what that might mean. "What are you saying? Will we get stuck here? Is that pilot not coming back for us?"

Weston shoots me a scowl. "Don't get crazy, Tori. He'll come back. It looks far away still. Like it might hit late tonight."

"He better come back," I say, mostly to myself.

"You got a hot date with him tonight?" And even though Weston's the master of indifference, it doesn't quite come out as indifferent.

I smile as the, "No," comes out of my mouth. I try to sneer as well, but I like that he's asking. It means I made him jealous when we were flying over. "I just don't want to be stuck here overnight, that's all."

"Hmmm," Weston says. "Stuck here with me?"

"Exactly."

"Well, I can think of worse people to be stuck on a tropical island with myself."

"Don't waste your time trying to flatter me, West. It won't work."

"Noted, Tori."

I sigh and walk over to the wall and flick the light switch. "We have power."

"I figured, since the water is running on a pump."

A pump? Wait a minute. "What does that mean?" I ask, getting nervous. "We'll lose water if the storm knocks out the power?"

Weston turns to face me, his confident smile shining. "Don't get ahead of yourself, OK? We're going to be back on the mainland before that storm hits."

"*If* that pilot comes back."

"He's coming back, Tori. He has no reason not to."

"The storm," I say, pointing my finger at the huge window and the purple clouds.

"So," Weston says. "That insecure girl is still in there, huh? Still a worrier, are you?"

"Fuck you." But my retort is weak and I know he sees it. I don't like the thought of losing power. I hate it when I'm away from the city. It freaks me out for more reasons than I care to remember at the moment. But the thought of being on this tiny island in the middle of the sea in the black of night with no power, and no water, and no one else besides my ex-boyfriend is a whole other level of freakout.

"He's coming back," Weston repeats.

But I'm not convinced. And now he's got that look on his face. That look he used to save for the moments right before I had a panic attack. That look says, *Get her off that ledge before she jumps.*

"Don't look at me that way," I say, angry. "I'm not that girl anymore, Weston. I don't need your shining knight services these days, so don't throw me those concerned, *She just got on the train to Crazytown* looks."

Weston chuckles and shakes his head. "You want to go back to the beach? Swim or something? Pass our time in paradise by relaxing on the white sand?"

"Do you?" I ask. And then, "I don't have a suit."

Weston takes off his tie and begins unbuttoning his shirt. My eyes open a little wider. I watch every move. The way his fingers flip each button loose. The way his tanned and muscular chest flashes me as the shirt comes apart. That stupid Corporate grin on his face.

I sigh with frustration just as he takes the whole thing off and starts going for his belt.

Will Weston Conrad strip naked to swim?

Oh, yeah. You bet your ass he will. I called him Naked Man back when we were together. He has a thing for it.

"Come on, Tori. Let's swim. You don't need a suit. I've seen your goods."

"First of all," I say, crossing my arms and maintaining eye contact as the pants come down, "I'm not 'goods.' Second of all, I'm not giving you the pleasure of seeing me naked after you've been such an asshole."

"When was I an asshole?"

He's kidding, right? "All the time."

"I'm just truthful, Victoria. You just can't handle the truth."

"I'm tired of fighting—" But I stop talking. Because yeah, he still looks amazing in those black boxer briefs he's partial to.

"Did you miss him?" West asks.

"Who?" I say, forcing myself to look up at his face.

"Naked Man?"

I almost laugh, but catch myself just in time. "Weston—" But before I can get anything else out, he's crossing the floor, I'm backing up, my hands are up, warning him to stay away, and I bump into the couch and fall back.

He stops in front of me, his goddamned bulge staring me in the face.

At least he's not hard.

Ooops. Spoke too soon.

"Weston, stop it."

"Come on," he says, extending his hand. "We're going to the beach."

"I'm not getting naked with you."

"I don't need you naked. Your fucking skirt is so short you could wade in up to your thighs." He shakes his hand at me, urging. "Come on."

I close my eyes so I can stop staring at the bulge, stop imagining his hard cock and all the ways I've been intimate with it in the past, and take his hand, letting him pull me to my feet. His arm slips around my back and he pulls me into his chest. God, I can feel his fucking dick against my hips.

"Victoria," he says in my ear. "You've missed me," he says, switching to the other one.

I wait for what comes next. It's a thing he always did with me when I was on the verge of something. Panic, or sadness, or whatever comes with all the things we went through.

He would stand behind me, both hands squeezing my shoulders. His mouth would go to work on my earlobe, and my neck, and my mouth. Then his fingers would dip down into my bra to squeeze my breasts and pinch my nipples.

We'd always have sex after that. Always. It drove me crazy.

But before I can say anything—*No, we're not doing that,* or, *Back off, mister, I'm not yours*—he backs away and he's heading for the door, tugging me along.

I sigh, missing his attention so much in that unused moment.

Outside it's got to be ten degrees warmer than it was when we first got here. Blazing hot. The house is not cool, not by any means. But it's tolerable. Outside, the fact that I'm in the tropics hits me in the face with the hot wind.

This cay, and all the other cays that I can see as we walk the ridge leading back to the beach, is about a mile long and half a mile wide. There are few smaller ones close by. Just sandbars sticking up from the sea, really. They don't count. But the biggest one is a couple miles to the south. It looks like it should be inhabited. But from here I can't tell. Most of the interior of the island is trees and brush.

West and I came to the Exuma Islands several years ago, but we stayed at a resort on Great Exuma and chartered a boat. This is nothing like that. Yes, it's stunning as far as the view goes. The beaches are all pristine white sand. The ocean is too many shades of blue, and green, and turquoise to name, and the palm trees are perfect. But the isolation... I'm OK for a few hours. A day is fine. But the thought of getting stuck here...

Well... I don't do alone very well. Not in isolation. I live in my building in the city. And there's so many other people living in that building with me, I don't ever feel alone. Plus, the city is filled with millions of people. Granted, most of them would not give a fuck if you were being stabbed to death on the sidewalk even if they were standing six feet away. But they're there. And not all of them are bad. Someone is always there to help if I need it. I can always call 911.

Here there is no one but us. And while I know Weston would never hurt me, it's the thought of *being hurt* that frightens me more. The thought of being hurt and being alone when it happens.

That fear consumed me when I was younger. It almost ate me up.

And Weston Conrad's perfectly toned ass isn't enough to stop me from worrying about it as I watch him out in front, eager to get to the beach. When we get back to the ridge near where the pilot dropped us off he jogs down the bank and dives into the small waves.

I look over my shoulder to the north. The purple clouds are still far away. The ocean seems calm and the wind is not crazy.

But those clouds…

"Come in!" West calls. "Stop looking at the sky and come in. It's fucking amazing, Victoria. It's warm and perfect."

That pilot is coming back. I know it. We were friendly on the flight down here. He was chatty and happy. There has to be some kind of logical mistake.

I walk down towards the beach and take a seat in the sand. West is smiling at me, shading his eyes.

"Maybe whatever was going down on this island was cancelled due to weather, West? Do you think that's why there's no one here?"

"He's coming back, Tori. Just relax. Come in the water and have a good time. I'm sure you could use a nice vacation. Think of it as a one-day vacation."

There is no logical reason for that pilot to *not* come back. If there was a storm coming here he'd know about it. He'd have warned us. Isn't that part of his job?

We don't even have food. And if the power goes out we won't have water, either. Hell, who knows how much water is even available now?

"Tori," West says, walking out of the water. At least his hard-on is gone.

"What?" I say, not looking up to meet his eyes.

"It's fine," he says, standing over me. "Just... come in the water and swim with me. It's fine."

"I don't want to get my clothes wet. I love this shirt."

West grabs my arm and pulls me to my feet. "I love it too. So just take it off and... and come have some fun."

CHAPTER TEN

WESTON

Victoria Arias is… complicated.

Everything about her is complex and convoluted. She's a maze of emotions and a labyrinth of feelings that requires careful navigation or the wild comes out and can't be put back.

"Tori," I say again when she ignores me. She's thinking about those clouds. Why the fuck did I even mention it?

When she stays lost in her head I just start unbuttoning her shirt myself.

"West," she says, both her small hands clamping over mine.

"Don't think about it," I say.

She takes a deep breath and looks up at me. Her violet eyes are so stunning, I want to get lost in them. Her lips are beautiful. Plump and luscious. And her skin is smooth and perfect. She reminds me so much of the girl I met that first day we spent together. Not the girl I met the night before when I was struggling with so many things and she was weighing her options.

The night girl and the day girl are two different people.

The night girl is strong, and resilient, and fearless. But the girl in the daylight is everything opposite of that. She is scared, and vulnerable, and weak.

The first night we met we sat together under those two trees in front of the administration building. Singing. God, was I really that dramatic back then?

It was a bad night for me. One of the worst in my life. Until, of course, two days later when life just went off the rails.

Tori was there through the whole thing. Our worlds fell apart together.

"I feel like…" She doesn't finish, but she doesn't need to. I can practically hear her heart beating faster.

Even with all her checks-and-balance tendencies, Victoria Arias is quick to come undone. There is a wildness inside her which cannot be tamed. She craves control because when she feels out of control the world had better watch out. And when she gets scared… well, that wild girl turns feral in all the wrong ways.

"It's an afternoon, Tori," I say. "One afternoon in paradise with an old friend. Nothing more, nothing less. That's all this is."

"But—"

I place my fingers over her lips and stop her words. "Just come swim. There's nothing we can do about it but adapt."

"I can adapt," she says, trying to sound confident.

But she can't adapt. She's never been one of those malleable people, one of those girls who goes with the flow. She *is* the flow. She is a current of electricity. She's dangerous and life-saving at the same time.

"I know," I lie to her. She needs the lie. Because if we do get stuck here she will panic. And I don't ever want to see that panic in her eyes again. The whole time we were together I tried to make it go away. I tried to force it out of her like a priest exorcising a demon. Will it with words, and actions that spoke louder.

And it never helped. People are a product of their experiences and the things Victoria had to endure happened long before I met her. And after dating her on and off for years... after chasing those demons away more times than I can count... I came to the conclusion that she doesn't want my help. She wants to do it all on her own.

And that was that. Especially after that contract she stole. Did it ever occur to her that stealing my seven-million-dollar deal was the same thing as taking the money I've been offering her since my business took off?

No.

And that is just stupid.

So I left.

I can't make her want me. I can't make her accept my help, or my protection, or my promises. I can't make her think I'm good for her. I've tried, believe me, I've tried.

And I'm not about to try again. I'm not stepping into that thankless role again. What I'm doing now is being selfish. I want to get through this day with her and then walk out the same way I did when we finally broke up for good.

I got the message loud and clear that night. She doesn't need me.

"You're good at adapting," I say, continuing the lie. "So let's just adapt to the fact that they changed the location of the retreat and live this day to the fullest. How about that?"

Victoria stops staring at her hand, still clamped onto mine, which is still about to unbutton her shirt and take it off. She looks up.

God, those fucking eyes. I can only imagine all the men who have looked into them and gotten lost. It doesn't make me jealous, it makes me angry.

"OK?" I ask, trying not to see what's behind the violet. I begin to unbutton her shirt again and this time, even though one hand is still on mine, she doesn't stop me. She holds on to me until her shirt is open and her lavender bra is the only thing between us.

I ease it over her shoulders and let it float to the sand, then reach around her back and unzip her skirt. She doesn't fight me at all this time, just lets me wiggle it over her hips and steps out once it too falls to the sand.

"The water is warm," I say, taking her hand and leading her down the beach. "And look at all the fish, Tori."

She's looking, concentrating really hard on the little flashes of color underneath the turquoise blue water. "Too bad we don't have snorkel gear," she says, as we enter the water and it splashes her legs.

"I bet that house has something. We can look later if we want. Come on," I say, tugging her deeper into the ocean. "Let's swim to that sandbar that thinks it's an island. There's a tree for shade. We can just relax out there for a little bit and I'll catch us something to eat."

"Please," she laughs. Then she squeals and jumps as the waves splash her belly and chest. "I can't even picture you catching us a fish."

"Well, maybe you didn't know this, but I worked on a boat setting lobster traps when I was a kid. I can catch us dinner, Tori. Don't you worry."

She laughs as we begin to swim. "Why do I have a hard time picturing you working for a living?"

"Shit," I say, spitting out some salt water. "What do you think I do all day? Sit on my ass and plan my tee times?"

"I mean real work, Weston. Like… hard work. Not desk stuff."

"Hmmm." She has no idea who I am. It would hurt, but I can't blame her. I never told her who I really am. "Just wait and see," I say. "We're gonna be eating good this afternoon."

She stays silent after that and we just concentrate on swimming out to the sandbar. I let her get there first so I can watch her walk out of the water. Her panties perfectly match her lavender bra and stick to her ass, which makes me have to close my eyes to stop imagining all the ways I'd like to fuck her again.

It's not good to start getting ideas, Weston. Just one day and then she's gone.

Victoria drops to her knees on the pristine white sand and then turns over and lies back, her hand coming up to her eyes to shield them from the sun.

It's her turn to watch me come out of the water. She doesn't hide this fact, either. Just stares at my chest, lingering there for a second before dropping down to my dick.

"Don't get any ideas," I say.

"About what?" she says, annoyed.

"I see that look on your face. You're wondering if my dick is still big."

Tori laughs and turns over on her stomach, her face propped up on her forearms.

I drop down next to her. Not too close. Because seriously, I can't fuck this girl today. I can't. It took me months to get over her. Probably close to a year to stop wanting her. And it's just one day. We're on some kind of break right now, but the reality is, we're trying for the same contract and I'm not gonna let her have it. Because if she gets it—if she takes that contract from me—my world as I know it ceases to exist. I can't let that happen. When we get back to the mainland I'm calling Mysterious and getting another location on Wallace.

I will have this shit wrapped up before midnight.

CHAPTER ELEVEN

VICTORIA

Why him? That's all I've been asking myself the whole swim over to the sandbar. Why did I have to get stuck on a deserted island with Weston Conrad?

I can say no to anyone. I'm good at it, actually. No is my favorite word these days. *No, I can't pay you, I'm broke. No, I don't want to date you, I'm celibate. No, you can't have my services for free, I have mouths to feed. No, there's no candy before bed, it will rot your teeth. And no, you can't stay out after dark because that's the law of moms everywhere.*

I have no on the tip of my tongue at all times. I hardly ever say yes. And if I was smart, I'd have said no yesterday when that stupid call came in. No, I will not play your little game and no, I will not try for this contract.

I might want West to think I've got a chance to beat him out of this little contest we find ourselves in, but the truth is, he *will* win. He always wins. I can't compete with him. These legs are not long enough, my skirt is not short enough, and my tits are not big enough to convince anyone to choose me over Weston Conrad. He has all the resources. He has all the contacts. And most of all, he has the reputation and power. Isn't that what they look for in people to do business with? Power?

I can't get enough of it to make things favor me. Or hell, enough to even the playing field.

It's hard to be a woman in business. People don't see

me as powerful, even though I am. I have quite a bit of power in certain ways.

It's just not enough compared to big, bad Mr. Corporate.

We will get off this island this evening and he will go one way and I will go the other and by the end of the night, he will have what he came for.

I'll be left with nothing. That's how it always ends. I'm used to it.

Maybe I had an opportunity before this little deserted island debacle. But that's if, and only if, I could get to Wallace first. Or simultaneously, at the very least. I won't get to him first now. He's not here. And West and I won't get to him at the same time either, because he has aces up his sleeve and I've got nothing but low-value cards with no chance at a straight flush.

"Hey," Weston says. He's lying on the sand next to me. Not touching me, of course. He's keeping his distance, I can tell. And the whole Naked Man joke earlier isn't enough to convince me I'm wrong. He saw the fear in my eyes. He could see that all the thoughts I was trying to keep at bay were whirling around in my head. He was talking me down off that ledge I often find myself on.

"What?" I sigh.

"Do you really think I'm not a worker?"

"What?" I have to laugh. "Why?"

He shrugs. "It bugs me."

"You and I come from very different families, Weston. It's no secret that I was brought up one way and you were brought up another."

78

"You're so sure of that?"

"Should I not be?"

"I'm just curious why you think it."

"Maybe because your parents have a house on Cape Cod? Or you drove a hundred-thousand-dollar car in college. Or the fact that you were at Brown and not on a scholarship."

"So that makes me lazy."

"I never said you were lazy. I just can't picture you working on a boat for money."

"How do you picture me working for money as a teenager?"

"I don't." I laugh. "I can't imagine why you'd need to work as a teen. Your father doesn't seem like the I'm-gonna-make-an-example-out-of-you type."

"He's not."

"So why work?"

"I worked for the same reasons everyone works. To make money."

"But you didn't need money, Weston. There's a big difference in working for a new custom paint job for your Aston Martin and what most people work for."

"That's not why I worked."

"Whatever. You know what I was working for when I was a kid, West?"

"Food," he and I say at the same time. "I've heard it all before, Victoria. I don't need a reminder. And I think lobster harvesting counts as working for food as well."

"Well, I can't wait to see this." I sigh. "I'm not going to turn down your offer of fresh lobster because I have principles."

"I have principles too. You say that like you're the only person alive with a moral compass."

"I'm one of the few."

"And yet you wore that skimpy skirt and low-cut shirt today. You were gonna bait Wallace with your clothes and your body. I'd have to call those morals questionable."

I get up and kick sand on his chest. "Fuck you."

West grabs my foot and I go down on my knees in the sand. "There's nowhere to walk to, Tori. So get off your high horse and just stick it out for once."

"God, I hate you." How dare he. I kick and he lets go, avoiding my punishment. "I'm swimming back. You can do whatever you want with the lobsters."

I crawl out of his reach and then get to my feet and walk back into the water. I'm not a strong swimmer, but the ocean is smooth, clear, and shallow over here. Our island is only about a hundred yards away, so I know I'll be OK alone.

Alone.

God, I hate that word.

I look over my shoulder, my heart fluttering for a brief second—hoping for an equally brief interval that West will follow me. But he doesn't. His eyes are closed and he's lying there in the sun like he hasn't got a care in the world.

Suck it up and swim, Victoria.

So I do. And it's uneventful even though my mind is a whirlwind of catastrophes waiting to happen. Sharks, or eels, or hell, whatever there is in this water that can hurt me. My imagination is in overdrive and I picture it all in my head until my feet hit the sand on the opposite beach and I walk out, shooting a look over my shoulder at Weston.

He's swimming after me.

Which makes me smile. Ha. It feels like a win.

I shade my eyes as I watch him. He's got his face buried in the water as his long arms reach through the small waves with as much effort as a fish. Then he dives under and disappears.

I start counting. One-one-thousand, two-one-thousand, three-one-thousand, four-one-thousand… and when I get to ten-one thousand I start yelling his name.

"Weston?" I scream, running back towards the water. I stand on the edge, wondering what to do. There's no one here to help me. My heart starts racing the second that thought enters my head. "Weston?"

I imagine his body floating up… or never appearing again. What if that pilot comes and West is gone? What will I tell his mom and dad? I will have to admit that I was here and I did nothing. And I can just see Mr. Conrad. I can almost hear his accusations. *He was always there for you, Tori. Why weren't you there for him?*

"West!" I scream it louder as I run into the waves. I dive under and almost choke on the salty sea as it pushes its way into my mouth, but recover and surface, drawing in a long breath of air.

West is looking at me, the biggest smile on his face. "Did you just… try to save me?" He laughs.

I open my palm and splash water in his face. "Fuck you! Just fuck you! I was calling your name! You were under for like twenty seconds!"

"Not twenty seconds." He chuckles, wiping the water out of his eyes. "Jesus Christ, Tori. I told you I worked in the ocean as a teenager. I can hold my breath for a minute at least. You don't need to freak out about a twenty-second dive." His hand comes out of the water and he's holding up a lobster. "They live in the cracks between the rocks. These warm-water lobsters aren't as good as the ones up in New England, but they'll do."

I let out a long breath and mutter, "I hate you."

"I know," he says, good-naturedly. "But I'll still take care of you if you're alone, Tori. Don't worry. I won't check out until you're safe."

He swims past me and covers the short distance back to the beach before I can even work out what those words might actually mean.

He's mad, I know that. Maybe because I thought he was lying about the lobsters. Or maybe because I pretty much accused him of being lazy. Or maybe because I don't think I'm safe here on this island and he's taking it personally.

It doesn't matter. Any and all of those reasons are good ones. And it just shows me that I was right to walk out on him three and a half years ago. I was right. I know what's coming. An entire day filled with Weston Conrad's caveman protection. Hours and hours of him insinuating that I'm helpless, or careless, or stupid. Or all of the above.

West is already walking back towards the little house when I get back to the beach. I pick up my shirt and skirt and carry them as I follow the little footpath.

My eyes are on West's back, his rippled muscles and his broad shoulders.

I have lots of reasons to hate him. I do. But only one matters. Weston Conrad is sexist.

He believes women should stay home and raise children. Not have both a career and children, mind you. But literally stay the hell home and raise children. When he told me that a few weeks into our relationship I thought he was kidding. I actually laughed.

But he was serious. And we fought over this all the time.

If West and I had stayed together I'd be a stay-at-home mother. My life would consist of children, having dinner on the table when he got home from work, and running the household.

This wasn't a guess on my part. I'm not making this up. He said this to me. Face to face, one year into our relationship. We had been fighting more and more about where we were heading as a couple. West was becoming distant and I challenged him. Accused him of cheating.

He denied it—I believed him—and said this was his major hang-up with me.

He wants a wife who is comfortable in her role.

Role.

That word still burns me. The moment that came out of his mouth I seethed. I saw red. I threw plates at him. I threw my stilettos at him.

I never actually *hit* him with the plates or shoes. But I did dump all his shit out on the lawn and make a scene in front of the neighbors.

83

The cops came—Weston was pissed off over that. And I don't blame him. Those charges were still hanging over him at that point in time. He was taken to the station and questioned. I had to go down there and admit that it was mostly me making the scene. They wrote me a ticket.

God.

This is what happens when Weston Conrad and I spend too much time together.

I'm not interested in fulfilling anyone's prescribed role. I'm not interested in being someone's subordinate. I'm not interested in marrying my boss. *I'm* the boss. I have my own company, failing though it is. I'm the boss. Not him. And I won't get caught in his trap again. Not even for an afternoon.

I'll keep you safe, Tori. I won't ever let anyone hurt you. You will never have to worry about that kind of stuff from me.

No. He's right. I wouldn't. Because I'd be his little trophy wife. Locked away in some fancy house with no real friends, only the awful girls from the country club to keep my mind off going mad. I don't even know girls from a country club, but I'm assuming they'd all be good little Stepford Wives as well.

I'd rather die than live that life.

Die.

CHAPTER TWELVE
WESTON

God, why do I let her get to me so badly? Why do I care that she thinks I'm some privileged rich bastard who needs to get his way at every turn in order to be happy?

I'm not like that.

I sigh as I pull open cupboards looking for a pot to boil the lobster in. There's no oven here, otherwise I'd just broil it. I find one in the last cupboard and drop it into the stainless-steel sink with a loud clang, then watch it fill up with water as I study the cuts on my hand from the lobster's spines.

The pain that comes with my prize feels good. It takes me back to all those summers I spent on the boat. I was only a little kid when I started harvesting lobsters and I didn't have a boat. No one hires a kid that age to help with their business. So I caught my own lobsters. I got busted for selling them the second summer. I didn't know it was illegal. I didn't even have a permit that first summer. I didn't know anything about harvesting lobsters. I just got lucky.

But the second summer I got caught and had to appear in court. My father was pissed off. But the judge liked my entrepreneurial spirit and told me to go find a guy named Rusty down on the docks near my house.

So I did. And I got hired. I was in charge of icing the lobsters once they were caught. I'd take the catch and dump it in the huge chests filled with ice water, dunking them until they stopped moving.

My hands were filled with the little pricks from spines that summer. Someone gave me a pair of gloves a few weeks in, but by then I'd learned how to avoid the spines and I didn't care for the gloves in the hot summer sun.

I liked that job. I liked the way it made me feel. Like I was independent. Like I was in control of my future. I still like work for those two reasons.

I spent seven summers working on that boat. Right up until I went away to boarding school in the eighth grade.

Victoria comes into the house, clutching her silk shirt and her short skirt in her hands. She looks at me, then my hands, which are still out in front of me, palms up.

"You're bleeding," she says.

"Yeah." I turn back to the pot and shut off the water. "They have spines. But don't feel bad for me, Victoria. I'm sure in your head I probably deserve the pain."

"Don't be a dick. Please. If we have to spend this day together, just don't be a dick."

"How am I being a dick?" I ask as I place the pot of water on the stovetop. "I'm not doing anything but being nice."

"I don't want to hear your pitch, Weston."

"I have no clue what you're talking about." I go looking for salt to put into the water but come up empty.

"'I won't check out until you're safe, Tori,'" she says, mimicking my voice in an unflattering way. "You never checked in, Weston Conrad. So you can't check out."

"OK," I say back. It's no use having a domestic fight

86

with a woman like Victoria Arias. I cannot win. Ever.

She huffs some air and mutters, "Patronizing asshole," just under her breath.

I choose to ignore that. I will not take her bait. I will not be the lobster in her pot. I will not have this fight again. Not ever. I'm so sick of it. And I probably should've given her this contract. Bowed out of the competition and just given it to her. Then I'd be somewhere else right now and we wouldn't be stuck here together all day.

But I can't afford to give it to her. She has no idea what losing this contract would mean to me. None.

Victoria disappears in the bathroom and the next time I look over at the pot, the water is boiling. So I check my watch and take this opportunity to plunge the lobster in the water headfirst, capping it tightly with a lid to avoid any splashing. I should've gotten two, I realize. One is not really enough to feed us both. But Victoria was screaming my name like she was in a panic when I came up and I forgot to go back down. It's just a snack, right? That pilot will come back in a few hours. We will get through this afternoon of uncomfortableness. And I can grab dinner after I get back to my hotel and reassess my strategy.

I could just ignore Victoria for the rest of the day. Let her spew her shit. But I'm not going to. Her insults are... well, insulting. So fuck her.

"Is it almost done?" Tori asks, reappearing. I check my watch and realize five minutes have gone by.

"We don't have any butter, or salt, or pepper, or whatever you like on your lobster. So yeah, I guess it's done."

87

She watches me as I take it out and do my best to cut open the shell with the dull knife I find in a drawer. Once the meat is exposed, I hand her a fork and she digs in.

"Aren't you going to eat?" Tori asks, when I don't join her.

"I'll go back and get another one later. I'm not hungry."

"Gotta feed the women first, right?" she says, the sarcasm not absent from her tone.

I look at her for a moment. A long moment.

"What?" she asks. "That's how you operate, right? Mr. Big Strong Man has to protect the weak little woman?"

"You know," I say, "I get why you're like this. I probably understand it better than most. But you're a real bitch, Tori. I don't know why you think I'm such an asshole, but that's your prerogative. So you're welcome to your opinion."

"Come off it, Weston. You know you hate that I'm here. That I'm making you fight for something you thought was owed to you. You know it burns your ass to have to compete with a woman."

"Right. I got all that the last time we fought. I'm a pig, you're a victim—"

"Fuck you," she says, almost choking on her bite of lobster.

"Hey, you're the one who wants it to be this way."

"You're the one who said I'd be your little stay-at-home wife if we continued to date."

"So?"

"So?" she sneers at me. "So I don't want to be someone's property."

"I called you property?" I laugh out loud, a real nice guffaw that echoes off the high ceiling. "I offered to take care of you and you practically spit in my face."

"I don't want to be taken care of," she snaps.

"Yeah, because you do such a good job taking care of yourself."

She slaps my face. Hard. She goes to do it again, but I grab her wrist. She tries to knee me in the balls, but I turn to the side, grab her other wrist, then walk her over to the couch and throw her down.

"Don't fuck with me, Tori. I'm not gonna put up with your shit. I'm not your fucking punching bag anymore, you understand?"

The tears well up in her eyes almost immediately. Not because I hurt her when I grabbed her wrists. Because I hurt her with my words. "I hate you," she whispers.

"I know," I say in a low voice. "You've made that abundantly clear over the years."

I walk to the door and I'm just about to pull it open when she says, "You loved it, didn't you?"

I don't even turn to look at her. "I loved *what?*" My shoulders tense up. My jaw clenches as one fist balls up hard and the other grips the door knob like I want to rip it off.

"The fact that you were right and I was wrong. You loved it because it fit into your stupid worldview that I couldn't take care of myself."

Now I do turn. Because I'm *pissed.* I point my finger at her face, look her straight in the eyes and say, "If you really think that I felt... vindicated, or triumphant, or whatever the hell it is you think I felt when I found out you got attacked, well"—I force a mean laugh—"then I'll just take this opportunity to walk out of your life and never come back."

So I do. I walk out, slam the door behind me, and keep going until I get to the beach.

I know there's an island with more structures than this one a couple miles away. There's three or four little cays between this one and that one, so it's not even going to be hard for a guy like me who grew up in the ocean.

I'm going to abandon Victoria Arias.

Leave her here to fend for herself, just like she wants.

Who am I kidding?

That bitch. She has a fucking hold on me that I can't seem to cut.

And besides, I reason, looking to the north, it's starting to rain and maybe that big storm isn't here yet, but the front of it is. And just as I think that thought, the sky opens up, the rain pelting me in the face.

Bitch.

I *know* damn well I'd never leave her alone, even if she doesn't.

CHAPTER THIRTEEN

VICTORIA

I'm still reciting all the reasons why forcing Weston Conrad out of this house was a good idea when the lightning strikes and the whole place shakes so hard, I scream.

I'm still screaming when West comes back yelling, "Holy fuck! Are you OK?"

"What happened?" I have to hold onto the kitchen counter because my legs are shaking.

"The fucking house just got hit with lightning! I saw it. That antenna isn't an antenna. It must be a lightning rod."

"Oh, my God. It's raining." No, not raining. It's pouring outside.

"I guess it's a good thing I didn't try to swim to the other island," West says.

"You were going to swim away?" That selfish fucker!

"Isn't that what you—"

But another lightning strike booms through the house and I startle again. "How many times can it strike that rod before it sends us up in flames?"

"Tons," West says, as he walks over to me and pulls me into his chest. "Like thousands of times, Victoria. Really. It's fine. It's just a good thing they have it, right? Otherwise the roof would be on fire right now."

I pry West's arms from around me and walk over to the window. That mass of purple clouds is still off in the distance, but that's not stopping the rolling thunderheads directly above us from doing their thing. What are the chances that the pilot will come back for us now?

I can't even go there.

"The power is out," West says, flicking the light switch on and off.

"We're stuck," I say quietly. "For real. We're stuck out here. What if that pilot guy thinks we got a ride home from someone else and just forgets about us?"

"Maybe the storm will blow over in a couple hours?" West says quickly. "Vlad will call the coastguard... or whoever the coastguard is in the Bahamas. Or our coastguard will call their coastguard and someone will come looking. Don't worry. We're not stuck."

"I'm not going to flip out, West. So you can just stop lying to me."

"Look, Victoria"—West laughs—"you flip out on a regular basis over the stupidest things. Do you really think I'll believe that this won't bring back your panic attacks?"

"Why are you so mean?" Really? Why does he have to bring that up every time something goes wrong?

West looks at the door and I realize he wants to walk out again. But he can't. He's stuck here with me. That's what he's thinking.

And can I blame him? I *am* a basket case when it comes to certain things. I have very good reasons for my panic attacks and I have very good reasons why I hate being alone. But I can be... a little... high-strung in certain situations.

I think I'm holding it together pretty well right now.

Until I realize my breathing is picking up and I'm sweating like crazy. The humidity in this house just went up like a thousand percent, so maybe that's all it is?

But my pulse is racing and my palms are sweaty, and then my head is pounding to the beat of my heart and things go blurry...

"Victoria," West says into my ear. "Listen to me," he says in the other one. I wait for him to squeeze my shoulders the way he used to back when we were together. I want it. I want him to do all those familiar things that comfort me. I want him to slip his fingers into my bra and squeeze my breasts while his mouth goes to work on my neck, and my earlobe, and my lips.

I'm certain that he will not continue, but I'm wrong. He cups the round muscle of my shoulders and kisses the soft skin of my ear.

"What?" I say. It comes out as a whisper, filled with so many things like want, and need, and desperation.

"We're fine. I'm here. You're not alone. People know where we are. And even if we do get stuck on this island tonight, we'll be back on the mainland by tomorrow. Do you understand?"

His hands lift off my shoulders, which just makes me want him more. "I want to believe you."

"So just believe."

I turn to face him, because if I don't he's going to back off and this moment will pass. I don't want the moment to pass. And not because of my racing heart or my spinning world. I don't want him to back off because... his *touch*. God, his fucking touch. It's something I've

93

missed so much and I didn't even know it until this moment right now. "Why is it always one or the other with us, West?"

He looks down at me and smiles. His hands come up to my neck and he gently drags my long dark hair off my shoulders, arranging it the way he likes to do when he's getting ready to kiss me. "Why are we so hot and cold? Why are we so on and off? So all or nothing? Friends or enemies?"

"Yeah," I say, placing my hands on his biceps. He's always been cut. His muscles have always been taut and his body lean. I stare at his eyes. Brown. They are brown, like his hair. So *nondescript* when I say the word in my head. But nothing about Weston Conrad is ordinary. His face is model-perfect, his jawline square and strong.

Even the stubble on his cheeks and chin is the perfect length to drive me crazy. I have felt that stubble between my legs more times than I can count. I have placed my hands on it to comfort him during those two years he was accused of things I know he's never been capable of.

I know him.

He knows me.

"Because we're equals, Victoria. You've never understood that. You've always thought I wanted to control you and I don't."

"Equals, huh?" I ask.

"On every level."

I sigh and remove my hands from his arms. Back away. Because he's pulling me into his spell. He's charming me with his words and promises, and I know they are lies. If we're equals then why does he have so many rules? If we're equals, then why don't I know everything about his past? He's told me some, but not all. He gets this vacant look on his face, like talk-time is over, whenever I push too far.

So we're not equals.

He wants the power and he only sticks around if he has it.

CHAPTER FOURTEEN
WESTON

"Hey," I say, reaching for her before she gets away. "Come here."

Victoria puts her hands up to my chest like she's going to push me back. But when they connect with my skin, they don't have any force to them. They rest there, flat on my pecs, fingers splayed. Her head bows like she's embarrassed and I take that opportunity to pull her into a hug.

God, the way she smells almost drives me insane. When she doesn't resist and places her head on my shoulder, I bury my face in her hair.

"I've missed this," I say.

She sighs. I know she's missed this too, but there are so many things between us. The sex was never the problem. It was our opinions and ideas about the future that came between us. Not to mention all her pushy questions about my past. Sometimes a guy just needs a few secrets. Why is that so hard to understand?

I'm just about to pull away, back off and give her some room, when she turns her head and kisses me on the cheek.

I turn my head too, just enough to find her lips. And then... and then... my hands have her face and my mouth has her tongue. Her hips push into mine and I walk her backwards a few steps, until she reaches the couch and has to sit.

I drop to my knees, my fingers eager to slip under the waistband of her panties. And then I am pulling them down her long—so fucking long—legs. I toss them over my shoulder as I lick my lips and stare into her eyes. She wants to close them, I can tell. She wants to close her eyes, and lean her head back, and let me lick her pussy until she comes.

But she wants to watch too. Her fingers thread through my hair, urging me to keep going. So I open her legs, lift her knees up towards her tits, and sweep my tongue up and down her pussy until she lets go of my hair and digs her fingernails into my shoulders.

"Keep going?" I ask. "Or am I smothering you with my expectations?"

"Shut up," she says, digging her nails into my skin. "Just shut up."

I laugh as I dip back down between her legs. "Tori," I murmur as I kiss her wet folds.

"No talking, West. I'm serious."

"Tori," I say again. "Tell me you missed this or I'm going to stop."

Her thighs squeeze together, clamping down on my face, and she bucks her hips, trying to get more friction, more tongue, more everything. "You're not stopping. You're just trying to be an asshole."

"Say it," I choke when she squeezes tighter. I lick her, flicking my tongue across her clit until her grip on my face loosens. "Say it or I'll rub my stubble all over the inside of your thighs."

Her foot smacks my lower back. "Why are you such a jerk? Stop talking and start licking, Mr. Conrad. Or I'm going to get up and walk away."

"No, you won't," I say, reaching up with one hand to squeeze her tits as my other hand dips between her legs. I push a finger inside her, making her moan. "I know every way to make you melt, Miss Arias. So don't challenge me during sex."

"We're not having sex. Because you're still *talking.*"

I pinch her nipple and her whole back arches.

"Say it," I demand, lifting my head up and withdrawing my finger. "Say it or we'll stop."

"Oh, for fuck's sake, Weston. Just shut the hell up!"

I pull back and let her legs drop.

"Don't," she says, pointing her finger at my face.

I smack it away. "What have I told you about that fucking finger?"

"I swear to God, West. If you started this to piss me off, I will never let you touch me again."

"Let me?" I laugh. "Shit."

"Yes, let you. I'm the one in control—"

She stops talking, because I've got my dick out and I'm thrusting it inside her before she can finish.

"Let me, Miss Arias? Say no. I dare you." I pump her hard three times. I lift her knees back up and lean my chest down onto her full breasts and kiss her mouth.

"I will," she whispers, her words nothing but a soft breath that passes between our lips.

"I dare you," I whisper back. "I dare you to tell me no. Because I'll stop. Don't think I won't."

She moans as I continue to fuck her.

"Say it," I command. "Last chance, wild thing. Last chance—"

She slaps my face, gets her foot in between herself and my chest, and kicks. I go flying back on my ass, my hands reaching out to prevent my head from hitting the hard floor, and she bolts.

I'm up, chasing her, before she even makes it to the kitchen. I grab her around her waist and lift her off her feet, planting her ass on the counter as she squeals.

She slaps my face again, but I grab both her wrists and hold them tightly together.

"Say it, Victoria. I mean it."

"I don't have to say it."

"Yeah, you do."

"I don't have to, Weston. Because… Because…" Then she deflates and softens. Her head rests on my shoulder and she whispers, "Because you know you're the only man I get off for."

Oh, I'm not even going there. If I start thinking about how many men she's fucked since we broke up, I might kill someone.

"So," she continues, "every time you make me come I'm saying it, West. Can't you just be happy with that?"

I let her win because that's the kind of guy I am.

Generous. Magnanimous. Benevolent.

And I want to fuck her hard right now.

So I lift her up and carry her back to the couch, placing her in front of me the same way she was before she ran. The couch is the perfect height for me to lick her pussy. It's the perfect height for me to ram her good while I'm on my knees. It's the perfect mixture of soft and hard, comfortable and cramped.

Just like us.

Victoria is all feminine fluff and I am every bit the dominant male she hates.

"I have the power here," I say, shoving my cock inside her again.

"Shut up," she moans. Her hands grip my neck and pull me close. Her mouth finds mine and we kiss it all away.

All the hate and all the fear goes out of her in an instant.

But I won't stop there. I like it the way I like it. And she can protest all she wants, she likes it that way too or she wouldn't be participating. So I say, "Tell me you missed this, Victoria. Or I'll bring you to the edge of ecstasy and leave you hanging."

"Whatever," she moans, bucking her back up, trying to stimulate her clit with friction against my lower stomach. "I missed you."

I pull out and come on her stomach, laughing.

"You asshole! You better not—"

"I'm sorry," I say, trying to stop the chuckles. "I'm sorry. I'll make it up to you. But all I wanted you to say is that you missed the sex. And you said you missed *me*. Which is a hundred times better."

She starts kicking again, but I grab her leg with one hand and reach for her panties with the other. I wipe them

101

across her stomach to clean her up, then toss them aside. "Stop," I command quietly. "I'm gonna make you come now, so stop."

CHAPTER FIFTEEN

VICTORIA

He infuriates me. I want to kick him away and slap his face.

But his tongue, and his hands, and his promise make me still. I don't even speak. I can't speak because his face is buried between my legs and I can't even be mad at him. He's making me feel way too good to be mad at him.

I moan.

He sweeps his tongue around in tight circles. His fingers push into me. His other hand is pumping his cock, making himself hard for me again.

"West," I say as my fingers find his hair and I grab fistfuls of it. He doesn't answer me. I shouldn't even want him to answer me. Because that would make him stop and I don't want him to stop. "Don't stop."

I look down between my legs as he looks up, his lips curled into a sly smile, his eyes filled with lust, and mischief, and power.

OK, he wins. I'll give him that. He wins.

I don't even mind that he won. It usually feels good to be next to Weston Conrad while he's winning a fight between us. It usually involves sweating, and writhing, and declarations of love.

I close my eyes and rest my head back. I just enjoy it. His win is my win right now. I let the shuddering pleasure sweep through my body as he works his mouth against my wet pussy. I allow the whole experience to build, moaning as he licks and sucks and then reaches up to squeeze my tits.

Everything is the same as it was.

Everything is completely different.

The whole world ceases to exist and the only thing that matters is him. And us. And now—right now.

"Tori," he murmurs against my clit.

"Oh, God," I say. "Don't start talking now, you idiot."

He pulls his face away and for a moment I have a shock of fear that he will deprive me. Punish me for being rude.

But he doesn't. He pumps his cock one more time, lets me get a good look at it—fully erect and as beautiful as a cock can be—and eases into me so slowly, I have to meet him halfway by lifting my hips.

"Now it's your turn," he says, lowering his chest onto my breasts and kissing my mouth. "God, I've missed you too."

That conversation seems years away from this moment. I can't even recall why we were fighting or what the stakes were. I can't recall anything but right now. This moment. I am drunk on his dick. I am lost in his world of carnal pleasures. He is the only thing that matters. He is the only thing that has ever mattered—

"Wait," I say, pushing back on his chest, struggling to get him off me. "Wait. Stop."

"What the fuck, Tori?"

He's *not* the only thing that matters. What the hell is wrong with me?

I get a foot between us and he knows what's coming. He tries to get off before I get in position, but he's too late. I flatten my foot on his pecs and—

He goes flying backwards, landing on his ass about four feet away.

"What the fuck?" West yells. "What did I do now?"

I shake myself out of the stupor his cock puts me in and get up, looking around for my clothes. I still have my bra on, and I find my panties covered in semen next to the couch.

"Good God, Weston. Did you have to use my panties as your come rag?"

West is on his feet again, his face filled with anger, and rage, and… regrets. "You're a crazy bitch, you know that?"

"I'm sorry, OK? I'm sorry. It's just… I can't do this with you, Weston. Not now. I have priorities and you're clouding my mind, as usual."

"Clouding…" But he lets it go. Just shakes his head back and walks over to his clothes, picks them up in a whoosh, and goes into the bathroom, slamming the door behind him.

It's then that I realize it's dark. Not, like, for real dark. It cannot be later than two in the afternoon. But it's dark outside. There is a raging storm. The trees near the small house are beating against the windows. Lightning is flashing off in the distance, but at least it's not trying to burn our shelter down.

I slide my skirt up my legs and zip it up in the back, then straighten my bra out. West had pulled the cups down so my tits were pushing up towards my chin. I put the silk shirt on, then take it off again when the heat and humidity inside this room—heat and humidity we surely created during our ten minutes of fun, even though it's got to be from the storm—threatens to suffocate me.

I just take my panties to the sink and—fuck. I can't even waste water washing them. If there's still water in the pipes we'll need it to drink.

I stuff them in my purse just to get them out of sight.

My lobster lunch is cold and rubbery, but I eat half of it anyway. I feel famished, but it's not fair to eat the whole thing since it's the only food we'll likely get today.

I know that pilot isn't coming back. I have a bad feeling about this trip. I have a bad feeling about that phone call I got. I have a bad feeling about why Wallace Arlington isn't here on this island today. I have a bad feeling about Vlad the pilot. That cannot be his real name. No one is called Vlad in the US.

The toilet flushes, audible even over the wind outside. West comes out of the bathroom, still only wearing those hot black boxer briefs and nothing else.

"You flushed the toilet?" I ask.

"Usually that's what you do after you piss, Tori."

"Stop calling me Tori. And I just decided not to wash my panties to conserve water. You don't know how long we'll be here. How dare you use that water—"

"Just shut up, for fuck's sake."

"Oh, fuck you. So I said no. Get over it."

"That's not why I'm pissed."

"Then why?"

He lets out a long breath and walks over to the kitchen to poke the half-eaten lobster with his finger. He does not eat what's left.

"Why?" I ask. "Why are you mad?"

"Forget it," he says, walking over to the door.

"Where are you going? There's a raging storm out there."

"We have to eat and I need to see how much water is left in the catch system." He looks at me with a sad face. I've upset him. And if it isn't because I said no, then what's up with that look? "And the storm is only going to get worse. So might as well do it now."

He opens the door and leaves me there.

CHAPTER SIXTEEN
WESTON

The rain pelts me, and the wind is so strong it feels like little stinging insects. I walk around the building and find the cistern I saw on the walk back from the beach. There has to be water in there. There's nowhere else for water to come from on this island except a rainwater catch system. Even if there isn't much, there will be enough with this storm. But it's better to know how much we have before we start using any more of it.

I climb up the ladder to the elevated tank and spot solar panels on the roof. Two of them are shattered from the lightning. But that's less than half. So hopefully there's some kind of restart button on the AC load controller that will kick the batteries back online.

"What are you doing?" Victoria yells over the wind.

I ignore her. That was a shitty move back inside and I'm quite pissed off at her right now. I get it, we're incompatible. But she's so fucking clueless.

"West!" she yells again as I reach the roof and grab hold of a solar panel to steady myself in the wind. "Weston! Get down, you're going to blow off the roof."

"Go back inside, Victoria. I don't need your nagging right now."

I don't hear her answer, but when I look over my shoulder, she's gone. Good. I've had about enough of her for one day.

I check the wiring of the panels, deduce that the two that were hit have pretty much fucked the system, and give up.

But when I climb down I notice a door on the back of the house.

Bingo. We have a generator.

Whoever built this place thought ahead and had plenty of money. I know how to run this shit—I had a lot of experience dealing with off-grid electricity when I was growing up in Nantucket—so I flip the switch to change the power source and start it up. Lights come on in the room and I notice there's a motion detector for that.

Nice.

But power is really the least of our problems. One half-eaten lobster isn't enough, not even if the pilot manages to come back late tonight. And that's *if* the storm passes.

So I go back in the house to get my shirt and my shoes.

"The power's on," Tori says as I pick up my shirt, slip my feet into my shoes, and head back towards the door. "Where are you going now?"

"Fishing, Victoria. We have to eat something."

"You're fishing with a shirt?"

"Just sit the fuck down and let me handle shit for once."

I slam the door behind me, but it's as anticlimactic as it sounds, because the wind is louder than any noise that door makes.

"West!" Victoria screams, coming out behind me. "Where are you going?"

Goddammit. I forgot she hates to be alone. "Victoria,"

I yell. "Just please, stay inside. I'll be back in a little bit."

"No," she says, defiant. "I'm coming too. I'm not staying there alone."

I know this is a losing battle with her. Alone is something she doesn't do. So I ignore her. Let her follow me. What do I care if she wants to get soaked and cold?

I don't go back to the beach. It's too long a walk in this rain and wind. Instead, I go over to the rocks near the house and carefully make my way down, thankful for the soft Italian leather shoes on my feet that will definitely be ruined in about five seconds.

"West, this is a bad idea." She's so close to me, I'm almost startled.

"Would you get the fuck back? Do you see these waves? Do you see these rocks? Would you like to fall in and be pulverized?"

She looks at me. Hard. Like she wants to tell me where to stick my orders. But then she looks at the rocks and her expression changes. "I don't need to eat. I don't want you to go in there, Weston. I mean it. Get out and come back to the house. Right now."

"No," I say. "Stay here and do not follow me in, no matter what."

I turn away and climb onto the farthest rock. This is her fear talking, not her concern for my welfare. She's afraid if I go in the water I'll never come back out.

And then she'll be alone.

The last thing I hear before I dive into the water is Victoria screaming my name.

111

CHAPTER SEVENTEEN
VICTORIA

He disappears. Dives right between two rocks as waves crash over them. I'm getting sprayed with the leftover mist even though I'm a good ten feet away.

"Weston?" I call out as I try to see below the surface of the water. "West?" It's no use. The water is agitated and murky even though two hours ago it was calm and clear.

I wring my hands and look up at the sky. The rain stings my cheeks and makes me blink. The clouds are gray and black and the purple ones are closer than ever.

That mass of swirling air has to be something bad. Something very, very bad. Like a tropical storm or a hurricane.

Oh, God. What if it's a hurricane?

I look around the island and realize how vulnerable we are. How many feet above sea level does the little house sit? Twenty? Thirty?

We could be swept away. This whole island could be swept away. Already the sandbar we swam out to is gone. The tree is gone too. Jesus Christ. The little tree got swept away! We're totally fucked!

Keep calm, Victoria.

I look back at the spot where West disappeared. He could've been bashed up against the rocks when he dove. He might be down there drowning right now. I'm going to get stuck here all alone. No one will ever come back for me. West will die and I will die and—

He pops up out of the water, gasping for air. But just as I'm about to let the relief wash over me, he dives back down.

"Weston!" I yell. "You asshole!" I'm so mad at him. So fucking mad at him. He's always been this way. Completely oblivious to how his actions affect other people. Does he care I'm up here ready to freak out because he feels the need to play provider? No. He doesn't. He has never cared about anything but his grand plan. He has never cared about anyone but his family.

And those stupid fucking friends of his. Those stupid men who dragged him into all that controversy ten years ago.

The Misters.

I hated them for making him into something he wasn't. Weston Conrad was good before those men in that house made him into this man today. He was good.

I want to cry right now. How the hell did this job I didn't even want turn into a life-or-death situation?

West pops up again and I hold my breath to wait and see if he'll go back under again. But he doesn't.

"I got them," he says, laughing like a boy who has never had a care in the world. What must it be like to be him? So confident, and powerful, and… *happy*.

"I got them." He laughs again. This time he holds up his white dress shirt. He's made it into some kind of catch bag and inside are… things. I guess lobsters or whatever it was he went down there for.

The waves crash over him and slam him into a rock. I gasp, but he ignores it, even though his head is bleeding.

He throws the makeshift sack towards me and I catch it instinctively, but almost drop it when the things inside wriggle and twist.

"If you drop that, Victoria," West says, pulling himself up out of the raging sea, "I will be pissed." He hops from one rock to another until we're on the same one. I look down at his feet. He's lost his shoes and there's blood pouring out of a wound on his ankle. "Come on," he says, grabbing the sack from me. "Let's get inside and dry off."

We are soaked. And the fact that we have no clothes to wear as we get dry doesn't escape either of us.

West is unfazed. He strips out of his boxer briefs and walks around naked like he's some kind of Jungle Boy. He even starts cooking the lobsters. He got two of them this time.

"Tomorrow," he says as I stand in the middle of the room, hugging myself and shivering like crazy, "I'll get us something different."

"W-w-we're going to be here tomorrow?" I ask through my chattering teeth.

"Would you take those fucking clothes off, Victoria? You're soaked. You can't warm up wearing wet clothes."

"You d-d-didn't answer my question."

"Well," West says, looking out the window as he deals with the simplicities of cooking lobster, "it's not looking good, Tori. We have to assume no one is coming until this storm passes. It could be a day or two."

"A day or *two*?" I take a deep breath. "Which do you think?"

"There's no way to tell. Take those fucking clothes off. There have to be towels somewhere. People who put up beach houses with off-grid electricity will definitely have towels."

I look around, still shivering. But he's right. There has to be more to this place. There are two doors we have not checked yet, so I walk over to the one closest to me.

I'm hoping for a bedroom with a nice soft bed when I open it, but no such luck. It's a closet and it does have towels.

"Cool," West says, reaching past me. But he doesn't pick up a towel from one of the shelves. He picks up snorkel gear from the floor. "I'll use this stuff next time. Then I'll be able to see better. The fucking visibility is shit right now."

"Here's a first-aid kit," I say, picking up the little white box with a red cross on it. "For your ankle. And your head."

"I'm fine," he says, walking over to the other door. He grabs the handle and pulls, but... it's locked. "What the fuck? They leave everything unlocked, including the house, but they lock *this* door?"

I've stripped out of my wet clothes, including my bra, and I wrap the towel around me before West can catch a glimpse. I take one for him too. I can't have Naked Man walking around all night.

He's not even paying attention to me, so I had nothing to worry about when I stripped. He's just staring at the locked door.

"What do you think is in there?" I ask, walking over to him and holding out the towel.

"Hmm," he says, taking the towel without looking at me. He wraps it around his waist and says, "Something good, obviously." He scans the room, finds something he likes, and walks away.

He grabs a fire extinguisher off the wall and comes back to the door.

"What are you going to do with that?"

He bangs the tank on the doorknob, bending it and breaking the lock.

"Oh," I say.

He messes with the handle for a few seconds and then pulls the door open. "Ho-lee shit."

"What?" I ask, leaning past him to see. "What's in there?"

West turns around and looks at me. "Guns."

CHAPTER EIGHTEEN

WESTON

I realize she's been wearing skimpy clothes all day, but goddamn. I can't take my eyes off Tori in this towel. She looks the way she did when we took that trip. That honeymoon practice trip. That's what I called it. I made reservations for that resort on Great Exuma Island and we spent a week just acting like we were the only two people in the world. Like honeymooners.

I turned her into Naked Woman that week. Two of those days we rented a sailboat and just took our clothes off and acted primal as we cruised around all the different cays.

It was probably the best two days in my life.

There is a nice collection of guns. Four AK-47's, two AR-15's—I lean in to get a better look at the pistols and see a .45, a 9mm, and a little .380.

"Why do you think this is here?" Tori asks as I notice a stash of tactical knives. I pick up one, unsheathe it from the nylon case, and find a serrated blade.

"Hunting. Probably."

"What do you hunt on a deserted island?" Tori asks, annoyed with my answer.

I want to say, *People.* But I don't want to freak her out. So instead I say, "Sharks."

"Sharks?" she asks, as I put the knife back and pick up another one, which does not have a serrated edge to it.

"Nobody hunts sharks with guns, West."

I shrug. "I'm sure there's lots of people who hunt sharks with guns."

"OK, whatever. Is this weird?" she asks. "That we have ended up on an island with a closet full of guns?"

Weird doesn't even begin to cover it. "Nope," I say, taking the two knives and closing the closet door back up. "I think whoever owns this place is..." I search for the lie I need. "Some kind of survivalist. This is probably like, a cache, you know? A place some paranoid freak might bring his family if the shit ever hit the fan. Probably some nerdy accountant by day and zombie apocalypse prepper by night."

"So it's not weird that we're here?" Tori isn't buying it.

"It was a mistake," I say, walking back to the kitchen to get back to the food. "That pilot probably dropped us off at the wrong cay. In fact," I say, looking out the window and pointing to the many scattered islands, "I bet Wallace Arlington is probably somewhere within a five-mile radius. I bet he's on another island and we're so close to him, we'd be able to smell his money if there wasn't so much wind."

Victoria follows me into the kitchen and plants a hand on her hip.

She's not buying it, Weston. Say something. Quick. "We're gonna laugh about this when we get back to Miami, don't you think? We'll probably still be laughing about this in ten years."

"I don't think it's funny. In fact, it's all very unusual. We get dropped off at the wrong cay on the same day a huge storm is supposed to blow in? Our pilot had to know the storm was coming, right? That's things pilots look into when they're flying around in a tiny, unsafe place in the middle of hurricane season."

"It's really... the end," I say. "Of hurricane season."

Victoria ignores that. "And then we get here to find this little house with some kind of power grid and a closet filled with weapons. And you expect me to believe that this is just overzealous preparation by a pencil-pushing family man?" She has one of those, *OK, buddy* looks on her face. "Really?"

I smile sheepishly. "Yes?"

"And it's not the end of hurricane season, we're dead smack in the middle of it—about to go into the most active part, actually. I might not be some kind of weather expert, but we have beaches in Brooklyn, West."

"Don't overreact, Victoria. We're only gonna be here a day."

I know what I'm doing. And I know what effect the word 'overreact' does to her. But it's all I've got left.

"I'm not taking your bait," she says. "And I know you well enough to see your mind working. What aren't you telling me?"

"What do you want me to say? Huh? I don't know who owns this island. I don't know why there's a closet filled with guns. I don't know why this house is here with a rain-catching cistern and solar panels on the roof. But it's an island in the middle of one of the most beautiful places on Earth. The Exumas are nothing but a playground for the rich, Tori. Rich people get bored and do weird shit like this. But I *do* know that you often overreact. And I *do* know that I'm not the least bit interested in dealing with one of those overreactions while we're stuck here. So you can wonder about all this all you want. I'm going to make dinner."

She walks away with a huff and I take my attention back to the lobsters. "I'm fucking hungry. I only got two, which means we only have food for one night. And if the storm gets bigger before it's over, then tomorrow I'm going to have to go fishing again."

Victoria says nothing. Just picks up all our wet clothes and starts hanging them over the chairs pushed up to the breakfast bar. "At least your pants are dry."

"And you have your scrap of a skirt."

"A lot of good that does me. Unless I want to go topless."

I shoot her a grin and a wink.

She doesn't grin back.

"Tori," I say, filling the pot up with water again.

"What?" she says, looking out the window at the purple clouds.

"Don't worry. We're fine."

She nods, but doesn't look at me. And I know her well enough to understand what that means. She doesn't believe me.

I'd give her more reassurance if I really thought we *were* fine.

But I don't.

We're fucked.

CHAPTER NINETEEN

VICTORIA

The power goes out again just as we're finishing our dinner. Lobster is not the same without butter. We don't even have salt and pepper. So it's nourishment, but nothing else.

"Shit," West says.

I don't even bother commenting. Something is wrong and he knows something is wrong. He's lying. He's keeping things from me. He's either not interested in having me freak out about it, or he's actually worried about the situation we find ourselves in.

I'm not sure which of those options is better.

If he's trying to prevent a freakout, well, then I'm pissed off that he thinks I'm so excitable that he needs to *manage* me. And if he's worried…

That's even worse. Weston isn't a worrier. He's a go-with-the-flow kind of person. It's one of the reasons we clash so much.

I'm not good at flowing.

"I'm not going out to try to fix the power," West says.

I say nothing.

"It's late. We should just try to sleep. I'll get to it tomorrow when it's light."

I don't know how we're supposed to sleep with the wind. It sounds like the roof might blow off any moment. And there's nowhere *to* sleep, anyway. Except the couch.

"I'll take the floor," West says, grabbing our plates and making his way to the sink in the darkness.

There's a little bit of light. I'm not even sure where it's coming from, since outside there's no moon and no stars. But it's not pitch black.

"Victoria?" West says, making his way back to where I'm sitting. He puts his hand on my bare shoulder—I'm still wearing nothing but this towel—and gives it a squeeze. "Come on, let's sleep."

He takes my hand and leads me over to the couch, then makes me sit. He sits next to me. "You're too quiet," he says.

"I'm thinking."

"About what?"

"All the ways this situation can go bad."

"We're fine."

"You're lying. Something is going on here and we're not fine. We need to get off this island."

"We'll worry about it tomorrow. There's nothing we can do now. Let's just sleep."

"I'm cold. We have no blankets."

"We have towels." He gets up and finds his way across the room to the closet with the towels. A few minutes later he comes back and starts draping them over me. Once I'm covered, he lays one on the floor.

"Stop it," I say. "You're not sleeping on that filthy floor. Just sit next me. Keep me warm."

I can almost feel his smile, even though he says nothing. When he sits his body is warm, but not warm enough. I curl into him, seeking more.

He puts his arm around me and sighs. "We are gonna be fine, Tori. I promise. You know I'd never let anything happen to you."

"I know." And I do. It's one of the things I both love, and hate, about him. His protectiveness borders on possessiveness.

"So…" he says. "What have you been up to the past few years? Your company was going so well the last time we spoke. I'm surprised you're in such bad shape."

"I got distracted. My father's…" But I stop. I don't want to talk about it. I *can't* talk about it.

"I'm sorry about him. You know I always loved him."

I nod. "I know."

"Do you have a boyfriend?"

Normally I'd lie about this. If West and I had met up in some random coffee shop in the city and he asked me this, I'd say, *Too many to count.* Or something else equally ridiculous. Just to piss him off. But I'm too distracted to lie, so I just say, "No."

We have a few minutes of awkward silence after that. "Do you have a girlfriend?" I ask, when the awkwardness starts to border on uncomfortable.

"Nope. I wouldn't have touched you earlier if I did."

I roll my eyes in the dark. Weston Conrad and all his high and mighty morals.

"It felt good though," West says, leaning into my ear. "Wanna do it again?"

His question has an immediate effect on me. I get a warm feeling between my legs. A tingle of possibilities. And every part of skin that is touching him comes alive.

"Tori?" he whispers, repositioning himself so he can lean into me more. "Tori?" he says again, placing one hand on my cheek and turning my face towards his. "Answer me."

"I don't know."

"Want me to talk you into it?"

I huff out a small laugh. That's what he always asked when he knew I wasn't in the mood.

"Huh?" he asks again, his hand twisting the little corner of the towel that's holding it closed against my breasts. It falls away and his hand is there, squeezing and kneading.

I know how this game is played. I don't have to say anything to make him keep going. He will persist in his quest to get himself inside me unless I say no.

But I don't feel like saying no right now. So I say, "Yes."

This one word coming from my own mouth has the same effect as his first question. Heat and a spark of desire.

"I'll make you come first this time," he says, kissing my neck.

I take a deep breath and reach for his cock. I push the towel he's still wearing up, and grab him in my fist. He's rock hard already. I have never made a play for his dick and found him anything else but rock hard for me.

"I know what you need, Victoria. You know I have those secrets."

"Shut up," I whisper. I don't want to hear anything about secrets right now. I just want the whole world to go away. I just want the darkness and the emptiness to become the same. I moan as West bites my earlobe. I just want him to make me forget everything for a few minutes.

I just want to be free of all this worry and stress.

"I already said yes," I say, my voice hoarse with desire. "So just stop talking and make me feel good."

"The way I used to?" he asks.

I could get lost forever in the memories of how Weston Conrad used to make me feel. It's like a slow fall into madness when I let those thoughts invade reality. So I don't go there now. I shake my head and keep silent. And he's moved on, anyway. His mouth is on my breast, his hands between my legs. He doesn't want an answer, he just wanted to make me think about how good it was.

And it was good. Great, most of the time. But the moments when it wasn't were unbearable. The lies between us are still there. We are still keeping secrets and I can't think of a single reason that I would give mine up now. They almost don't matter anymore. It's practically over for me.

I can't imagine that Weston Conrad, after getting away with keeping his, after all he went through, would ever hand over the things he's got locked inside him either.

Those secrets have served him well.

He's winning this game.

He is the winner.

CHAPTER TWENTY

WESTON

Victoria Arias does not play games during sex. She does not want me to slap her ass and call her bad. She will never roleplay, or let me tie her up, or crawl across the floor on her hands and knees for the privilege of sucking my cock. She won't watch porn with me, have sex outside in the mud, or let me stick my dick in her mouth after I fuck her in the ass.

She is not looking for some dark side of herself. She has no inner submissive locked up in her head. She doesn't want to be jolted into the present with a slap to her tits, or her pussy, or her face.

No.

When Victoria Arias has sex, it's because she wants to be loved.

That's it. That is all she's after.

Love.

It's not as boring as it sounds.

At least, to me, it's not.

Because this was my first clue that Tori was my future wife. She's… normal. She likes normal. She *wants* normal. So it really pissed me off that she couldn't see our grand future together back when we started talking about it.

"West," she moans now. "Don't stop."

I kiss her stomach as I make my way down her body, pushing all that other stuff out of the way for now. It's only fair that I give her my full attention after I lied about what those guns probably mean. There's going to be enough time tomorrow to worry about all the problems we have.

So tonight, we're just going to forget.

When I get to her belly button I reach under her knees and push her legs up and open. My tongue is there and she is wet. She was always ready for me when I came to her and she's still ready now.

I suck her clit for a moment. Let her enjoy the sensations. She likes to go slow and I don't have anything against slow. The only time I get to slow down is when I'm making love to Victoria. But I live life hard and fast. So naturally, that's my default setting in the bedroom as well.

Oddly, that's something I didn't mind giving up for her most of the time.

Tori's hands are in my hair, twisting it and fisting it as she starts to breathe hard. Her arms in this position squeeze her breasts together and I look up from my place between her legs to catch the view before I miss it. They are just an outline in the dark, and that should be a tease. But it's not. The outline is all I need because holy God, she is so beautiful.

"Your pussy tastes as beautiful as you look, Miss Arias."

I can't see her smile in the darkness, but I can feel it. And the little breath of air that escapes her lips lets me know she's got a laugh inside her.

Her hands fist my hair a little tighter. Her back arches

just the slightest bit more. Her breathing kicks up a level. Sex with Tori isn't boring because, while she does like to be worshipped, she also likes to hear my dirty mouth as I do it. It turns her on so bad, she gets animalistic and wild. Just like she is in real life.

Everything about Tori and me is real.

Except all the things that aren't.

Push it down, Corporate. Time for that later.

"Licking you between your legs, Miss Arias... well, there's enough sweetness in your pussy to give me a toothache."

She giggles this time. But her thighs also come together and squeeze against my shoulders.

I push my tongue inside her, sucking on her desire, and then withdraw and crawl my way up her body. Her lips are already there, meeting mine so she can kiss me.

She likes to taste my mouth after I lick her.

We kiss for a few moments, one of her hands letting go of my hair so she can reach down between my legs and wrap her palm around my thick cock. Our tongues are seeking, and pushing, and twisting as she pumps me— slowly at first, then with a regular rhythm.

"What comes next?" I ask. She might not like the kink, but she has always loved the talking. Sex with Tori has always been about the foreplay. We've had whole conversations during sex. We've had fights during sex. We've made plans during sex, and plotted vacations, and told each other just exactly what would happen on said getaways. We've even had philosophical discussions during sex.

131

And it has always turned me on that I can make her come while discussing politics, or an art exhibition we saw the night before, or our grocery list.

"Next…" Tori says, tracing a fingernail down the curve of my bicep. "You probably want me to suck your cock."

I smile and let out a small laugh. "I would not turn it down," I say, pushing a finger between her legs so I can continue to play.

"I bet the only reason you're sorry there's no lights is because you won't be able to see my lips as they wrap around your tip. You won't be able to see my tongue as I lick you like candy."

"We're going to do this again tomorrow morning, so I'm not the least bit worried about it."

"You're a cocky bastard," Tory says. "Thinking I'll just be here for you whenever you want me."

"Nah," I say into her mouth as I kiss her again. "I don't think that. I think every time is the last time, Tori. So I'm going to make the most of right now and hope for the best tomorrow."

She's silent. But she never stops kissing me. Her palm never stops squeezing my cock. Her hand never stops fisting my hair.

I want to fuck her so bad right now. But I already messed up the last time by not letting her come first. And I won't do that again. She might get the wrong idea about my intentions tonight.

So I break our kiss and take my lips to her breasts. I gather one together, squeezing. They are so big, my hand barely fits around them. And even though I can't see her nipples, I know they are large, and round, and just a shade or two darker than her skin. I bite, her back arches, her fist leaves my hair and her hand comes to rest on the side of my stubbled face. Her other palm squeezes my dick.

"I missed you," she says in a low somber voice.

I pause from licking her nipple and place my lips on hers. I kiss her words away. I kiss her fear away. I kiss it all away and say, "I'm still here. I will always be here."

Her legs open for me, just a little. But it's a signal I know well. So I ease forward until my cock is pushing against her entrance. She draws in a deep breath as I enter. Slowly stretching her to make room for me. Slowly penetrating her to connect us together.

Both fists are in my hair now, and she's tugging me down. My face to her face. My lips to her lips. We kiss as we start. This is how she likes it. Slow, and soft, and filled with silent words of worship and promises.

"I think I'll keep you forever, Miss Arias," I say, when she takes a breath. "I think I own you."

"Don't be a caveman, Mr. Conrad. You know I'm nobody's property."

"You're wrong," I say, starting to pump her harder. "You've always been mine and you know it. You just hate the fact that I'm right and you're wrong. You just hate the fact that you love me, even though I'm pushy, and controlling, and want you to wear an apron—"

She slaps my face, but she moans as she does it. "Stop talking," she says.

But what she really means is… keep going.

"I'm gonna come inside you tonight. I'm going to get

133

you pregnant, and marry you, and then make you walk around the house naked."

"Except for that apron, right?" she breathes into my mouth.

"Except for that apron. And your belly will get big, and your tits will get bigger, and your pussy will be swollen and sensitive as I bend you over the dining room table and fuck you from behind as you arrange the place settings for my dinner."

"You're a pig and that is never—"

But I'm fucking her harder now. Her tits are bouncing against her chin and she can't go on.

"I'm going to fuck you during dinner. And then I'm going to fuck you as you do the dishes. Bend you over the counter. Let you look out the window at the neighbors as I take your ass. And let you scream to the world as I make you come. Domestic life with me, Miss Arias, won't be what you think."

I grab her under her ass, hoist her up, and walk her over to the wall. I push her back against it as she wraps her arms around my neck and her legs around my hips.

Every time I've done this, my dick has never slipped out of her pussy. It's like her personal mission is to keep us connected. And she has never let me down.

"You're gonna come now, Victoria," I say, pushing my dick deep inside her as I whisper in her ear. "I'm gonna fuck you against this wall…" My finger slips into the tight pucker of her ass and she gasps. "And I'm going to come with you. Inside you. Get you pregnant, make you mine, keep you forever. You belong with me. Say it."

I'm pumping my cock into her hard now. It's the only way to finish off a caveman fuck. Pressing her against a wall. Smothering her with my power and my body. Telling her all the things she wants to hear and all the things she doesn't, at the same time.

She will never admit it, but she likes my version of her future and that's why she pushed me away. She wants it. She just won't admit it.

CHAPTER TWENTY-ONE

VICTORIA

"Shut up, shut up, shut up," I say, over and over again as West continues to fuck me. Why does he have to say these things?

"I'm gonna put a ring on that finger, Tori. I'm gonna give you the wedding of a lifetime. I'm gonna fuck you like I've never fucked you before that night. And then I'm going to take you to an island, just like this one, and rip your clothes off. Make you walk around naked with me for days, and weeks, and maybe forever. I will eat your pussy everywhere we go on that island. On the rocks, in the waves, lying in the hot sun. I will taste you and then I'll kiss you, just the way you like. Let you taste it too."

"I'm not marrying you," I say, almost breathless. His finger in my ass is driving me wild. I just want him to put me down, bend me over, and fuck me from behind. I want to feel the weight of him as he collapses onto my back when we are spent. God, why can't he just do that instead of all this damn talking? "I'm never getting married, I've told you that a hundred—"

But I can't continue.

Because he's reading my mind. He's carrying me back to the couch. He sets me down and I whimper when his cock slips out from inside me. He bends me over the back of it. Not hard and demanding. Just matter-of-factly. Like my wish is his command.

137

My body is weak and I bend when he tells me to bend. I open my legs when he tells me to open them.

And I wait. The seconds seem like hours as I wait for his dick or his fingers, or his... oh, my God, his tongue.

He licks me. His fingers are inside me. His hands spread my ass cheeks open and his tongue probes my ass, slips down to my pussy, and... holy shit.

"You will marry me," West says as he thrusts his cock inside me again. I'm so wet, he just slips right in.

But his finger is still playing with my ass and that is what I love. He knows it. I love it, I want him in there too, I want him everywhere, inside me every way. And in that same moment he's withdrawn and relentless. His cock is painful as he thrusts forward. My back arches and I scream as his dick goes in my ass. His hand is on my hip, and then it's not, it's between my legs, strumming my clit.

I throw my head back and see him. Looking down at me. As I come.

There is that moment when we are looking at each other. And then there is that moment when we have to close our eyes and see nothing.

He pulls out and spills his semen all down my back.

And then he completes my fantasy. He bends forward and covers me with his weight. We are breathing hard, almost gasping for air. And he says, "I'm still gonna come inside you, Miss Arias. I'm gonna get what I want from you. But right now, I think we need to sleep."

West gets off me and I miss him immediately. But he's only gone a second. He's got a towel when he stands me up. He cleans off his chest, then my back, and we sink into the couch cushions together.

"I love you, Victoria. I have always loved you."

"I know," I whisper back.

"You should rethink your life. You should try to imagine the life I'm offering you. Not as a trap, like you always said. But as a... a sanctuary. From all the bad, and all the stress, and all the worries that come with being alone. You don't have to be alone. You don't have to be in charge. You don't have to be in control. It's really not all it's cracked up to be."

I can see his point. I hate to admit it, but all these years later, after being in charge, and being in control, and being single... I can see it.

I'm lonely, and scared, and stressed out. I am on the brink of losing everything. People are counting on me and I'm about to let them all down. I am in a bad, dark place.

But I am also wrapped up tight in Weston Conrad's arms.

And I can't help but wonder if this is what it would be like for real.

If I was his good little wife.

CHAPTER TWENTY-TWO

WESTON

"Wake up, Tori." I give her a little nudge and go back to packing the dry bag I found in the closet with the snorkeling gear.

"What?" she asks, sitting up and rubbing her eyes. Her hair is wild, her face is flushed from the humidity and heat that is making this place feel like a hothouse, and she's still naked from last night.

Jesus fucking Christ. I should not have done any of that yesterday. It's going to be so hard to walk away from her again. But I can't help myself. She's so familiar. So easy to fall into. So... perfect. It really sucks that we can't get along. That we have almost nothing in common when it comes to future plans. That we are both so stubborn.

She agrees with me during sex sometimes. She slows down and gives it some thought, at least. But I know it's just the sex talking. She's in a state where she has to give in. But the next morning she's always back to her old self.

We just don't want the same things in life.

"What are you doing? What's going on?"

She's so goddamned cute when she wakes up. All confused and innocent. It's the only time of the day that she lets her guard down.

"We're gonna leave," I say, grabbing her bra and panties and throwing them to her. "Get dressed. I washed your panties, so put them on. I've got your skirt and blouse

141

in the bag with my stuff so we'll have dry clothes once we get there."

"Get where?" She's irritated now. "Where the hell are we going? Is the storm over? Did the pilot come back?"

"No. But there's a lull in the storm so we're going to try to swim over to another island. I saw it when we landed. There's a building over there. Maybe they have a radio."

"Why can't we just stay here?"

I ignore her and just continue packing the bag. I've already got the handguns in the bottom. I don't want her to know I'm taking them. And I've got two towels, because I have no clue if that other building even has necessities.

"West? What's going on?"

"We just can't stay here. I have a feeling that storm yesterday was only the beginning. The purple mess is still off in the distance. Like it's hovering or moving very slowly. But it's even bigger than it was yesterday. I think it's a hurricane."

"Hurricane? For real?"

"Yeah, this place is no good, Tori. We need to leave. It's low, only like thirty feet above sea level. This house will probably flood. That other island was bigger. Higher up. We need to make for it while the break in the storm lasts."

"But what if—"

"It's not far, Tori. We made it to the sandbar yesterday, right? Well, I know it's a neap tide right now. The full moon was last week. So even though the water level is higher because of the storm, it's lower than it should be because of the alignment of the moon and the sun. I think that sandbar is probably submerged a few feet at most. We should still be able to walk on it. I'm betting all those sandbars are like that. We won't have to swim far. Think of it like a causeway."

Tori sits up, looks around, then stands and plants her hands on her hips. "You're serious? I'm not going in that ocean."

"You are. You don't have a choice."

"I have plenty of choices. I think that if there's a lull in the storm they will be looking for us. We should wait here and—"

"No one is looking for anyone until that hurricane passes. Don't you get it? We're fucked." I didn't want to scare her, but I have no choice. We don't have time for a fight. People could come back. And I'm pretty sure that's the worst possible thing that could happen. There's a reason we're here. And there's a reason that closet was packed full of guns. I'm trying not to think too hard about it yet, because I don't want to face some inevitable facts. But none of this is good. It's bad. Far worse than I first thought before we found those guns.

"You don't know that," she says, still defiant.

"Do you want to stay here alone?" I don't want to threaten her with that, either. It's a low blow and she feels it immediately, because she recoils. But I have no other option. We need to get the fuck off this island. "Because I'm leaving. So if you'd like to stay behind all by yourself, that's your choice."

Tori huffs out some air, silent, but defiant. I let her stew. She's coming. I know she's coming. She won't stay here alone.

"What if they come looking for us and we're gone? I think we should leave a note."

"We'll deal with that later. And no," I stress. "We're not leaving a note. Just do what I say and things will be fine."

"What do you mean, later? And why no note? No. No, no, no. That makes no sense."

"It does make sense, Tori. You just don't have all the information."

"Then tell me," she growls. "What are you keeping from me?"

"I'm making a decision and that's the end of it. We're leaving. So put on your bra and panties and let's go. The low tide will be here in like an hour. We don't have much time if we want to take advantage of that."

"How do you know all this shit anyway? Since when are you an expert on tides?"

"I told you," I say, starting to lose my patience. "I worked on a boat for seven years. This is common knowledge for sailors. The pilot said it was low tide when we landed yesterday, and the tides are regular. They come at regular intervals each day. Can't you just do what you're told for once? I mean, unless you've got some secret tidal training I don't know about. But I'm guessing not, because if you did, you'd know I was right and we wouldn't have to argue about it."

I stuff the last of the gear into the bag and seal it up.

"You're taking one of those knives?"

"All of them," I say. "We need to hunt, right?"

She huffs out more air and rolls her eyes. "You're some kind of survivalist now? Please."

"Yeah, well," I say under my breath. "I've been in survival mode since I was seven. It's nothing new for me. Now let's go."

I'm only half right about everything I told Tori, but it's enough. The trek from our island to the new island takes four hours. It's not more than two miles away and it takes four hours. She balked at the edge of the beach. So I pointed to the storm, still stirring in the northern sky, and threatened her with a high tide if she didn't get her South American ass in the water.

She swam to the first sandbar, which was more than a couple feet submerged, so I was wrong about that. But she was still able to touch the bottom for about two hundred yards, so the part I was right about was the only thing that counted.

It kept her going, and that's all that matters.

But once we got to the edge of that sandbar and she realized the moment of truth was upon her, she panicked. I'm talking full-on panic attack with hyperventilating and fearful eyes, and claims that she was going to die.

It's been a long time since I've seen her this way.

I hate it.

I'd rather see her with another man than see her so scared.

We had to stand there on the edge of the ocean, the water swelling higher and higher as we waited for the episode to pass. I had to coach her constantly while we swam to the second island, which still had land above water, but the low tide was over by then and the ocean was rising fast. When I pointed back to our island she was shocked that so much of it was hidden under the waves.

"See," I said. "We would've died over there."

She got her fear under control after that and swam to the third island without comment, even though it was a struggle from start to finish. I was actually scared that time. She's not a strong swimmer. Nothing like me. I know what to do with an angry sea.

I wasn't sure she could do it. I really had doubts. All I thought about as we swam, the waves tossing us and pulling on us, was that I would never be able to live with myself if something happened to her. But there was an inflatable floatation belt in with the scuba gear, so I put it on her, tethered us together, and pulled her to the last island.

So here we are.

"Where's the building?" Victoria asks. It's raining again. Really starting to come down hard, but we're soaked anyway, so it hardly matters.

"It's in the middle of the island." We're sprawled out on the beach waiting for our heavy breathing to even out. "I'll go look first. You stay here and then when I know it's safe I'll come back for you."

"Like hell," Tori says, standing up. "I'm not staying here. And if you try to make me, I'll follow you into those trees. I do not care what danger is in there. I'm not staying here on this deserted beach alone. Fuck that."

I have to laugh at her defiance. Even though I want to get to the building first so I can try to figure this shit out, I know she's firm on this. So I just say, "Suit yourself. But when the natives attack, don't blame me."

Tori grabs my arm, squeezing tight. "Do you think there are *people* here? That we're... like... trespassing?" Her eyes search mine, looking for reassurance.

"No. I don't. I think whoever owns this place has a lot more sense than we do. This hurricane has to have been on the news. People who own islands keep track of that shit. No one wants to be stuck out here during a hurricane."

She lets out a long breath. "Yes. That's probably true."

I hold out my hand and Tori looks at it for a second. "Come on," I say. "Let's go together then."

She smiles, rolls her eyes. But she does take my hand. We walk the beach in the worsening storm looking for a footpath. The trees and brush are thick, so there's no real chance of making a new path. Not with the mud and the rain, and the gusting wind.

We find one a little way down the beach, half hidden in the blowing palm trees. And once we get in under the windbreak canopy of leaves, we follow the narrow trail in silence. It leads to a lagoon with an empty boathouse, and from there we find the path to the main house.

Which is a lot nicer than the piece of one-room shit we just came from.

And the power works.

"Why does the power work here?"

"People with money, Tori. They can do whatever they want."

"Must be nice," she says, irritated. "But that's not an answer."

"I'm sure there's an explanation."

But I'm humoring her. The power is on because a motion sensor porch light activates when we come up to the front door. Which means people were here not too long ago. They have a sturdier system than the last island, that's all. It lasted a little longer.

At least that's what I tell myself.

"There's a radio!" Tori says, her voice excited after many hours of sadness and fear. "Look!"

And yes, there is a radio right there in the mud room. I scan the area for leftover shoes or coats. Something, anything to tell me if people are here or not.

But I see no signs.

Tori runs over to it and is about to turn it on when I grab her hand away. "What are you doing?" she asks.

"We don't need to call now. They can't help us and it will just make people worry."

"You're crazy. People are looking for us, West. We need to let them know we're OK."

"We will," I say. "But not yet. Let's just check this place out first."

She huffs some air and squints her eyes at me. But I didn't say it as a command. It was a suggestion. So she's not mad. I think I just set all her little alarm bells off though.

148

"It's pretty nice, right?" I say, trying to get her mind off my new anti-radio stance.

Tori looks around and takes a few steps towards the great room.

It's like any well-furnished room you'd find in a vacation home. High-beamed ceilings, dark wood tables, built-in cabinetry, and dark marble-tiled floors. There's even a flatscreen TV, for fuck's sake.

I look around, warily. Something is very, very wrong with this trip. Why was Victoria brought in for this contract? Was Liam behind this? Is he getting even for some old wound between him and my father? Was it the pilot? Who does he work for? Mysterious?

This is where the panic starts to take hold of me. I've had that thought in the back of my head since yesterday and I've been pushing it down and pushing it down.

But there it is.

Mr. Mysterious.

I think this is about him. Maybe even worse than that. Maybe he's the one behind all this bullshit. He did refer me to that pilot. He did give me that tip about Wallace. The house back on that island had Paxton Vance written all over it. The set-up, the seclusion, the guns.

I look over at the dry bag on the floor and wonder if I should get rid of them. What if he's used them in some crime? What if they are murder weapons? I mean, all us Misters play it cool about him. *Oh, he's so mysterious.* Like we're rolling our eyes about his quirky eccentricities and not wondering how many people he's killed since college.

But I know what I'm thinking every time Mysterious shows up, so I know Nolan has to be thinking the same thing. He's a suspicious bastard. Even more than me. Something is off about Pax and we all know it. I would not put it past him to sell us out.

Hell, maybe he *did* rape that girl back in college? Maybe it was him all along. And then when the arrest warrant came who was there? Match and his stupid friend Five. Is it a coincidence that Match and Mysterious are the best of friends these days? Really? Pax has always been a man who hates people, but now he and Oliver are BFFs?

I don't buy it. Those two are doing business.

And I've been suspicious about Match for a while now. What kind of man runs an online dating site and never has a girlfriend? No. They are up to something and this trip proves it. I'm stuck out here—Victoria Arias is stuck out here—because Paxton Vance gave me bogus information.

"What are you thinking so hard about?" Tori asks from across the room. She's got a remote in her hand and the TV comes to life. "Holy shit. We've got HBO and everything. Whose place do you think this is? Some rich movie star? Silicon Valley tech mogul? What if we're in Peter Thiel's doomsday bunker?" She laughs like this is ridiculous.

I don't laugh. Somebody went to a lot of trouble to set this place up. Except I don't think it's the PayPal billionaire's island. I think whoever owns this island probably owns the other one too. And I think I'm on a first-name basis with whoever that is.

"Jesus, West. What are you daydreaming about?" Tori puts the remote down on the coffee table and walk towards me.

I paint on the smile and head for the dry bag to keep myself busy. "Nothing, really. Just thinking about how lucky we are to have found a safe place to ride out the storm."

"Shit, do you think that hurricane is still coming this way?"

"I hope so," I mumble under my breath. Because if it's not, someone will come looking for us very soon.

"What?" Tori asks. "What did you just say?"

"I said I hope not. I hope that fucking pilot has called the coastguard for us and they're arranging some kind of pickup."

"Yeah, me too," Tori says, sighing as she crosses her arms. "I'm cold. Does it feel like this place is air-conditioned?"

I look up at the tall ceiling and see massive fans hanging down by long poles. And sure enough, there are vents on the ceiling.

How much money does it take to run this place? Who would leave all this going if they left the island?

"What if someone's still here?"

Tori and I come to the same conclusion at the very same moment. We look at each other and I see the fear in her eyes as I start shaking my head. "Nah," I say, playing it down. "Where would they be? The wind is blowing hard now. And it's been raining most of the day. If people were here, this room is where they'd be."

Tori looks around like she needs a moment to talk herself into my lie. For such a wild girl, she sure does have a sweet, vulnerable side.

"Want to check it out?" I ask, reaching to the bottom of the dry bag and grabbing the guns. "Together?" I pull them out one at a time and set them on the floor beside me. When all three are there I look up at Victoria.

"I knew you took them."

"Yeah? And?"

She shrugs. "Something's wrong, isn't it?"

I shrug this time. "I'm not sure yet."

"Do you think it's about Wallace? I mean, that was all pretty strange, right?"

I have no answer. "I don't know, Tori. I'm not sure if it's Wallace or the people behind the job to get Wallace."

"Like Liam?"

So she's been thinking about this too.

"Maybe."

"But isn't he a good friend of your family? Why would he set something like this up, West?"

I open my mouth to tell the lie. The lie I've been telling since I was seven years old. But I can't bring myself to say the words.

"West?" Tori prods.

So I make up a new one. "Not good friends," I say. "Not exactly."

CHAPTER TWENTY-THREE

VICTORIA

He's lying. I've always known he's been lying about who he is and where he came from. But I figured it was some small lie. Like, his father wasn't in the import-export business. I mean, come on. I'm from Brooklyn. I know that import-export is code for mafia.

But I don't think this is what he's lying about. It's something deeper. Bigger. Badder.

"Then…" I say, trying to reason it all out. "Why would Liam set us up?"

"Maybe he didn't."

"Then who?" I ask.

West picks up the smallest gun and stands up, offering it to me. "You know how to shoot, right?"

"Sure." My father was a policeman. He taught me to shoot when I was fourteen. About a week too late, unfortunately. "But I'm not taking that gun."

"Tori, look. You're right. Something weird might be going on here. I need to know you can fight back."

I shake my hands in the air and laugh. "I am a lethal weapon, Mr. Corporate. Don't you worry your pretty head about me."

He lets out a long breath and smiles. It's the first smile I've seen on him today, the only time his forehead wasn't creased with worry and exhaustion. "I know, Miss Arias.

But you can't karate-chop someone from across the room."

I chuckle back. Karate chop. He's so cute. What I am capable of doing to a man is nothing short of torture. "I feel safe here," I say. "I can't explain why, I just do. I don't think we'll need guns. But we should look the place over thoroughly."

West's smile drops on one side, making that lopsided grin I love so much. He doesn't do it often. Only when I'm right and he's not mad about it.

To me, that look says, *OK. We're OK.*

"We're OK," I say, to give him the same comfort he's been giving me these past two days. "We're fine. We'll wait it out here and figure it out when the storm ends. And we have a radio now. So… we're fine."

"Yeah," he says, barely audible. "Let's look around. Maybe they left food."

We do look. But there is no food. There's pots and pans and a real oven—gas even—a refrigerator—empty—and a microwave.

All of which is useless.

There is a massive set of stairs which go down on one side and up on the other. We go up first, and find three bedrooms.

"I guess we won't have to sleep together tonight," West says.

"I guess not," I agree. I glance up at him really quick to see if he's got any regrets about that, but he's moved on to look at the bathrooms. I wait in the hallway as he flushes all three toilets, and then I follow him down to the basement.

"Well," West says, once we're down there. "This is... interesting."

There's a safe that spans an entire wall. Complete with one of those round wheel things that you use to open it, and a computer pad where a combination needs to be entered.

There's a silver envelope taped to the ginormous door. West rips the note off the door like he's taking it personally, then looks at me with raging eyes.

"What?"

"Do you know who wrote this?"

I feel all kinds of defensive. "Why would I know that?"

"No," he says, taking a deep breath and combing his fingers through his tousled hair. "No, I mean, Mr. fucking Mysterious wrote this! I fucking knew it!"

"What? Your friend? This place belongs to your friend?" I look around, take it in with a new set of eyes.

"I'm pretty sure that last one did too."

"So that's who that guy was at the table with you?" I didn't see him. I've never actually met any of the Misters in person before. West and I went in a whole different direction after those charges. I never saw any of them unless it was on TV.

"What?" West's eyes are blazing. "What guy I was with at the table?"

Shit. *Good going, Victoria.*

"You were listening, weren't you? When Pax gave me the heads up on where Wallace would be yesterday."

"It's not as bad as it sounds," I start.

But West cuts me off. "You were trying to steal that contract, Tori."

"You don't even need that contract. You're rolling in money, Weston. I need it. And not for selfish reasons like you. Like your stupid cars and your stupid houses."

"Way to get defensive and nasty when you know I'm right," West counters.

"It's all true though. You've always been greedy, Weston Conrad. I'm trying to save people and you can't let me have one stupid contract to keep that stuff afloat?"

"Save who?" He practically snorts. "Cut the shit, Tori. The only person you're trying to save is yourself."

"Well, fuck you. You know? Because you're wrong. You're totally wrong about me. I'm trying to save my father's legacy. He's dying, Weston. He'll be lucky to live six more months and all he's ever wanted was to keep that trust fund afloat."

He looks shocked. "You have a trust fund?"

"Not me, you idiot. The kids."

"What fucking *kids*, Victoria?" Now he looks pissed.

I'd forgotten I'd never told him. Jesus Christ. I never told him. It's been so long since we spoke. Three years at least. And that was only a drunken one-night stand. We went to my place in Scarsdale because it was closer to the bar we met up in and my Manhattan building was still being renovated. West was gone by the time I woke up in the morning. Probably sorry he let things go so far. He was still very mad at me about that seven-million-dollar contract he thought I stole a few months earlier. There was no call, no text, not even an email saying, *Thanks for the fun.* Just here and then gone.

I didn't take it personally. I was a little bit relieved. Because there's no room in my life for a man like West. One night of sex is fine. Like last night. That's OK with me. It was fun, felt good. But once we're off this island there's no way in hell we'll ever see each other again.

"What fucking kids?" West repeats.

"Look, it's a long story—"

"Did you have a fucking baby?"

"No." I laugh. "Don't be ridiculous."

"Then what kids are you talking about? You don't have any siblings."

"Well, it's a funny thing. Really. And it *is* a long story. But I was adopted, West. When I was fourteen. I grew up in foster care and my father, the man you *know* as my father, well, he saved me after..." Shit. I never had any intention of talking about this again.

West takes a seat in a nearby chair. "Are you shitting me right now?"

"No, why?"

"You're serious?"

"Yes. Why would I lie about this?"

"So you were never going to tell me your backstory?" He stands up again, begins to pace.

"Are you getting attitude with me about my personal life? Please. You pop off with this little hint that you're some kind of reformed blue-collar worker yesterday. 'I worked on a boat, Tori.' 'I know how to catch lobsters with my bare hands, Tori.' 'I have memorized the fucking tides, Tori.' And you think you're allowed to get mad at me for not telling you about my past? Fuck *off*."

He grabs me by the arm before I can spin around and leave, but instincts kick in and I deflect his wrist, kick forward toward his balls, and—

I'm down on the ground face first. "Nice try, Miss Arias," Weston breathes into my ear. He's got my hands behind my back and... and... I'm stunned.

"What the fuck—"

"I'm a third-degree black belt, Victoria. So you can cut your tough-girl shit, OK? I'm not in the mood." He lets go of my wrist, gets up, then pulls me to my feet.

"Since when?" I huff. "You never took martial arts when we were together."

"Wrong. I've been taking classes since I was seven. I earned my black belt when I was nineteen."

"But... you never fought back. When I used my moves on you!"

"You're a girl, Tori. Why the fuck would I fight back?"

"You're such a dick."

"Why?" he snarls. "Because I'm a gentleman? Come off it. I'm not going to hurt you. I only took you down this time because I'm sick of your shit and we don't have time for this."

"You're sick of *my* shit? Ha."

West just stares at me. He's so pissed off right now. He points his finger in my face, the same way I've done to him, over, and over, and over. "You're hiding things from me."

"You're hiding things from me! So I guess we're even."

"You're adopted. Where are your parents?"

"You've met my father."

"Your real parents," he snarls.

"None of your goddamned business."

"It *is* my business. We're here because someone *put* us here."

"Yeah, your stupid friend, Mr. Mysterious."

"Maybe," he says.

"What do you mean, maybe? You just said this is his place. And how did you know that by that note? Huh? Is his name on it?"

"No," West says, picking the silver envelope up off the floor where he dropped it. "This," he says, opening it up so I can see a series of cut-and-paste letters that look like an old-fashioned ransom note, "is his calling card."

"He's a kidnapper?" I laugh.

"It's not funny. None of this is funny. You don't understand. My friends have been having trouble with people from their past in the past six months. One by one, all us Misters are being targeted again. And this," he says, waving his arms wide, "appears to be my turn."

"So your friend, that Mysterious guy, he's the one fucking with you?"

West sighs and turns away. "I don't know. I don't know what to think. But you're here, you see." He turns back to face me. "You're here and you're a girl from my past. This is exactly how it's been happening. Mr. Perfect got a visit from Allen. Remember that asshole? Romantic's half-sister reappeared in his life before she tried to fuck with him. And now *you're* here."

159

"You think I'm the one who's fucking with you? You're an asshole." I grab the note from his hand and read it. There's a bunch of numbers and one sentence. "'You'll know what to do.' What's that mean?"

West grabs the note back. "I guess I'll open the safe up and see."

He walks over to the keypad and punches in the numbers. There's a loud click and some weird sounds, like something is moving inside the door. The huge wheel thing starts moving by itself and a few moments later another click, and the safe opens about an inch.

West looks at me, then opens it up.

CHAPTER TWENTY-FOUR

WESTON

It's a room. Like a whole other room. Like a studio apartment. The walls are solid rock, like it's all built into the side of the island. There's a little kitchenette in the back with a small dinette table, a door that leads to a bathroom immediately to the left, and a living room filled with a couch and two chairs.

Tori walks towards the kitchen and I try to figure out what Mysterious meant by, *You'll know what to do*. Was he referring to the numbers and the safe? I'll know to open the safe?

OK. I've gotten that far. Now what?

"Hey," she says. "Here's another one of those silver envelopes."

I walk over to her and take it from her hand. Fucking silver envelopes.

"'When the time comes, lock yourself inside. I'll be in touch.'"

"He'll be in touch? How? And why the hell would we lock ourselves inside a fucking safe? Would we even be able to get back out? What the hell, Weston?"

I take a deep breath and let it out. What the fuck is happening? Now I know how Nolan felt when that shit started to go down with him. But Mysterious was involved in that as well. He was right there when Nolan got in trouble.

Do I trust him?

What choice do I have? It's easy to forget there's a raging storm outside down here. I can't even hear the wind right now. But the truth is, we're stuck. There was no boat. There's no hidden helicopter. And I can't fly one of those, anyway. There's the radio, but... I'm not sure calling for help is the right move. And if Mysterious left us this safe room—literally, that's what this is—then that's a good reason to stay put.

"West," Tori shouts. I realize she's been talking this whole time while I was thinking. "What the hell is going on?"

"I'm not sure," I say. "But he wants us to stay here for a reason, so we better do as he says. At least for one night. We're not using that radio, understand?"

She just stares at me.

"Understand, Victoria? I don't need you pulling your feminist card out now. Something bad is happening and we need to work together on this."

"You are such an asshole. Two minutes ago you were accusing me of being involved. Now you want me to trust you?"

"Just... forget that. You're not involved. I know that. We better go find food—"

"No, that's what I was saying. These cupboards are stocked with packaged food. There's milk in the fridge, West. It's not even expired. Which means we don't need to find any. There's plenty. Weeks' worth, probably."

Milk. Not something you keep on hand over long periods of time. Which means someone was here very recently, just like I suspected. "We're not going to be here for weeks." Good God, at least I hope we won't be. "Maybe we should just eat and go to sleep."

"In here?" Tori asks. "Or the bedrooms out there?"

I look over at the couch and picture last night. It was nice to be near her. I miss her body next to mine. I miss the scent of her hair as I sleep. I want that for another night, but I'm not sure how to insist on this room when there's a whole house above us and no chance anyone will come looking tonight. "Upstairs, I think. We can take this food upstairs. The first note said I'd know what to do with this room. And right now I don't. So we must not need it yet."

"I'm not locking myself in that room, Weston Conrad. No matter what happens. So fuck yeah, I'm sleeping upstairs."

And then she walks out, a box of crackers and a block of cheese clutched in her hands.

Fucking Tori Arias. Why, of all people to get stuck on an island with, does it have to be her? The only girl I want but can't have?

And this new revelation about her past. It intrigues me and sends my Mr. Corporate cynicism into overdrive at the same time. Because I see what's coming. She's gotten a little glimpse into my lies as well. And if I want more of her, she'll want more of me.

Something I cannot—will not—give up.

So we are doomed. Again. I hope that big asshole in the sky in charge of irony is enjoying himself right now. Or maybe it's *her*self? I bet the god of irony is female.

163

I leave the weird-ass room Mysterious has set up and make my way back upstairs. Tori is sitting on the couch with a plate of cheese and crackers propped up on a pillow, watching an old rerun of *Seinfeld* on the flatscreen.

Can this trip get any weirder?

"I love this episode," Tori says, cheese slicer in hand as she carves off little slivers of cheddar. "George Costanza is showing off that fake picture of Jerry's man-hands girlfriend to gain access to the Forbidden City." She laughs at the TV. "He's so stupid."

"So you're OK with this?" I ask, taking a seat next to her on the couch. She offers me a cracker, but I shake my head. "With just being told what to do by my mysterious friend while a hurricane rages outside."

She shrugs. "I'm not thinking about it. I'm going to eat and enjoy myself until the power goes out. And then I'm going to bed. This place is much better than that last one. Things could be worse."

This is not a typical Victoria Arias answer. "Since when did you get so Zen?"

"Since now," she says sharply, looking over to stare me in the eyes. "I'm done with you. And your asshole friends. And your secret life as a lobster fisherman. And whatever else you're keeping locked away up in that head of yours." She brushes her hands together to get rid of her cracker crumbs, then sets the plate on the coffee table and stands up. "I'm going to get out of these wet clothes and forget all about what's happening outside in the real world. How's that for Zen?"

She walks over to the dry bag and picks up her skirt

and blouse. I expect her to go change in the bathroom, but she sets them on the kitchen island bar, her back to me, and reaches behind herself to unclasp her bra.

Fuck. My eyes are glued to her body. The small muscles in her shoulders, the way her long hair—which is starting to dry now—ripples along her back as the lavender bra slips down her arms and drops to the floor. She grabs her silk blouse and puts it on, pulling her hair out from the neckline as she lowers her head to button it up.

"Shit."

"What?" I ask, still mesmerized.

"I lost two buttons and there's a rip in my shirt." When she turns around I can see her peaked nipples through the thin silk. The two missing buttons are the ones near the top, so her breasts practically hang out. She pretends not to notice that I'm staring and just wiggles her skirt up her hips, then zips it up, and begins pulling her panties down her long, tanned legs.

"Are you getting a nice look?" she asks, still concentrating on her wardrobe change.

"Well, you're certainly putting on a nice show."

She angles her head to look at me with a sly grin.

Yes, the god of irony is definitely a goddess. If I was back in the real world, I'd just walk out and get as far away from her as I could. As fast as possible. In fact, this would've never gone this far because I know how addictive she is.

"Black belt, huh?" she asks, coming back to the couch and grabbing her plate of cheese and crackers.

"I'm not talking about it."

165

"Well, that's fine." She slices off another sliver of cheese and props it on a cracker. I watch her take a bite and wish her perfect lips were wrapped around my cock.

Stop it, Weston. She's not real. She's some illusion of days gone by. She's not even nice. She's a total bitch, remember? Slaps your face every chance she gets. Plays games, and throws fits, and generally acts like being wild is a gift and not her own desperate attempt to cover up all the bad things in her past.

"We can talk about you instead," I say. "About *your* little black-belt experience. Even though I know why you act the way you do."

"Do you?" She eyes me, daring me to keep going down this line of questioning.

"I was there, remember?"

"You weren't there," she snaps. "You came afterward, Weston. Just like my father. You were late, just like everyone else."

"So it's my fault? Not his?"

"I didn't say that," she whispers, concentrating on her food. "And if it came out that way, well, I didn't mean it, either."

"But you never told anyone."

"Just shut up, Weston. You have no right to give me the third degree about running away."

"Maybe not, but what you did was wrong. You let him get away with it. How many other women has he attacked since that night?"

"Fuck you. It's not even like that, so—" But she abruptly stops talking.

"So? What's it like?"

She smiles that smile she does, the one that says, *If you want something from me, I want something back.* "Why were you working on a boat when you were seven?"

I consider her question. It's not a dangerous one to answer. Not really, if I keep all the important details out of it. And the reason she never went after her attacker that night has been eating away at me since it happened.

So I answer. "We were poor. We needed the money."

"Poor? Ha!" She belts out a laugh. "You were poor when you were a kid?" She laughs again. "Well, I bet that rags-to-riches tale must be very interesting then, right? Because when I met you, your closet was filled with thousand-dollar suits, you were driving an Aston Martin— even though that's about the most pretentious car you can own in America, aside from a Rolls Royce—and you bought me a twenty-thousand-dollar engagement ring."

"Yeah, I still have that ring."

Her brows knit together as she frowns. "I refuse to feel guilty about that."

"I'm not asking you to. I'm just stating a fact."

Tori huffs out some air and tosses her hair the way she does when she's trying to get over something that bothers her. "So how did you go from poor pathetic lobster boy to paying cash for an Ivy League education?"

"Tell me why you never turned that guy in and I'll tell you how I got here."

She squints her eyes at me, looking for the trap. Oh, I've laid one. I'm very careful about my past and there's no way in hell she's gonna get that out of me so easily.

"OK," she says, after considering my offer for a few

moments. She takes a deep breath. "OK. If I tell you something, then you tell me something."

"Deal. Why didn't you turn him in?"

The muscles in her jaw clench for a second and then she takes in a long breath of air and lets the words out on the exhale. "I knew him."

"You knew him? He was the guy you broke up with the night we met?"

She nods.

"Jesus, fuck, Victoria. What the hell?"

"Don't *judge* me," she snaps. "I have my reasons."

"What possible reason could you have to protect an asshole like that? After what he did to you, Tori? Holy fuck!"

"He was threatening my father's legacy."

"Legacy?"

"I'm not telling you anymore. I answered your question, now you answer mine." Her expression goes flat, like hard, cold steel. "How did your family go from dirt poor to filthy rich?"

I have had this answer ready since I was seven years old. I've just never had to tell it before. So I'm careful as I consider my words. Very fucking careful. "My father ran a salvage business."

"Salvage?" Tori asks, trying out the new word. "What's that mean, exactly?"

"You know, treasure hunting. In the ocean."

"Really?" She smiles, picturing it.

"Yeah. But he sorta sucked at it. Until he didn't. We found some treasure. In the ocean. In international waters.

168

It was a big find and it was a fishing boat, not a ship. From a long time ago. So we didn't have to surrender it. We kept the find, cashed it in, and the rest is history."

"Hmmm," Tori says. "That's it? That's how your family went from so poor, you had to catch lobsters to pay the bills to…"—she points at me—"to this?"

"Yup. That's it. Your turn. What's your father's legacy?"

She hesitates. Why? It's not like this information can't be discovered. I mean, if she doesn't want to tell me, and Mysterious and I are still on speaking terms when this is all over, I can have him dig up her dirt. It would be very easy to get whatever information she's hiding.

"He saved me. My father, the noble policeman. He saved me and taught me how to defend myself and took care of me. But I'm not the only one he saved."

"Go on," I say.

"He runs a charitable organization. For kids like me. And when you started the headhunting business I saw an opportunity to make money."

"So you copied me."

"Does that piss you off?" she sneers. "That a woman could do the same job as you?"

"Don't be snide, Tori. I'm not a misogynist. I don't hate women or think they are incapable of contributing. I just want my *wife* to be my *wife*."

"I think it's the same thing."

"Well, it's not." We stare at each other for a moment. "So what does his legacy have to do with your ex, the rapist? And by the way, it never escaped my attention that

169

I was accused of rape twenty-four hours later."

"Now it's your turn to stop being ridiculous, Weston. We both knew you were innocent. I saw the whole thing. You were never going to jail for that. You had a witness."

"But my friends could've. They didn't have an alibi like me."

"I don't think it was him," she says, with more thoughtful consideration than this guy deserves.

"Why are you defending him? He raped you. You let him get away with it. And you have no idea who was behind those accusations. No one does." I stop for a second, considering this. "Unless you *do* know and you never told me."

"I don't," she seethes. "And if you accuse me of that again, I'll walk out of your life when this is over and *never* come back."

I should be more concerned with the facts at hand, with all the secrets that might come spilling out of this very dangerous conversation, with the reason why she's too afraid, or too proud, or too *something* to tell anyone what really happened to her the night after we met. But my thoughts are consumed with the possibility that she *won't* walk out on me. That we might have a chance at a second chance. That she might rethink the answer she gave when I asked her to marry me—six fucking times.

CHAPTER TWENTY-FIVE

VICTORIA

West is silent for a few minutes and I try to pretend I'm more interested in *Seinfeld* than I am him until I can't stand it anymore.

"I don't know who set you up, Weston. And it hurts me that you think I'd keep that from you if I did."

He's staring out the window when I look over at him. It's like a hurricane out there. But maybe not really a hurricane. A bad storm for sure. But my fear of blowing away or being swallowed up by the sea has abated. This house is in the middle of the island surrounded by all kinds of trees and brush, and high up on a hill. I can see the ocean, but it's not twenty feet outside the window, like the other island. And we have power, satellite TV, and food downstairs. His friend put us here, for whatever reason. So this is... controlled. I like controlled.

Which is funny, I suddenly realize. Because West has been trying to control my life since we met and I rail against it with all my being.

Why?

Why do I feel the need to refuse him?

"I'm sorry," West says, leaning his elbow on the arm of the couch to prop up his chin.

I let out a sigh. "I accept your apology."

He looks over at me, opens his mouth to say something, thinks better of it, then shakes his head and looks out the window again.

"What?" I ask. "What were you going to say?"

"Never mind. I will respect your privacy. Obviously you don't want to discuss your past with me, and I should've realized that a long time ago and dropped it. So I'm gonna drop it now. Fuck it. I probably don't know anything about you, do I?"

"I feel the same way." I try not to sound defensive, but I'm not good at hiding my feelings. "You never told me you were poor. Or anything about finding treasure. That's kind of exciting, don't you think? That's something a man would tell his girlfriend, right? Yet you never told me."

"I let you believe what you wanted to believe."

"What did I want to believe?"

"That I was some born-and-bred rich asshole." He shrugs. "Whatever. I don't care if you think of me that way. It's better than people thinking of me as some poor kid who had to work since he was seven to climb out of the hole his parents put him in."

I think hard about that answer. "I thought you were on good terms with your parents?"

"I am," he says quickly. "Why?"

"Well, you sounded a little… bitter just then."

"I'm not bitter. I'm over it."

OK. I need to drop that. The past needs to stay in the past. That's my story and I'm sticking to it. I want my past to stay hidden, so how can I blame him if he wants his to stay hidden too?

"Do you want to have dinner with me?" West blurts out.

172

"Dinner? Like, when we got this island and get back to our real lives?"

"No," he says softly. "Like, tonight."

"I don't think I have a choice." I laugh.

"You have a choice, Victoria Arias. It's always been your choice. But that's not what I mean. I mean, would you like to have a nice dinner with me tonight?"

I laugh. "Like a date? To where? The rainy, windy beach?"

"How about downstairs? And it's not really a date. Just a nice dinner. I'll go get us something out of the ocean. I know where to find lobsters in a turbulent sea."

I just stare at him. "You're serious?"

"I'm serious. I feel like maybe our relationship can start over now. Like we've come to some kind of conclusion and I'm ready to just... be friends. That's what you've always wanted from me each time we broke up, right? Just to be friends."

Just friends. I roll the words around in my mind. I did want us to remain friends, but West was always the one to pick up and leave. A new contract, or a new apartment, or a new state... whatever. Girlfriends, probably. I'm surprised he doesn't have one now. How does a man who looks like that *not* have dozens of girls hanging off him at every moment?

"Well?" he asks.

"I don't want you going out into the ocean again, so no to the seafood. But if you can whip up something better than cheese and crackers, I'm in for that. I'm starving."

"OK," he says, standing up. I let my eyes linger on the

muscles in his bare legs for a moment, before tracking up his perfectly toned body and finally meeting his gaze. He's got a little devious smirk on his face. "I'll get right on it."

And then he grabs his wrinkled clothes from the dry bag, which is still on the floor where I left it when I changed, and disappears downstairs.

It takes me several minutes to realize what he just did.

Took control. God, why does he have to be like that? And why does it make me so defensive?

Don't go there, Tori. Just don't go there. Leave it alone. Let him make you a friendly dinner. Tomorrow the storm will be totally gone and we'll find a way out of here—either with the radio or his friend will show up. And we'll go back to our separate lives.

I need to come to terms with the fact that my business is bankrupt. I need to tell my father that I've let him down. And I need to call that guy who sent me on this job and let him know I failed.

I will not be able to deliver what he asked for.

"Hey," West says, shaking my shoulder. I sit up a little and look around, confused. "I guess you were tired," he says.

I sit all the way up and take him in. He's wearing his clothes again, which are dirty. The shirt is ripped from the lobsters and it's stained a nice off-white color now from the sea water. Still, he's looking quite put back together compared to the wild boy persona he's been sporting the past couple days. "What's happening?" I ask.

"Not much. The storm is dying down. Just some hard rain now, but not much wind. And dinner's ready."

Dinner. I forgot about that.

"Are you hungry?" West asks, when I stay silent.

"Yes," I say, getting up and wriggling my too-short skirt down my legs. I should put my bra and underwear back on. They are probably dry. And it would go a long way towards not having sex with West tonight like I did last night.

But... if we have to go back to our normal lives tomorrow, what's one more night down memory lane?

I leave the bra and underwear hanging on the barstool where West left them and start down the stairs.

"I don't smell anything."

"Well." He laughs behind me. "I had to make do with what we had."

When I get to the door of the safe I stop and smile. He has the small dinette table set with paper plates and plastic dinnerware. Paper towels are being used as napkins and there are two emergency candles lit between the place settings. There's even a red flower sitting in a mug acting as a vase.

"You really know how to impress a woman," I say, walking over to the table. "Where did you get that flower?"

West pulls a chair out and motions for me to sit. He always did have manners. I smile and sit, letting him help me scoot the chair in. "There's a tree, just outside the front door."

I sigh. He's kind of charming, right? In his own way.

"What are we having?" I ask.

West has an old frying pan lid covering a plate on the table. He lifts the lid and says, "Tonight, Miss Arias, in celebration of our temporary reunion and the good luck of being stuck on a deserted island with you, I present… emergency food ration pack number two-three-seven. Otherwise known as macaroni and cheese."

"Oh, dear," I say. But I'm smiling. It's sweet. "Did you try it yet?"

"Uh, no. I might skip dinner and just enjoy the pleasure of your company."

"Oh, no, you don't, Mister Corporate. You're eating this shit."

He opens his mouth like he has a quick comeback, but then he shakes his head and looks down as he takes his seat.

"Did you just blush? You were gonna say something dirty, weren't you?"

"No," he says, placing his paper towel napkin in his lap. "But I love that you were thinking I'd say something dirty."

"You're lying," I muse, taking the little cup of mac and cheese from the plate. I peel back the plastic that covers the top and inhale. "It doesn't smell too bad." I pick up my plastic fork and take a bite, immediately spitting it out. "Oh, my God!"

"It's terrible, right?"

"The worst!" I laugh. "Someone would really have to be starving to eat this."

"We can eat cheese and crackers if you want. Or have

a glass of milk—"

"No, no, no. I'm gonna enjoy the hell out of this mac and cheese, Weston Conrad. You made it, and you set the table and lit candles. So I'm eating it. It's the least I can do."

"Do *I* have to eat it?"

We both start laughing.

"Come on, Weston. Where's that boyish spirit you had hunting treasure as a kid?"

"You're gonna make me eat this, aren't you?"

"It's not that bad, I swear. Take a bite."

He grimaces as he forks some mac and cheese into his mouth, but then smiles as he chews. "Hey, it's pretty good. I'm not a bad cook after all. But you, Miss Arias, you can cook the hell out of some pasta."

"I do make a pretty nice homemade mac and cheese if I do say so myself."

"God, yeah. I think I fell in love with you when you made that prime rib at Christmas that first year."

"Remember that apartment? It was nice, you know? I sorta loved that you were out of school. I know that's pretty horrible, considering you had those bullshit charges and that was the only reason we got to shack up together five towns over. But it was nice coming home to you after classes. And waking up with you."

Holy shit, what am I doing? I should not be talking about the past like this. Least of all about how great it was to sleep with him every night.

"Yeah. I had it easy compared to the other guys. I never really thought I'd be found guilty. I mean, you were my secret weapon."

I have to smile at that. "I was, wasn't I?"

"You made it all better, Tori. For real. I don't think I've ever properly thanked you for sticking by me."

I shrug. "You saved me, West. That night I stumbled onto your self-pity party out in front of the administration building changed my life."

"Remember when we got that turtle?" He draws in a deep breath as he laughs.

"Sheldon." I start giggling. "We were practicing being parents."

"I think you took it a little too far when you started sewing clothes for him. Especially since you made him dresses."

"Turtles can't wear trousers." My smile is so big my cheeks might crack.

"You were good at it, you know."

"My grandma… *adopted* grandma. She taught me how to knit dolly clothes, even though I was too old to play with dolls when I met her. She said every mother needs to know how to make dolly clothes for their little girls. I bet she'd have loved to see Sheldon in his dresses."

"Well, yeah, you were good at making turtle dresses. But what I meant is, you were good at all that stuff, Tori. That home stuff. *Mom* stuff."

"West, please. Why do you always have to bring it up? I don't know what to say to you about it. I don't want to stay home and be some good little wife."

"You could've been my *wild* wife." And he says it so seriously, and he looks so sad as the words come out… I

178

want to put my arms around him and apologize. "You could've been my crazy, wild wife, Victoria Arias. And I'd have fucking loved it. I would've let you throw plates at me. I'm pretty good at ducking."

I take a deep breath and look down at my plastic carton of food. "It would've gone wrong fast enough."

"Why?" he asks. "Why do you say that?"

"Because that's what happens when you get married." I look up at him. "You fall out of love. It might not happen right away but it always happens."

"Says who, Victoria? There's no time limit on love."

I swallow hard and shake my head. "It's inevitable. Nothing lasts forever. You have these perfect weeks of honeymooning and enjoying wild sex, and discovering everything about each other. But we already had that, Weston. And it was never enough for you. Why do you need that piece of paper?"

"Why *don't* you need that piece of paper?"

"Because it's meaningless—"

"It's not meaningless. It's got so much fucking meaning, Tori. It means you're my wife. It means you're my partner. It means you get everything of mine if I die. It's a promise to each other, to our future kids, to the world."

"It might mean that to you, but to me it means we're on a time limit. It means the clock is ticking until we fall apart. It means we have an expiration date."

He stops to consider my answer. It says a lot about me. Things I should probably not let him in on. "Is that why you always said no to me? Because we were doomed from the start? Because you're afraid of falling out of love?"

"Sheldon couldn't keep us together."

West smiles, but it's sad. "I have more faith in you than you have in me. And I hate that."

"Why couldn't we just stay the way we were? I mean, look at how much we fought, Weston. It was ridiculous."

"Our fights were about the future. We never fought about day-to-day things. You never bitched at me about my socks on the floor or leaving dishes in the sink."

"You're a neat freak, I never had to."

"I never bitched at you for spending money or cleaning the house."

"You're filthy rich, Weston. And we had a maid clean the house."

"See how perfect we were?" He's got a smile on his face, but there's a lot of uncertainty in that smile.

"Do you want to get back together with me?" I ask. "Is this what you're doing right now? Courting me for a renewed relationship?"

He stares at me for a moment, then shakes his head. "No. I just want you to realize that we were good. And the reason we fell apart was because you were afraid." I'm about to say something, but he continues. "Besides. We can't go back anyway. I feel like we never even knew each other."

I start picking at my food. "Well, that's true. How could I ever be with a man who refuses to tell me about his past?"

"Do you want to know my past, Tori?"

I shrug, but, "Yes, of course," comes out of my mouth.

"I want to know yours too. Let's tell each other our pasts. Tonight. Let's pretend it's that first week we met and that rape charge never happened. That you weren't reeling from a bad breakup and that asshole didn't rape you the next night. That we didn't get distracted and just meld together into a team before we were ready. Let's try that beginning again. I want a do-over."

CHAPTER TWENTY-SIX

WESTON

"You know what's funny?"

"What?" Tori asks, looking down at her plate.

"All the other Misters had to keep that night a secret from everyone. Remember that guy, Five? Who told us not to talk to each other?"

"Sure," she says, her voice small and sad. "I remember you telling me about him."

"Well, none of the other guys ever got to tell their side of the story. Not to the rest of us, or their parents, or even their lawyers. Because Five came in and took over. Sent us on our ways. We talked on the phone, sure. But not about the case. It was always about what we were doing. What we'd do next. How we might help each other. But I always had you. And I didn't have to tell you what happened because you saw the whole thing. So I guess I made a mistake back then."

"How do you figure?" She looks up at me, those brilliant violet eyes wide and watery like she might cry. She loves me. I know she does.

"I let you down. I didn't mean to let you down, Tori. It just happened so fast."

"I know." She sighs. "It did happen fast. That's why I wasn't sure if we were real."

"We're real, Miss Arias. And maybe I didn't start this trip with getting to know you better in mind, but it's not a bad way to end it, right?"

"I don't want to talk about it." She says it in a very firm voice. There is no way she will tell me what's hidden behind those eyes. No way. Not tonight.

"OK," I say, giving in. "But are you willing to listen? Because I think I *do* want to talk about it. My past, I mean. Not yours."

She blinks at me. "How much more is there?"

I shrug. "A lot more."

She considers this for a few moments, but remains silent.

"Are you interested?"

She nods. "Yes."

I stand up and walk around the small table, extending my hand. "Then come with me."

I lead her back upstairs—all the way upstairs—to the bedrooms. And then I take her into the master bedroom where the view out the massive floor-to-ceiling window is palm trees thrashing, rain pouring down so hard that rivers are running down the glass, and the angry ocean that wants to eat this island alive. I've got a blanket on the floor in front of the window and I motion for her to take a seat.

She does, and I do as well.

"Put your head in my lap, Victoria. And look up at me as I talk." It's an order, and she hates orders. But for whatever reason, she complies. I stroke her hair, loving the softness of it. And the smell. Even though it smells like salt, and rain, and wind, and it hasn't been brushed in two days.

I love this version of Victoria Arias. The wild one. Not

just on the inside, but the outside too. She never lets herself be wild in appearance. She is always tailored, and polished, and put-together.

"My father was a drunk." I look into her eyes to see how she takes this, but she just nods her head for me to keep going. "Not the harmless kind, either. The wife-beating kind. The kid-beating kind. The kind who takes his paycheck at the end of the weekend and buys enough beer to put him into a stupor for the weekend. My mom left when I was six."

"She left you *behind?*"

"She had no choice. She was committed for trying to kill herself."

"Oh, my God, West. That's terrible. Where is she now?"

"Oh, she succeeded. About six months after they took her away. I think she was always mentally ill, you know? Always on the verge of suicide. They let her out on a weekend furlough because she was getting better. So my dad and I went to the mainland to pick her up. And he told her she wasn't going back to the hospital. He was taking her home. She told him how happy she was about that. And we all went to lunch before taking the boat back to Nantucket. And before you ask me how we got to live on Nantucket if we were so poor, that house was a shack. It was in my father's family for six generations. It had an outhouse, for fuck's sake. So that's how."

"Jesus, West."

"So we got to the restaurant and we all ordered our food. And my mom said she had to use the restroom. She

185

never came back. She slit her wrists in the bathroom with a steak knife. And do you know what my father said the next day, when we were finally back home?" I don't wait for an answer. It's a rhetorical question. "He said, 'She could've done it before she ordered the food so I didn't have to pay her bill.'"

Tori sits up, her eyes wide and her mouth open. "Your *dad* said that?"

"Yeah. He couldn't care less about her. And even I knew, at the age of six, that she killed herself because he was taking her home."

"I just can't picture your dad saying that. He looks so normal in those photographs. So that's your step-mom with him? How do you even talk to him still?"

I just keep going. Why not? I'm on a roll now. "The next year I got that job with another boat company. My father had a fishing boat, right? But he never worked regularly. He was too drunk to get out of bed four days of the week. And I started making money to pay our bills. So you see, Tori, you pegged me all wrong. I'm not the guy you think I am."

"And then you found that treasure? When was that?"

"I was fourteen. I was a straight-A student in school because I saw the rich kids on the island. They were only summer people, but I saw them. Met some of them. Learned about them, and their lives, and what kind of futures their parents planned for them. And I wanted to be just like them. So I made it happen. I was fourteen when my dad and I found that treasure. It's funny how money changes your life. It certainly changed mine. I took that money and got into a private school on the mainland. And the rest just sort of worked itself out."

She looks out the window as she thinks about my story.

I wait. I wait for her to come to a conclusion, or ask another question, or tell me she's so sorry.

But she does more than that.

She starts with the words I so desperately need to hear.

"Lucio Gori Junior was the first boy I ever had sex with."

I think I stop breathing.

"And it wasn't consensual. Not in my eyes. I was only eleven." Tori looks up at me. "He was seventeen." She looks out the window.

"Jesus fucking Christ."

"He called me his girlfriend. He took me on 'dates.' And I use the term 'dates' in quotation marks because they were trips to the woods, or to the back of his father's garage, or wherever he could find that got us alone together. He'd say— He'd say, 'Come on, *Vicki*.' God, I hate the name he used to call me. 'Come on, Vicki. We have a date today.' And I'd go. Because my mom worked for his dad." She looks up at me again. "His dad is a dangerous man. You don't fuck with Lucio Gori Senior."

She doesn't need to spell it out for me. I can read between the lines.

"But... when I was fourteen Lucio Junior found out I liked another boy. My mom had already told Senior I'd marry his son. I was promised to him. That's why we lived in one of their houses for free. You wouldn't think this kind of arranged marriage thing happens in America anymore, but it does. It does when you're a girl with a mother like I had. So Junior beat the shit out of me. I was so badly hurt they had to take me to a doctor. Not a hospital, but *their* doctor, you know?"

I nod, even though she's not looking at me. I know.

"And they had to leave me there overnight. And I knew that if I didn't take a stand, right now, in this moment, while everyone was sleeping in the little makeshift hospital, while the Gori family was back at their house, and while my mother was off doing drugs or selling her body, or whatever the fuck it was she did... that I'd be stuck. So I ran away. I ran to the police station and found the man who would eventually adopt me. He was the detective in charge of organized crime in another part of New York. He took me there, out of Brooklyn. And that's where I stayed. Safe. Brand-new life. A brand-new girl. A smart girl who tried hard and did all the right things.

"And then I got into Brown. On scholarship, thanks to my dad. And I forgot who I was and where I came from. Until one night Lucio Gori Junior showed up on my doorstep and I took another stand and told him we were done forever. That if he didn't leave, I'd call the police. My roommates were home, so I guess he felt he had no choice. He left."

"That's what happened to you the night you met me?"

She nods. "Yes. And the next night, when I was attacked and raped after I spent the day with you, that was Lucio again. It happened in an alley, in broad daylight. It was always in broad daylight when he took me. Like he had nothing to hide. Like he was untouchable. He said,

'You're mine and I'll take you whenever I want.' But by some stroke of luck, he never came back. I thought maybe it was because I was dating you? And you were so high-profile at the time? I don't know. But he never came back after that last attack."

Fuck. This shit breaks my heart. I don't know what to say except sorry. "I guess we both had it pretty tough growing up. I'm so fucking sorry, Tori. I wish you'd have told me sooner."

She shrugs. "I think it worked itself out, you know? Why bring it all back up?"

I lean down and kiss her lips. Softly. Like I love her. And I do. I love her. "I would never do that to you," I whisper. "I'd kill anyone who hurt you, Tori. I'd never rest until I got them back."

"I know that, West. But I can't help the way I feel. When people start talking commitment I get this panicked feeling in my chest and my heart starts racing. I was a piece of property to him, West. I cannot let myself be someone's property again."

I kiss her again and say, "I would never treat you that way, Tori. I don't want to mow you down or keep you in line. I just want to grab your hand and bring you along for the ride."

A tear leaks out of her eye and runs down her cheek. "I've never told anyone that story."

"I'm so glad you told me."

"I'm glad you told me your story too."

My hand slips underneath her shirt and I caress her breast. She closes her eyes and I get this feeling of...

power. Not power *over* her, power to make her feel better. I hate that she still has panic attacks, but I'd be lying if I said it doesn't make me feel good when I'm the one who calms her down.

I just want her to need me.

"We could try again," I say.

She takes a deep breath, never opening her eyes.

"We could drop off all this baggage and try again, Tori."

"I love you," she says. "I've always loved you. I want that so bad, even though I hate to admit it."

"Why do you hate to admit it?" I ask, as I start unbuttoning the two buttons she has left on her silk blouse. "Why is it so terrible to have a partner in life? We could be good together, Tori. We could make so many good things together."

Her eyes open and she places her hand on my stubbled cheek. Just the heat of her palm makes me want her so bad. "I want to believe that, but—"

I place a finger over her lips. "Just let me show you how much I understand what you need. OK? Just let me show you how well I *know* what you need."

CHAPTER TWENTY-SEVEN
VICTORIA

I don't even have to answer because we both know we belong together. It was so obvious ten years ago when we first met back in college. That night under the trees. The day after, when he showed up outside my class. It was all so perfect before Lucio came back and did his damage. But what would it cost me to give in again? Really? What would it cost me to let him back in? To let us be together? To trust him?

If it doesn't work out, maybe a broken heart. But they say it's better to love and lose than never to love at all. And even though I never believed that, I *want* to believe that.

"I think," I say softly. He smiles down at me like I am the only person in the world. Like we are the only two people in the whole world. "I think I know what you need too."

I might lose this bet. It might be great for a year, or two, or ten. And then it might all go to shit. But I'd have that year, or two, or ten to hold in my heart. Years we'd probably be very happy.

"All I need is you, Miss Arias. I fell in love with you so long ago. And the only thing I want back is your trust. Just give in a little. Just let me guide you through life, Victoria. When you let me take control you get to think less, worry less, panic less."

"I don't know if I want that, Weston. I really don't. I

feel like I do a good job most of the time. I don't want to be an extension of you. I want to be your partner."

My blouse falls open and his lips find my nipple. His fingers find the other one and he sucks and squeezes, sending my mind into that floaty existence that comes with lust. His mouth is on my mouth, kissing gently at first, then he takes my lip between his teeth and bites with just the slightest bit of pressure.

"You have it all backwards. Giving in to me has nothing to do with losing yourself. Giving in to me just makes us flow. Like a river, Victoria. With no rocks in the way. No bends to wind around. No cliffs to fall over. I'm pretty good at success, you know. I've done pretty good so far. Just trust me. And just start doing that right now. Let me take control here. Let me show how I know what you want… what you need."

God, my whole body is tingling from these words. I've never heard him talk this way. Maybe he's not the guy I thought he was? I have been wrong about so many things.

"Say it, Tori. Say you'll give in."

He positions his body on top of me, his hard cock pressing against my bare stomach. One hand hikes my skirt up, grabs my leg under my knee, and he pulls it out from under him, exposing my pussy to his pressure. I close my eyes and moan as his hips begin to grind against me.

"Say it," he croons in my ear as he props himself up on top of me.

I open my other leg, spread myself for him, grant him full access.

His mouth dips down to nibble on my neck and I can't

help it, I grab his muscled shoulders and dig my nails into his skin.

"Wild girl," he says in my ear. "I know you're a wild girl. Let me show you how wild we can be together."

"Oh, God," I moan.

"Just say OK," he whispers softly. So softly it makes my nipples peak and my pussy wet. "Tell me to take control and we'll try things my way for once. You won't know if you like it until you try."

I don't think I could say no, even if I wanted to. And right now, I really don't want to. "OK," I say.

"OK, what?" he asks, his voice less soft now. Rumbly. Fierce. "I what to hear you say it."

"OK, you're in control."

He's got his hands wrapped around my wrists and my arms above my head before I can even think.

"West—"

"Shhh," he says. "Don't worry. I'm not gonna hurt you. I'm not trying to scare you. I just want you to you explore this new way with me."

New way? I think I know what that means, but I don't really think I know what he means. Weston Conrad has always been gentle with me. Like I'm something he might break. We don't do rough sex. Not really. That sex against the wall yesterday was about as rough as we do it. Bending me over the back of a couch. I like that. But we don't do anything really rough. Is that what he wants?

He's straddling me now. His hands leave my wrists, but he says, "Leave them there," just as I think of regaining some control by touching him back. "Don't. Move."

It's not mean. He's not rough, either. I'm not scared.

I try to breathe deeply as he stands up, his feet planted between my legs, and begins to unbutton his shirt. He smiles at me the whole time. And then his fingers nimbly undo his pants and he pulls them down. They get kicked off to the side and he kneels, his long cock all hard and thick, resting right at the entrance to my pussy.

"God, I want you," I say. "I want you inside me."

"I want you too," he says, moving forward until his dick is positioned in front of my face. "But I want to be inside your mouth first. I want you to suck my cock like you missed it, Miss Arias."

"Can I use my hands?" I ask, so unsure of what he's after.

He closes his eyes and moans. "Fuck. Keep asking me for permission like that, Tori, and I'll come on your face right now. My answer is no. Now open your mouth and suck my cock like you've been dreaming about it for three years."

I feel a gush of wetness between my legs as he tells me these things. Do I like it his way?

"I don't like to ask twice, Victoria."

He says my name like he's talking business. Like the negotiations are over and it's time to sign the contract.

I open and he moves forward, his hands planted on the blanket on either side of my head. I feel the smooth tip first and swipe my tongue around it in a little circle.

"Keep your eyes open," he says, using that same even tone that makes it sound like a command. "I want you to look me in the eyes as you suck my cock."

I have to tip my head back some in order to meet his gaze because he's leaning forward, and as I do that, his fingers find my throat.

They don't squeeze, but it startles me.

"Trust me," he says.

I can't talk back because he sinks his cock into my mouth a little deeper, pressing my tongue flat and opening up my throat.

I've sucked his dick plenty of times. I can take him about halfway on a good day. But I know he's already there and I know he's not going to let that be where he stops.

I seal my lips around his shaft, sucking on him like nothing in the world tastes better than his dick. His eyes begin to close, but he catches himself and smiles.

My head begins to bob with his rocking hips and it turns me on to think of what he's doing. Face-fucking me. God, I want more of this. I cannot believe I'm so turned on. Am I supposed to be turned on? Am I supposed to like this? Or am I supposed to hate it and just do it because he tells me to?

"Tori," he says. "Eyes on me."

I hadn't realized I'd closed my eyes. And I find it very difficult to hold his gaze while I suck him off.

"You're so pretty," he says, fingers sweeping under my hair. "Your lips look so pretty wrapped around my cock."

I moan and close my eyes again. But he fists my hair, pulling it just enough to get my attention back where it belongs. On him.

"I want to come down your throat, Miss Arias. I want you to open wide and let me stick my cock deep inside your throat so I can make you swallow me. Make you choke on my come."

Again, I'm surprised at how calm he is. How soothing his words are. Even though his words are filthy, he's says them like they're sweet.

I'm even more surprised at how calm *I* am.

He's deep, deep inside me. His hips are still rocking. Not hard and fast, but slowly. Way too slowly.

"Take one hand down," he says. "And put it between your legs."

I do it. Immediately. But my arms aren't long enough to reach around his body and find my clit. I moan in frustration as I wriggle to change position.

Weston Conrad smiles at my struggle. And then he thrusts forward one more time, grabs my hair, pulling hard, and comes inside my mouth.

"Swallow," he growls, fighting to keep eye contact with me. "Swallow or I'll never let you come tonight."

I'm practically choking on his semen, and lots of it drips out of my mouth and down my chin.

But I do as I'm told. I swallow as much of him as I can.

CHAPTER TWENTY-EIGHT

WESTON

I flip her over before she's even done, press her face into the blanket, lift her hips up until she's on her knees, spread her legs wide, and dive into her pussy. She is so sweet. Everything about her body makes me think of dessert. I have her wriggling and moaning seconds into giving her my full attention.

"Tori," I say, coming up for air. I grab her hips and hold on tight. "Do you want me inside you?"

"Yes," she says, her eyes closed tight, her head turned sideways with her mouth open. God, I want to fuck her every which way right now. I can't get enough. "Please," she begs.

I want to go slow, I really do. I want to make this last forever. So I lean back and push my fingers inside her slick pussy. Her back arches and her legs begin to tremble and shake.

"You want it, don't you?"

"Yes," she says. "I want you *now*."

"Not yet, wild girl. Not until we lay some ground rules."

"What?" she asks, opening her eyes and lifting her head up. "Rules? Don't fuck with me, Corporate!"

I laugh. "That's *Mr.* Corporate to you, baby."

"Weston," she says. But I wiggle my fingers inside her and one finds her G-spot, so she takes a time out to moan and enjoy that.

"Yes?" I ask, totally amused.

"Just fuck me, you asshole. You already got off and left me hanging. This better not turn into a pattern."

"What if it does? Will you say no next time?"

"I mi—" But she can't even finish because I'm teasing her clit now.

"What was that? I didn't catch the end."

"Stop it, you jerk. You're not allowed to negotiate during sex."

"Well, if you were the one making the rules, I'd agree with that. It's unreasonable and unfair to negotiate in the throes of passion. But I'm gonna do it anyway."

"So shut up and get to it!"

"First," I say, easing my fingers out and leaning forward, so my chest is pressed against her back. "I want some concessions."

"No," she blurts. "No. We fuck, then we talk. That's my new rule. No more talk-fucking."

"I make the rules, my violet wild child. But I don't want much, so just be quiet and listen. I just want you to make me a promise."

"No," she whines. "That's not fair. You already got off!"

"Listen, Victoria. Just give me ten seconds and listen. All I want is your promise that you'll see me again when this is over."

She shoots me a wary look over her shoulder. "That's it?"

"That's it, babe. That's all I want. We're gonna have a

real date when this is over and we're gonna have a real discussion. We're gonna come to an agreement about making this work. So promise me."

"Fine," she says. "Fine. Just step down off your high horse and put your dick in my stable!"

I laugh so loud, it echoes off the ceiling. But then I spank her ass and say, "Listen, missy, the only wild talk happening when you have sex with me comes from my mouth. Your mouth does what I tell it to do. Understand?"

She's about to reach back and punch me in the face so I grab both her wrists and bind them behind her back in a firm grip.

"And no hitting when I talk like this. It's playful, Tori. Just let me be the big strong man I am and play your part as my softer, better half."

She struggles to get free of my hold, but I grip her tighter. "I'm going to make you pay for this."

"You can try," I say, releasing her hands and slapping her ass.

She looks at me like I'm really gonna get clocked now. "Do not *slap* me."

I slap her again. It cracks so loud, she yelps as her body tries to twist and turn. But my body is there, covering her. I've got my hands underneath her now, palms squeezing her breasts. "Someone has to tame you, Miss Arias. It might as well be me."

"You're in so much trouble after we're done."

"I look forward to negotiating that proposal with you. Now, focus." My dick is pressing against her asshole, and even though I'd love to fuck her ass right this moment, I want her pussy more. Right now, I just want to hear her moan as she comes all over my dick.

So I ease inside of her and all that ferocious attitude disappears with a sigh.

"See," I say. "I know what you need." I pull out, almost all the way. Her ass tries to follow my lead, to prevent my cock from withdrawing, and in that moment, I thrust forward. Hard. And again. Harder. Her whole body is pushed forward on the blanket as I continue to fuck her from behind.

A slapping noise fills the room. The evidence of our skin-on-skin contact. Her moans fill the room. Evidence of her arousal. I am grunting, my jaw clenching. My hands are gripping her hips so hard, I might leave bruises.

"Ohoo," she says, each time I pull back. "Uhhhh," she groans, each time I fill her back up.

I lean down, fucking her doggie-style as I cover her back, my hips thrusting and pumping. I reach around to her mouth and I put my fingers to her lips. She begins to suck and lick them, just like she did my cock.

It's too much.

That little bit of action is the pinnacle of her desire.

"Come," I whisper in her ear. "Come right now, Victoria. Come all over my dick and then I will flip you over and eat your—"

She explodes. I stop, enjoying the contractions of her pussy against my shaft. And when they begin to lessen, I do exactly what I said I'd do.

I flip her over and eat her pussy.

She comes again. I could do this all day. My little wild woman is multi-orgasmic most of the time, and I feel like putting that little skill to the test. I reach up and squeeze her tits. Hard. Her hips buck against my mouth, directing my tongue to her clit. I take it between my teeth, nipping it just hard enough to make her wiggle to get away, and then I suck it in, let go, and swirl my tongue around it like it's a sweet piece of candy and I can't get enough.

She comes again.

I am in fucking heaven.

I pull back and lie down next to her on the blanket. "Get on top," I command. "Now."

Tori scrambles up from her position on the floor and straddles me, placing her pussy directly over my hard cock. She eases down, throws her head back, and I fill her up once again.

Her tits are in my face and I lean towards them, my mouth seeking the large, round outline of her nipples.

My hands are there, wrapping around her full breasts, kneading them as she pushes herself to the brink. Her hair sways, dragging along my chest, the long dark waves teasing me as we move in rhythm.

Her back is arched, her eyes are closed, pointing towards the ceiling. I take one hand off her tit and palm her throat.

She comes again, the wetness inside her pussy coating my dick with her hot release.

And then I fuck her so hard, my balls slap against her ass. I fuck her so hard, she has to put her head down on my shoulder and just give in.

We come together the next time. And even though I know I should, I don't pull out. I meant what I said. We're moving forward with *my* plan now. I'm never using a condom or pulling out again.

We lie there, sweating, and hot, and slick, and satiated in the aftermath. Our hearts are beating together. Thumping like crazy. Just thin skin and hardened muscles separate us.

And she says, "You're a dick."

And I say, "I know. But fuck it. I want what I want. And I know you want it too, you're just scared to admit you need someone like me in your life. So fuck it, Tori. I'm just gonna take, and take, and take until you make me stop. And that's where we'll stay forever. Just like that. I'll get as much as I can from you. And you'll give as much as you can *to* me. And that's our happy place, babe. That's how we meet in the middle."

We fall asleep. On the fucking floor. Sprawled out. Arms and legs tangled together.

Happy.

For once.

CHAPTER TWENTY-NINE

VICTORIA

The sun is hot and blazing through my closed eyes when I begin to wake up. No pounding rain. No whipping wind. No insufferable humidity hanging in the air.

"Hungry?" West asks, kissing me on the lips. "I made us ready-to-eat survival pancakes for breakfast."

I smile and open my eyes. He's still Naked Man next to me. He will stay that way all day if I let him. God, I kinda miss the fucking exhibitionism we used to share.

I think about all the words he said to me last night. All the ways he made me feel good. And I give in. For now.

"Yeah," I say, sitting up to look at what he brought me. "Starving, actually. I don't think I'll complain if you want to go catch us some seafood for dinner tonight."

"We're going home today. Mysterious will come get us."

"How do you know?" I ask, feeling a little bit of regret over that news.

"He said he would. I don't really know what the fuck is happening, but I can't afford not to trust him right now. We're sorta stuck. He'll be here. We'll go back to the mainland and I'll figure it out."

"What about Wallace?"

"You're still thinking about that fucking *job*?" West laughs.

"Aren't you?"

He makes a face, which I know means yes, he is. But he says, "Later, Tori. We'll talk about all that stuff later."

"Why later?"

"Can you just relax and eat the fucking pancakes?"

"Don't be a dick to me. I just want to know where we stand in that department."

"Department? You mean business? Tori, come on. We both know your business is bust. If Wallace is still available to be hunted, I'm the one who's going to hunt him. Not you."

I stand up and go looking for my clothes. I pull my skirt on first and then slide my arms into the thoroughly ruined lavender silk blouse.

"And now you're going to throw a tantrum? Even though you know I'm right?"

"You're not right," I say, pissed off. Why do I ever think he'll change? Why do I ever think he'll stop being a controlling asshole? Why do I ever give in to him at all? He is who he is. "In case you haven't noticed, Mr. Corporate, I'm a fighter."

"Oh, I've noticed. You throw that fight shit in my face every chance you get."

"Why are you being an asshole? Was last night just another one-night fuck to you?"

"Don't cheapen my actions and words just because you're too stubborn to face facts. I really don't appreciate that, Victoria. Everything I've ever said to you was sincere."

"Yeah," I say. "Including that whole 'You're a loser' shit you just spewed."

"I never called you a loser."

"Then do not insinuate my business is bust! It's not. I'm fully capable of bringing it back from the brink, Weston. I've got tricks up my sleeve."

"You've used up all your tricks, Tori. You have to stop relying on tricks."

"Fuck you." I head towards the door, but West grabs my arm. I grab his arm with my opposite hand and disable the hold in one smooth motion. He backs off, hands up in the air, his clothes in one hand. "Don't grab me," I snarl.

"I'm not grabbing you," he says, pulling his pants on. "I'm just letting you know I don't want you to walk out. And you know your jujitsu magic won't work on me anymore. You know I can fight back."

"But you won't," I sneer. "Because you think I'm too weak to bother with."

And then I spin on my heel and walk out the door. I go down the steps, West following me downstairs, taking them two at a time. And he's in front of me before I get to the door.

"Where the fuck do you think you're going?" He's still buttoning his pants and his shirt is hanging open.

"To the beach to wait for the rescue. I'm just done with you for now. If you want to talk to me once this Wallace Arlington job is over, I'll talk. But until then, you're my opponent."

"You can't win, Tori," he calls, as I leave the house and find the footpath that will take me back the way we came. I ignore him and just keep walking.

I'm sure there's probably a closer beach, but the beach we came from is the beach that faces the other island. And if people come, they will probably go there first. I need to be there so I can figure out a way to signal that we're here.

I'm not sure about Corporate's friend Mysterious. I have no idea who that guy is. But I'm pretty sure that Vlad the pilot has alerted the coastguard. It's got to be like… a float-plane pilot's creed or something, right? If they drop people off who expect a pickup, and a massive storm prevents said pickup, the pilot has to alert people.

Right?

I'm going with it. I really need to get off this island. My clothes are ruined, I don't even have underwear on, my tits are sweating like crazy, and I need a shower. I smell like the fucking ocean right now. And I feel gross. All that salt is stuck to my skin.

"Tori," West calls, a little way behind me on the path. "You're going to get lost."

"Oh, fuck you. There's a path here, Weston. I'm following it, the same way we did yesterday."

"Tori," he says again, jogging up next to me. "Just fucking calm down. Why are you so mad about this Arlington thing? You know it's not enough. You know that one job won't be enough to dig yourself out of the mess you've made."

The mess I've made? I can't even speak right now. So I ignore him and all the stupid words that come pouring out of his mouth as we make our way back to the beach.

When we get there, I've had enough of him for a lifetime. Plus, he's still fucking talking.

"I'm not listening," I say, shaking my head as I walk out onto the white sandy beach and scan the horizon.

I can just barely see our island. It looks a lot farther away than I thought it was.

Did I really swim from there to here?

I smile at that.

I guess I did. I'm here. I made it. I'm a survivor.

Never mind that West had to put that lifejacket on me for the last leg of the trip. I'm not an ocean swimmer and I made it three quarters of the way with almost no help.

"Goddammit, Tori," West yells. "Stop fucking ignoring me!"

"What?" I say, reeling around to get his hands off my shirt. "What, goddammit?"

West puts his hands up like he's surrendering. "Can you just be calm for a minute?"

"Why should I be calm? You have no faith in me, Weston. None. I can take care of myself and you should want me to take care of myself. You should say, 'Hey, Tori, you're just as good as me, so take your best shot and best of luck. We'll see who get the contract in the end.'"

"That's what you want me to say?" he asks.

"Yes. Something like that. Something uplifting and positive."

"Here's something positive for you. How about I just give you the money you need, you let me get the contract, and then I'll fucking kill Lucio Gori and we'll all live happily ever after?"

"What?" He did not just say that. "What the hell are you talking about? You're not doing anything to Lucio Gori, let alone *killing* him."

"He raped you. Do you really think I'm just gonna let that asshole get away with that? You are fucking out of your mind."

"I didn't tell you that story so you could go avenge me, Weston. I told you in confidence."

"Well, you should know me better."

I am so angry, my head might split right down the middle. "You planned that little heart to heart conversation, didn't you?"

"Don't be ridiculous. I didn't plan anything. You told me because you wanted me to *do* something about it."

He's serious. He really thinks my confession was code for, *Go kill him for me.* "I told you because you confessed something personal about your childhood. I thought we were trying to earn each other's trust." I stare at him for a second. "That's not why you told me, was it?"

"Tori, why do you have to be so—"

I punch him in the face. His head snaps to the side and a little trickle of blood runs off his cheek. He turns back to me and smiles.

I punch him again.

He laughs. "I'm gonna hate-fuck you, Victoria Arias. If you hit me one more time, I'm gonna throw you down on the sand and—"

I move on him. My leg sweeps behind his ankle, I grab his shirt and thrust him sideways as I twist my hip. He lands on the hard sand, still laughing.

I stand over him, seething.

"I hate you, Mr. Corporate. How about that? I fucking hate you right now."

"Hey." He smiles. "Like I said, hate fuck's a-coming. I'll play along, how about that? I hate you too, Miss Arias. And just to keep things going, I'll go one step further. I hate you more."

I stand over him, ready to... to... I want to scream! "No, you cannot hate me more. I hate you more and I want you to admit it, right fucking now."

CHAPTER THIRTY

WESTON

"Say it." Victoria Arias looms over me, her feet planted on either side of my hips, seething. "I want to hear you *say it.*"

She looks like the storm that just passed. That poor lavender shirt is rippling in the remnants of the wind. It's ruined. And out of nowhere, like God was playing a trick on us earlier, it starts to rain. Hard, pouring-down rain.

"What's your fucking problem?" I ask. "Just what the fuck, Tori?"

She drops, her ass sitting on my dick, but nothing about this moment says seductive. She slaps me six times in the face. Both hands, one after the other. Six times. *Bam, bam, bam, bam, bam, bam.*

"Say it!" She yells it this time.

I taste blood in my mouth and reach up to wipe it away as I look her in the eyes.

Those beautiful violet eyes. That wild dark hair is sticking to her face as she rages. And her breasts are practically bursting out of her shirt—those last two buttons have no hope of containing them.

Another slap, and this time it stings.

"Stop it," I say, grabbing both her wrists and pulling her down onto my chest. "Just fucking stop it."

"I hate you more, Weston Conrad." Her voice is low. Even. Controlled. "I hate you more than you will ever know and I want to hear you say it."

"Why should I give in to you? Why the fuck should I? Do you really think this badass attitude you have is cute, Miss Arias? Well, it isn't. It's fucking old, OK? I'm sick of it. I'm sick of you. And I'm not giving you what you want. Ever."

I push her off me and get up. I'm wet, I'm covered in sand, I'm hungry, I'm thirsty, and my dick has been hard for three days.

"You're a coward," Victoria says, her South American accent appearing. "You're a coward and a cheat."

"That makes no sense. And I'm not a cheat. You're the fucking cheat. How the hell did you get here, huh, Victoria? You *cheated*!"

She's on her knees now, that goddamned lavender shirt blowing open. "Well, just give me what I want, Weston Conrad. And then we can part ways and never see each other again."

"I'm not giving you this contract. Fuck that. I earned it. You're the one who tried to steal it from me."

"I don't just want the contract, you idiot. I never wanted the contract. I wanted *you*."

I just blink at her. "What?"

"Did," she clarifies. "I don't want you anymore. I wouldn't want you if you were the last man on Earth!"

"Or a deserted island?" I say, laughing.

She throws a handful of sand at me, but the wind catches it and it goes in her eyes. Her hands fly up to her face as she doubles over in pain.

Fuck.

"Victoria," I say, dropping down to see if she's OK. She's not. She's crying.

"Victoria," I say again as I try to pry her hands off her face. "Let me see."

She shakes her head and starts to sniffle. "Just tell me what I want to hear."

"What?" I ask. "What the fuck are you after? I can't ever make you happy for more than a few hours. I don't fucking know what you want!"

She drops her hands and looks me in the face. "I hate you more, Weston Conrad. I hate you more than you hate me. And I want to hear you admit it."

"Fine." I shrug. "Whatever. You hate me more. What the fuck do I care?"

"What the fuck *do* you care?" Her makeup was washed off in the rain days ago. There's no leftover mascara to stain her perfect cheekbones. And her lips are naturally pink and plump. I can't stop looking at them.

Her.

I can't stop looking at *her.*

"Why are you doing this?" I ask.

"I want that contract."

"No. I told you no. How many times do I have to explain this to you? It was my contract to begin with. You fucking cheated!"

"But I need it more!" she yells.

"I said I'd help you, Tori. I already said I'd help you, for fuck's sake!"

"Don't call me that *ever again*!"

Jesus Christ. Why does she have to be so wild?

"If you give me that contract, I will give you something in return."

"What?" I ask. "What do you possibly have that I want?"

"Me."

Her eyes search mine. Back and forth. Back and forth. I do want her. I want her so fucking bad. But I can't give her that contract. That contract isn't even enough to fix her problems. But it's mine. It's *mine*, dammit. If it's still available, I cannot let her have it. I just can't. If she ends up with this contract, my world shifts. And not in a good way. She can't have it and I'm tired of talking about it. Thinking about it. So I change the subject. "I thought *you* wanted *me*?"

"Not anymore," she says, tipping her head up to regain some of her dignity. And even though most of the people on this planet wouldn't be able to conjure up some dignity while sitting half-naked, half-starved, and half-satisfied at the tail end of a hurricane, Victoria Arias manages. "I mean nothing to you, West. You used me last night. You used me just like you use everyone else." She pokes me in the chest to emphasize her words. "And you know what? I'm tired of you, too. You checked out ten years ago and never came back. Turned into Mr. Corporate and said, 'Fuck you, Rhode Island. I'm going to LA.'"

I'm just about to open my mouth and tell her off when it hits me. She's been mad at me this whole time. Not because we broke up. Not because we couldn't make the long-distance relationship work. But because she thinks I left her behind.

214

But I don't get the chance to say any of that. Because the sound of a helicopter comes into range.

"Here!" Victoria yells, jumping to her feet and waving her arms. "Here! Here! Here! We are here!"

She bolts down the beach, her perfect legs stretching out into a full run, her dark hair flying out behind her like a banner that dares me to follow her into war.

I want to follow her. I want to think so anyway. I want to believe that I can fight her battles, and take no prisoners, and come out on the other end a winner.

But I don't believe it.

Because she doesn't need anyone to fight her battles. She's made that perfectly clear.

And I don't believe I could match her passion and commitment anyway. I don't believe I could keep up with her, to be honest. Or hold on to her, or even make her the slightest bit happy. I don't believe I can do anything right when it comes to Victoria Arias.

And it's not because I feel like sulking against the wall at my own pity party.

It's because I've hurt her so many times in the past, it's become a habit.

It's because we're in this endless pattern of destruction. We're a trainwreck. A plane crash. A hurricane of nothing-will-ever-come-of-this.

Ever.

"Here!" Tori screams. Her voice cracks, that's how loud her yell is. But there's no way in hell they can hear her. So I get to my feet and jog after her. Her arms are flailing in the air as she tries to get their attention.

215

"Tori," I yell over her noise, and the wind, and the rain. "They can't hear you. Just stop!"

She does stop. Like… immediately.

It's a fucking miracle. I'm just about to ask her what's up when she points to the island behind me. "Do you think that helicopter is unusually large for a rescue mission?"

"What?" I whirl around and look over at our island. "What the fuck are they doing?"

"What is that hanging down? Do they have cargo or something? Are they not here for us, Weston?"

"Jesus. Maybe not. But what are they lowering?"

"Men," Tori says. "I'm counting them as they lower down. That's twenty so far."

Twenty guys? To rescue two people from an island? She counts the rest of the guys and stops at twenty-eight.

"Twenty-eight men. Do they look like soldiers to you, West?"

I think it's funny she's suddenly so calm. And if she had never said the word 'soldier' I might take a moment to enjoy her stillness.

But yeah. "Soldiers," I say, repeating her word.

"Do you hear that popping noise? Is that shooting? Why is the helicopter hovering, Weston? Do they always have two of those propeller things on a helicopter?"

Everything about this is suddenly wrong.

"I think we should go back to the house, Tori. I don't think they're here for us." I want to say, *I don't think they're here to save us.* But I keep that part quiet. "I think we should just go back to the house and wait for Mysterious to figure

216

shit out and show up. If they're looking for us they won't know we're here. And if they're not, they won't see us out on the beach when they go to leave."

"Look, they're running back to the helicopter."

"Shit. We better go. They won't come here. We're fine."

"Um, Weston. Do you promise not to get mad at me if I tell you something right now?"

My stomach sinks. "What?"

"You have to promise." She looks up at me and smiles that smile when she wants something from me and I'm not giving in.

There's a time and a place for that. This is not either of those things. "I promise. Now what?"

"They *will* come here looking for us. Because I left a note."

CHAPTER THIRTY-ONE

VICTORIA

I expect him to yell. I expect him to scream, and tell me I'm a selfish, stubborn woman who thinks she's always right. I expect all the things I've gotten from him in the past.

But he doesn't do any of that. He doesn't even frown.

He takes my hand and drags me through the trees, pulling me along with him, so hard I think my shoulder will come out of the socket.

"West," I say, trying my best to keep up. "Slow down!" The branches and leaves are drenched with rain, which has stopped just as suddenly as it started. But they slap me in the face and water gets in my eyes so I have to close them and hope I don't fall as West continues to freak out and drag me along.

He says nothing until we get to the boat house on the lagoon. Then he stops and looks me in the eye as he places both of his hands on my shoulders and squeezes. "Victoria. I need you to listen to me. OK?"

I nod.

"You're going to stay here. You're going to hide in the trees until I come back. And if any of those men from that island come while I'm gone, you're going to run in that direction as fast as you can."

He points off to the left and my gaze follows.

"There's no beach on that side of the island. OK? There's no beach so it won't be easy for them to find you. So you make your way through the brush, as fast as you safely can, and then wait until I call for you before coming out. Do you understand?"

"Where are you going?" I ask, suddenly very frightened.

"I'm going back to the house to close up the safe. Maybe they'll think we're in there and it will give us enough time to find a good hiding place."

We both look up as we hear the sound of an approaching helicopter.

"Do what I say, Tori. I mean it. These people are not fucking around and they are here for us."

"Why, though? Why are they after us?"

"We can think about that later. Right now, we just need to hide. Don't come looking for me. I'll find you. Now run. We don't have much time and I'm not going until I see you run."

"West—"

"Run, Tori. I'm dead fucking serious. And don't stop until you can see the ocean."

I want to kiss him or hug him. Or say I'm sorry I didn't trust him and left that note and now he has to clean up my mistake.

But I don't. I figure the best way to show him all that is to follow his directions.

So I take off into the trees. There is no path. Just underbrush and tree trunks and bugs. I have no shoes on, so my feet are bleeding almost immediately as I step on

220

rocks, and sticks, and all the tiny disgusting things that live on this island.

It takes me minutes to be brave enough to look behind me. I didn't get that far. I can still see the red roof of the boathouse through a break in the leaves.

The helicopter is louder. So loud I have to clamp my hands over my ears. It's circling the island above. I stop when I get to a small clearing with a tall tower in the middle, afraid to move for fear of being seen from the air.

So I hide under the tree cover and watch it. Whatever cargo it's carrying is hanging by ropes or chains. It's nothing but a box.

What's in that box?

I crawl on my hands and knees to the tower, then climb up as fast as I can. It's only about thirty feet high, but that's higher than the tallest trees, so I have a good view.

The men are being dropped down by a line, one after another. There must be no good place to land here. "Please, let West already be leaving the house. Please, please, please." I chant it over, and over, and over.

Men are yelling on the other side of the island. Shouting, then shooting.

Holy fucking shit.

"Please, please, please," I say, climbing back down the tower. It's my mantra and I chant it as I run. There's a small trail, but I don't take it. What if they fan out and start looking down all the trails?

I keep to the brush, trying to put some distance between me and the shouting.

A branch catches my shirt and it rips as I keep going. Red lines appear on my arms and legs as the thin branches of young trees slap against my body.

The helicopter circles overhead again. Like they are searching for someone.

Me?

Or West?

I don't know, I just cower in the brush and hide under long fern fronds. When it moves on to another spot, I continue my run. A few minutes later I can hear the ocean, then see it. And I've run out of room.

This is where I'll have to stay.

This is where I'll have to hide.

CHAPTER THIRTY-TWO

WESTON

I lose precious seconds looking for the guns I don't have on me. I didn't expect Tori to walk off. I should've fucking put them somewhere close the moment I woke up.

But I didn't.

I totally fucked up and now I need them and I don't have them. And these fuckers are here to kill us. I just know it.

I don't want to think of the how or the why. I don't want to think of the number one suspect on my very short list who might've sold me out. I don't want to think of Tori, out there in the trees, running for her life.

I just need to get those guns.

Last night I woke up and stared out the window, planning what we might need to do today. None of those plans included a Chinook helicopter filled with mercenaries.

That's what they are. I know it. They're not soldiers. This is most definitely a private operation.

The sound of the helicopter becomes deafening and I know they are hovering over the house. The guns are at the bottom of the dry bag, and the bag is... where is it? Where the fuck did I put it? I left it—

There. I grab it off the kitchen counter and run for the stairs. I practically leap down them, five at a time, and rush towards the safe, slamming it closed and arming the lock. I'm just about to leave when I see the silver envelope, slide on the smooth floor as I pick it up and stuff it into the bag, and then, just when I think I'll get out of here in time...

They kick the front door open upstairs.

My body freezes but my mind is filled with thoughts.

There has to be a way out of the basement. *Think, Corporate.*

It's not my voice in my head, it's Paxton Vance's. Mr. Mysterious would not have a basement with no exit. He's far too paranoid for that. And I know—I just know—this is his house.

I have twenty, maybe thirty, seconds before they come down here.

Think!

Why the fuck didn't we explore this whole house yesterday?

Oh, I know why. I was too busy trying to fuck Tori. Me and my goddamned cock are gonna get us killed over that mistake.

Think!

I don't see any windows, so that means it has to be a door. I open the first one I see. Bathroom. Next is a closet, then a bedroom. The last one is the utility room that houses the generator. It's humming along. Well, not humming, exactly—that fucker is loud. And we never heard it. Which means these walls are soundproof.

I close the door and flip on the lights. Another door, on the other side of the generator, has light leaking through the bottom. I glance at the machinery, find what I'm looking for, and flip the switch.

The power goes out and my whole world goes silent and dark.

Get out now, Corporate.

I feel my way along the wall towards that sliver of saving grace light near the floor.

Are they out there? They have enough guys to surround the house. I press my ear against the cool metal and listen.

Nothing.

I place my hand on the door handle, push. Nothing. Pull. Nothing. Fucking locked. I feel along the door for the lock, flip it, then try again.

Just a crack.

The helicopter is suddenly there, right on top of me, that box of cargo swinging in the air as it circles the house. It lowers, hovers, and then I hear a man shouting instructions.

A man whose voice I recognize.

CHAPTER THIRTY-THREE
VICTORIA

The shooting. They are shooting. More and more and more shooting.

He's dead, Tori. And you killed him. He's dead and you're stuck here without him. And you're going to die too.

No.

I stand up in the brush.

No.

I start making my way back. Fuck that. They are not getting him. I will not live the rest of my life knowing that he died to save me and I did nothing to help. Even if I have to kill them with my bare hands for revenge only, I'm going back.

I get about fifty feet when there's a loud *boom*!

Instantaneously I'm on the ground, my face pressed into the wet grass and dirt.

What the hell was that?

I get up and start running again, not stopping until I reach that little clearing on the hill. I climb the tower as fast as I can, praying that these people are too busy to be looking. Too busy with their mission to notice me.

And when I get halfway up, I cling to the metal rungs, unable to believe what I'm seeing.

A tall pillar of smoke a couple miles away.

They blew up the house on the other island.

That's what was in that box.

Explosives.

Holy shit. What the fuck is happening?

I climb down and start running again. The shouting is loud and I can hear one voice in particular giving orders.

Why does it sound familiar?

Who cares, Victoria? Just do something!

I slow down when that commanding voice gets closer. "He's dead," he yells. "Let's get the fuck out of here before the whole thing explodes!"

No. No, no, no.

I stand up and rush towards the voice, making so much noise in the underbrush, I cannot believe he can't hear me when he comes into view.

Everyone else is running away, back towards the hovering helicopter. They are lifted up, one at a time, and still that one lone man waits, the back of his head swiveling from side to side, like he's the lookout.

When he turns his body in my direction, I duck and pray that he didn't see me.

"Vance!" someone yells. "Vance, we gotta go! We only have one minute!"

I don't want to think of what will happen in one minute, but I know. They are blowing up this house too.

This guy's name is Vance. Paxton Vance.

He set us up.

"I see you," he says, the underbrush crunching under his boots as he draws closer. "And you're going to do exactly as I say if you want to stay alive, Victoria Arias."

I stand up and shake my head. "I'm going to kill you, Mr. Mysterious. I'm going to kill you and get you back for what you did."

"Vance!" the guys yell again. "Vance!"

"No," he says calmly as he extends his hand. "You're going to come with me and do as you're told. Because in thirty seconds, that house is gonna explode."

"Vance!" His friends are frantic now.

"Stop, Tori!" Weston yells.

There's shooting in response. Not from Vance, who is standing still when Weston's bullet hits him in the center of his chest. But from the other guys.

"Drop!" West yells. "Drop!"

I do it on instinct. My face hits the ground again as bullets fly past over my head.

He was alive.

He was alive.

And now he's standing in the middle of a rainstorm of bullets.

The shooting stops and the helicopter whines, circling over the top of me, but the trees are too thick for them to aim.

And just as quick as all this started, it ends.

The helicopter tilts, and flies off.

I wait for the silence but it never comes.

Because that's when the house explodes in a fireball.

I stay where I'm at for minutes, at least.

"Miss Arias?"

That motherfucker is not still alive.

"Miss Arias? Are you hurt?"

What is happening?

"Answer me, goddammit."

229

"Tori," West calls. "Tori! Where the fuck is she, dude?"

I stand up, unable to believe it. But he's there. West is there, standing next to his friend, who has a bullet hole in his chest.

"What the fuck is going on?" I scream.

I run up to Paxton Vance and punch him in the face. He grabs hold of me by my arms, but West is there, tackling him to the ground.

I fall with them, and the three of us struggle.

I grab Vance's rifle and pull, but he jerks back. "Tell her, asshole. Tell her before she gets us all killed!" Vance yells.

"He's on our side, Tori. Just calm down! He's on our side!"

I stop struggling and just lie there, panting. "What is happening? What the fuck just happened?"

"It's OK," West says, pulling me up off the ground. Vance gets up, pulling the barrel of his rifle out of my grip as I stand.

"I'm the fucking cavalry, Arias. So quit your bullshit and give me a fucking minute to explain."

CHAPTER THIRTY-FOUR

WESTON

"This had better be good," Tori growls.

"We don't have time for that," Pax says, one finger probing the hole I left in his armored vest. "Our ride is at the boat house right now. We need to go before those assholes start feeling guilty for leaving me behind and come back."

I can't argue with that. Because I can't answer her question.

I have no idea what's happening. All I know is that we have no choices here. We either stay on the island and hope for some kind of real rescue when people show up to investigate the explosions, or we go with Mysterious.

"Come on, Tori. We can talk about it once we're safe."

I expect a fight. I mean, what are the chances that Victoria Arias will ever go quietly?

But she says nothing.

Pax starts heading in the direction of the boathouse and she simply falls in line behind him. I take up the rear, and can't help but be pissed off that her shirt is ripped open and Pax got a good view of her tits just now.

We walk the half a mile back to the lagoon in silence and even though I'm not expecting anyone to be there, there is someone there. A guy I'd like to punch in the face for many, many reasons.

Vlad the pilot is grinning like an asshole as we walk up to the boat.

"I count three living, breathing bodies," he says. "So looks like this one went off without a hitch."

"Don't count the living just yet, Five. We're not even close to being done here."

Five. I *knew* that guy looked familiar.

Five was our fixer back when we were charged with rape. Five was the guy Match called to swoop in and tell us what to do.

"What the fuck is going on?" I ask, looking straight at Mysterious.

"Just get in the boat, man. I'll explain along the way."

"Nice to see you again, Vlad," Tori snarls as she moves forward. But I grab her hand and turn her around to face me.

"Are you OK?" I ask, taking off my shirt and holding it open for her, so she can slip it on.

She sighs and looks down, like the tough girl just flew out of her with that exhale.

I button the shirt up so she's covered again. "Are you hurt?" I ask.

She shakes her head and looks up to meet my gaze. "No. But I'm scared to fucking death right now."

I pull her close and wrap my arms all the way around her body so I can hold her tight. "We'll be all right. We'll figure it out. OK?"

And even though it took a hit squad and two explosions to get what I've always wanted, I'm happy anyway.

Because she looks up at me and says, "I know. I trust you. Just get me out of here."

Pax waves his hand towards the boat. "Get in, you guys. We've got a plane waiting for us back in the US. So we're gonna go there, get on, dump the boat, and go to San Diego by air."

"Why San Diego?" Tori asks as I help her into the boat.

Pax looks at me and says, "I got a place and we need to stick together until we sort all this out."

I stare at him, not quite sure what to make of all this. OK, so he's admitting he's behind some of this. But how much? How much is him? And who else is involved?

"You got a problem, Corporate?" Pax asks.

I look over at Five—he's telling Tori to go down below—then look back at Pax. "Where's Oliver?"

"He's waiting in San Diego. We're meeting up with him."

"And Nolan? Mac? Are they coming too?"

"No," Pax says. "Not yet."

"What do you mean, not yet? Why the fuck not? If this is connected to Nolan's bullshit, he needs to be in on it."

"Maybe it is. Maybe it's not."

"What's that mean?"

"Did you tell her?" Pax nods his head in the direction of the boat.

"Tell her about what?"

"Who you really are?"

I study him for a moment. My jaw is clenching. "I told her."

233

"You did, huh?" Pax says, laughing a little. "You told her everything?"

"Define everything."

"Because I know everything, asshole. So did you or didn't you tell her *everything*?"

"You don't know shit. And whatever it is you think you know, you're wrong. So get the fuck out of my business and back off."

"So she knows who your real father is?"

I squint my eyes at Mysterious.

He squints back.

"What the fuck are you doing, Pax? Did you set me up? Did you set all this up? Was that whole thing with Wallace a lie?"

"We'll talk about it in San Diego."

"No, we'll talk about it—"

"Not now, Corporate," he says, cutting me off. "Unless you want me to go down in that boat and tell your girlfriend all the things you've been leaving out of your life's story."

I am so pissed off right now.

"Get. In. The boat."

"We're not done," I say, bumping his shoulder as I go past.

"Not even close," he says, following me.

I take a seat next to Tori, who is huddled up on an l-shaped sectional with a sleek teak marine table in front of her. She looks at me when I enter and takes a deep breath.

"You all right?" I ask, taking a seat next to her as she scoots over to make room for me. We suddenly feel like a team now. Us versus them.

"Yeah," she says, wrapping her hands around my bicep and leaning into me. "Are you? I thought they killed you."

"I'm fine," I say, leaning down to kiss her head. I'm not going to worry about what Mysterious thinks he knows about my past. There are a lot of moving parts there. Best to let him spill before I come out swinging with a defense. "I went in the house, closed the safe. But by that time, those guys were already there. I found a backdoor and ran right into Pax, who sorta…" I look over at him as he talks with Five about whatever. "He sorta had a plan. I mean, he was expecting us to be in that safe room. And when we weren't, he went outside looking, found me by the back door. We had to play it right to the last second so his team would leave him behind."

"Who is his team?"

"I don't know yet. I guess we'll find out when we get to San Diego."

She sighs. "I don't want to go to San Diego, West. I just want to go home. I'm hungry, I'm tired, and I need a shower. I just want to go home."

"You can't go home, Miss Arias."

Tori looks up. Paxton is standing in the entryway that leads to the control room. "Why not? What is going on?"

"I'll tell you the same thing I told Corporate. I don't know yet. But whether you like it or not, you and this asshole are the reason this is happening. I can't, in good conscience, cut you loose just yet."

"Cut us—" Tori starts.

But I hold up my hand. "We'll just wait, Tori. OK? We're fine. Whatever is happening," I say, throwing a look at Pax, "we'll figure it out and be home in a few days."

"Maybe," Pax says. "Maybe not. I wouldn't promise her anything you're not sure you can deliver, Weston. And we've got a lot of come-to-Jesus moments ahead. For both of you. So if you're tired, Miss Arias, I suggest you claim one of the cabins and get settled. We're sailing to West Palm Beach first, then we'll get on the jet and land in San Diego. So you've got plenty of time to rest up."

Pax turns his back to us and goes back into the control room, like this conversation is over.

"Well, he's an asshole," Tori says.

I smile. "See, I'm not so bad."

Her body shakes with a small laugh. "I'd like to take a shower. Do they have showers on these things?"

"I'm sure they do. Come on, let's go check it out and claim a cabin."

I wait for her to fight. *I'm not sleeping with you, Mr. Corporate.* Or, *Don't order me around, you controlling pig.*

But she doesn't even put up a small fight when I take her hand, and stand up, and lead her past the galley and down the stairs to the cabins. I check the first door—occupied. Then the second—also occupied. We turn around and try the starboard side, open the next door and find it empty. "I guess we'll take this one, huh?"

"I don't care. Do you think they have any clothes I can wear?" Tori looks up at me. Everything that has happened in the last few days has finally caught up with her in this

236

moment. She looks exhausted. Her eyes are ringed with dark circles, her arms and legs have red welts and scratches from running through the underbrush, and she's got a cut on her cheek that looks painful.

"I'm sure I can find something. Look," I say. "I bet this cabin has its own en suite." I let go of her hand and walk into the cabin, which is spacious. The salon was well-equipped with a TV, a bar, and ample seating for at least twelve people. The cabin has a king-sized bed with luxury bedding and six pillows. There's two doors—the first one, I discover when I open it up, is a closet. "Look, clothes."

Tori walks up to me. "So they planned this whole thing?" She looks up at me, frowning. "They have clothes for me, West. What the hell is going on?"

"I'm not sure yet. Just... let's... we just have to trust him, OK? I don't have a good reason, I'll admit it. I'm suspicious too. But we're stuck here until we get to Palm Beach. I'm sure the jet he's talking about is the one we share. So I'll have more options once we get to the US. But for now, let's just rest and keep our heads down. OK?"

I'm expecting a fight. Some protests at least. But Tori just hunches her shoulders and nods her head. "Is that one the bathroom?" She points to the other door.

I walk over to it and pull the door open. "Yup. And look, it's got a tub. Why don't you take a bath and just go to sleep?"

"Where are you going to be?"

"Feeling needy, Miss Arias?" I give her that crooked smile she loves so much.

237

And she cracks a small one in return, but it's brief. "A little bit. But you can't go too far, so I'll be OK."

"Go take a bath and I'll be in after I grab something to wear from Pax. OK?" I kiss her tenderly on the lips and pull her into a hug. "We're fine, Tori. Just fine."

She nods and turns to the bathroom, closing the door behind her.

I head back up to the control room and find Five and Pax sitting at the bar getting drinks.

"You want one, Corporate?" Five asks.

"Sure, Vlad."

He shrugs. "Hey, man, it's not my fault you fell for it. This is just business."

"Right." I take the shot of tequila Pax slides across the sleek teak bar, and down it. "Fuck, yeah," I say, slamming the shot glass down. "I needed that. We found the clothes for Victoria in one closet. But there wasn't anything for me. You guys got something to spare for me?"

"Your stuff is in the other cabin, Corporate," Pax says.

"Stop calling me that, asshole. It's a fucking insult and you know it. I don't call you Mysterious unless I'm pissed off about something."

"Maybe I'm pissed off about something. You ever think of that?"

"What the fuck do you have to be pissed about? You're the one who set us up. You're the reason we're here in the first place."

"Try again, *Corporate*." Pax does a shot and slams his glass down on the table too.

I look over at Five, who simply shrugs and says, "I'm the hired help, so don't ask me."

"Frankly," Pax says, "I'm surprised she's even considering rooming with you tonight. You might want to double-check your sleeping arrangements."

"Thanks, Mysterious. But I highly doubt I need relationship advice from you."

He shrugs. "You know she's gonna find out."

I say nothing.

"You gotta know that. So the sooner you come clean, the easier it's gonna go, my friend. Because if you don't tell her who you really are... I will."

My eyes narrow into slits as I consider his threat.

"And by the way, I'm gonna go ahead and call our debt even since you got both of my fucking islands blown up out there today. In fact, from the way I see it, I think you owe me right about now, *Corporate*. So let's make a deal."

CHAPTER THIRTY-FIVE

VICTORIA

The tub is small and round. Not oval, like they normally are so people can stretch out and relax. It's big, don't get me wrong. But it's round. How does a person relax in a round tub? Obviously whoever designed this ship didn't ask a woman's opinion.

So I opt for a shower. And the water is wonderfully hot and soothing. The steam relaxes my muscles and I relish in this new calm we have settled in.

I know there's more to the story than anyone is telling me at this point, but I can't afford to make a big deal about it. The last thing I need is that scary Mr. Mysterious asking me how I got involved in all this.

I frown.

It's gonna come out. There's no way I'm not gonna get asked that question.

I'm just rinsing the conditioner out of my hair when the bathroom door opens and West walks in. He's already naked and he says nothing as he steps into the shower with me and lets the water pound down on top of his head.

I grab the soap and start washing his chest, which makes him open his eyes and smile. "I'm OK," he says.

"I know you are," I say back. "Just trying to make it easier."

He smiles bigger at that and starts shampooing his hair. I rub the soap up and down his arms, scrubbing away the dirt and grime, then bend down and get his legs, starting at his feet and working my way up. I look up at him and he's got his head tilted to the side, with a big questioning grin on his face.

"Really?" he asks.

"What?" I say back, blinking my eyes innocently. "I'm just trying to help you out here Mr. Conrad. Get you nice and clean."

"Miss Arias. If you get on your knees in front of my cock, I'm gonna come up with some expectations."

I laugh. "Something like this?" I ask, taking his dick in my soapy hands and lathering it up. My motion is slow, way too fucking slow for what he's thinking about right now. I look up at him as I do it. "Or am I reading you wrong here?"

"I'll take that first," he says, with a chuckle.

I'm relieved that he's not as tense as he was when we first came aboard. I know something is going on between him and his friends. Maybe something he doesn't want me to know. But I'm too tired to worry about that right now. I just want a night of peace. Just one night next to him in a bed with his arms around me.

Tomorrow can wait. Everything else can wait.

West lifts the shower head off the holder and starts spraying the soap off his body. The white frothy bubbles run down his abs, his cock, his legs.

I smile up at him as I bring the tip of his head to my lips, licking him as the water trickles into my mouth.

He inhales deeply, his hands automatically on the back of my head. And the next time I look up, he's got his eyes closed.

I go back to work. Sucking him, my hands pumping up and down, his skin slick and smooth from the water.

"Let's get out," he says, reaching for my arm and urging me to stand. "Come on, let's get out and finish this in bed. I just need you next to me right now."

I stand up and we both rinse the leftover soap off us real fast, and then West shuts the water off. He reaches past me for a towel hanging on a rack and begins to dry me off. First my hair, ruffling it up. And I don't even care. It will be a wild tangled mess when it dries, but I don't care.

He likes me wild, right?

I grab another towel and dry him as he continues with me. I rub it down his perfect chest and hard abs, bending down again to dry his legs. When I come back up, he bends down to dry mine and I ruffle his hair too.

"That's super-sexy," I say.

"Why do you think I did it to you?"

We smile, and I might even blush a little.

How long has it been since we were this comfortable?

Years. Maybe even ten years. It was like this in the beginning. Everything was fun and new. He could do no wrong in my eyes and he never complained that I wasn't listening or didn't understand his point of view.

We just… accepted each other the way we were.

Maybe that's the secret to a long-lasting relationship? Acceptance.

People say those vows when they get married. For better or worse and all that. But do people really mean

243

them?

Maybe I'm just cynical?

Maybe I should be less cynical?

"What are you thinking about?" West asks.

"You," I say. "Us."

"This fucked-up shit I got you into?"

"It's not your fault, West. If it's anyone's fault, it's mine. For fucking up your job."

"Nah. I have a feeling this shit was coming no matter what. I told you about my friends, remember? Something is happening, Tori. And I'm really not sure how it's gonna all shake out."

"It's gonna be fine, OK? I know it."

"You can't know that."

"I know. But I'm gonna go with it anyway. I can't do this anymore, Weston. I really can't. I'm tired of making decisions and putting out fires, and worrying about every little thing. And maybe this is the absolute worst time to make this change? Maybe this is the perfect time to keep doing what I'm doing, considering what we just went through. But I don't care. I'm tired. So just take me to bed, Weston Conrad. I feel safe here. As long as I'm in your arms tonight I know we're going to be OK. I'm just glad we're together."

West has a very serious look on his face when he nods and puts his hand out for mine.

I take it and he leads me into the cabin, turning off the light as he passes a switch on the wall.

He pulls back the covers, only partly visible in the low light coming through the portholes, and I climb in, relishing the softness of the sheets and the warmth of his body as he presses himself up to me.

"We're safe here," I say. "I can feel it."

CHAPTER THIRTY-SIX
WESTON

Are we safe here? Or did we just jump into a whole other pot of problems? Are Pax and Five here to help us? Or help themselves?

"What are you thinking about?" Tori asks me.

"Nothing but how great it feels to be here with you. I'm sorry for all the shit that's happened between us, Tori. Really. I am. I feel like I might've missed out on a lot of great years with you just because I didn't take the time to see your point of view."

"Ditto," she says.

"Or get to know you properly."

She turns her body so she can look me in the eyes. "I'm sorry too." She sighs. "I think... I think I have no idea who you really are."

God. This sucks.

Because I really want to tell her the truth.

But not now. Not tonight. Tomorrow. I'll tell her tomorrow. Or... maybe the next day. Or maybe when all this is over. Then we can sit down and talk about it all. All the things I left out. All the things that still haunt me. Pax thinks he knows, but he knows what I already told Tori, nothing more.

"Are you... too tired?"

"Huh?" I answer, absently.

"West!" She giggles. "Are you going to make me beg for it?"

"Oh." I laugh too. "No. No." I move closer, position myself on top of her. "There's no begging." Our eyes lock. Like we don't want to miss a moment. I kiss her on her mouth, her tender lips reaching for me, the tips of our tongues touching and then… I just can't get enough. Everything that has happened over the past few days melts away and leaves nothing but desire in its wake.

"I need you, Mr. Conrad," Tori says, pulling away just far enough to get words out. "If you want to be my prince, then fine. Because I really need a prince."

I just stare at her. How to describe the feelings? How do I put into words the depths of hell I'd walk through just to get to her?

I only know one way and it's not something I want to talk about tonight. So I let that go. I drop all that hate and anger I've got for the person who's hurt her. And I just… be here.

My fingers weave into her hair as I take her mouth once more. Our touch is soft, and our kiss is long, and there is no rush to get to other places, or other parts, or the release.

The world just suddenly becomes slow. Like every moment with her lips against mine is a year we'll spend together. I'll make everything right and we'll find our way through this maze, this labyrinth of wild emotions, as a team.

"Say it," I mumble.

Her eyes have never left mine. They stare straight at me. Straight into me.

"Say it," I command.

"Do you need to hear it?"

I nod. "Badly, Victoria."

She tries not to smile, but it's no use.

"I want you," she breathes into my mouth. Her eyes flutter, like she really wants to close them. "Inside me. Please," she says.

But that's what not I'm looking for.

She spreads her legs wide for me, her breathing kicking up a notch. I'm there, giving her what she wants. Easing into her, the way I have hundreds of times before—but a completely different way too. She wraps herself around me, wraps me inside her grip, gripping my shoulders like she needs something to hold on to.

The sex is not the only reason why I love Victoria Arias.

It's not just because I love slipping my fingers into her silky hair, or the way my tongue likes to traces circles around her nipples.

It's not just the fact that her pussy is sweet and my cock fits inside just right.

It's not just the way she arches her back in response. It's not just the primal feeling she brings out inside me. That feeling of pure lust and longing for more of this, and that, and everything we've ever done.

It's not just because she's beautiful on the outside. I love her for the person she is on the inside. Flaws and imperfections. Fears and insecurities. I love her for her weakness and strength. Her beauty and pain. I love her because there is no other person on this earth who can make me ache for something the way she can.

I'm after that love in return. That's all I've ever wanted from her.

We move together like our love-making has been choreographed. Like we are dancing our way through the last act, and no one is watching but us. And we don't care. Because we don't do anything for the accolades, we only do things for us.

The slow begins to wear off the way it does and the world begins to catch up. Tori is moaning and her hips are pressing against mine, urging me to take her harder. Push deeper inside her. Give her more.

So I roll us over and let her take control. She laughs, breathlessly, her smile contagious. And she begins to move her body in a different way. She's gripping the hard muscles of my biceps like she needs them around her. She needs me to hold on and never let go.

I reach up, place my hand on the back of her neck and force her down onto my chest.

"Yes," she says, her heart racing against mine. They race together. Like we are both trying to get across some imaginary finish line. "Yes," she moans as I grip her hair, keeping her in place. I don't want her to get too far ahead of me. She might take off and never come back if I let her do that. So I hold her prisoner there. In my grip. My cock buried deep inside her pussy. My lust out of control, my desire off the charts, my want… God, why does it feel this way to want someone so much?

"West?" she says.

Fuck. Stop being so damn dramatic, Corporate, and fuck your girlfriend the way she wants you to.

"West…" she says again.

"Come," I say, pumping harder. So hard my balls slap against her skin. I reach down and play with her asshole. "Come, baby. I need to feel it. I need to feel your love so bad."

We come together, that final rush of adrenaline the shot I need to put my fears aside. Put the last few days aside and just give in to her completely.

"I love you," she says a few moments later when we are hot, and sweaty, and breathing so hard, it feels like our hearts might explode. She places my hand on her breast to feel the thumping. And then she places hers over mine.

We lie there, looking up at the ceiling of a six-million-dollar yacht, as those final thoughts of the day race across that finish line.

Victoria Arias walked into my life on my darkest day. Even though everyone thinks the darkest day came two days later with those rape charges, that was nothing compared to the kind of soul-crushing defeat I had to accept under that tree as I tried to drink my problems away. And this girl… this *angel*… appeared with a sweet voice and a talent for listening.

I think I won.

And it scares me.

Because someone else thinks I won too. And that's why all this shit is happening. It's not Perfect's fault we got charged with rape. It's not Romantic's fault we got charged with rape.

It's mine.

CHAPTER THIRTY-SEVEN

VICTORIA

The closing of our cabin door jolts me out of my sleep. West sits down on the edge of the mattress, making it dip from his weight. He's got his head in his hands.

"What's wrong?"

"Nothing," he says, turning to look at me over his shoulder. "We're at the marina in West Palm Beach, so we gotta get up and get dressed now. The jet is about thirty minutes away. We should be in California this afternoon." He gives me a half smile. "You've got a dress in that closet. It's not purple, which sucks. But it's clean, which is a plus. My clothes are in the next cabin over, so I'll meet you up top, OK? Don't be long."

He gets up and walks out.

Hmmm.

Not even a kiss? Does my breath stink or something?

I sigh, then throw off the covers. "Fucking Weston Conrad. He's back to his usual self, I guess."

I'm still not sure what to make of this whole trip. Of all that stuff that happened back in the Bahamas. Or the rescue. Or his friends, for that matter. Mr. Mysterious does not exactly come off as a friendly guy. No. He would never be called Mr. Friendly.

And I have no idea what to think of Five. As Vlad the pilot he came off as some kind of slacker in a tropical shirt.

Some guy who lucked out with pilot lessons when he was young and won a cool float plane in a poker game.

Yeah, that's how he came across. But I've heard stories of Five. Not in a long time, mind you. But West called him 'a privileged asshole who is too smart for his own good.'

Vlad didn't have that vibe at all.

So. Five is a man of many faces.

Good to know.

I open the closet to the clothes I've been provided. Just as West said, there's a pink sundress. Pink is not my color and I frown as I pull it off the hanger and check the tag. I hope my tits will fit in this thing.

I go into the bathroom, wash up, finger-comb my wild hair, then give up. It's no use. I am stuck with the feral look today. Which might come in handy if I have to set these men straight when they start getting bossy. I want to know just what the fuck is happening.

I wiggle my girls into the dress and slip my feet into the sandals at the bottom of the closet, and grab the light sweater off another hanger, just to hide the fact that I'm not wearing a bra.

My poor purple bra was blown up.

It hits me then.

Someone tried to kill us yesterday.

"Don't think about it yet, Victoria." And I don't. It's no use worrying. I wasn't kidding last night when I said I feel safe. So far, anyway. There's more to this story than I know and all the answers come from the three Misters who will call their little meeting to order this afternoon.

So I'm gonna wait them out. Just sit tight and listen. Watch everyone as they talk. See how they act. And then I'll start to worry if I feel it's necessary.

I'm a fighter. I'm not some weak little girl who bends over to get fucked.

Well… haha. I laugh. I do that too. For my man.

Is he my man?

Jesus fucking Christ, Victoria Arias. Get a hold of your wandering stream of consciousness.

I leave the cabin and find my way to the stairs. This thing is huge for a boat. I've never been on a yacht, so maybe they all look like this. I wouldn't know. But I'm impressed.

I have been on Weston's jet though.

And I'm actually looking forward to that kind of luxury today. Even if it ends with a serious meeting I might not want to be a part of.

I wonder if Jerry and Jonathan still work on the jet?

"Well, finally," Mysterious says as I climb the stairs and come out in the main living room.

"Fuck off," West says to his friend.

Vlad—Five—smiles at me and says, "Ready?"

"Are you going to fly the jet too?" I ask, walking over to West, letting him take my hand. I look up and smile. He smiles back, but I can tell there's an uneasy tension in the air and I just interrupted a conversation.

"No," Five says, walking towards the doorway. "But the car is waiting and we need to get the hell out of Florida before they realize we're back."

255

I look up at West, but he mouths the word, *Later*, to me.

I shrug. What am I gonna say? I don't even have a ride home to New York. I was supposed to call my secret boss for the return ticket once the whole Wallace Arlington thing was over. I'm stuck with these guys whether I like it or not.

We leave the boat and it's still dark outside. The sun is just barely starting to think of coming up in the eastern horizon over the ocean.

The car is long and black and we all slip in, silently. Mysterious and Five are on one bench, West and I are opposite them.

We stare at each other in uncomfortable silence.

I try to ignore that and look around the interior. It's nice. Two leather bucket seats are built into the benches, so it really only seats four people. There's a bar, which no one makes a move for, even though Mysterious strikes me as the kind of man who has a drink before breakfast. And the accents are all in that upscale sleek burl wood pattern that you only see in luxury cars.

"So," I say. "Aside from traveling to San Diego, what's the plan?"

"We could start with the truth," Mysterious says.

I raise my eyebrows at him. West grabs my hand. "Don't listen to him, Tori. He's an asshole even on a good day. And I think he's having a very bad day right now."

"Because of you," Mysterious says.

"I thought you guys were friends?" I ask.

256

"Friends, enemies..." Five says, closing his eyes and leaning back. All three of them have suits on. Black suits with black ties. "It's nearly the same thing with this team."

Hmmm. "Is this your uniform? When you guys are in Mister mode?"

Mysterious narrows his eyes at me.

I narrow mine back.

"Miss Arias," Five says. "I think we'll get through this trip a lot easier if you don't pry too much." He opens his eyes and stares at me. "Until we ask you for your side of the story, that is."

"My side of... what story?"

"How you got involved in this whole Wallace headhunt," Five replies.

Oh. I clam up fast.

"Yeah," Mysterious says, looking over at West to my right. "I thought that might shut her up."

"Don't talk to her," West growls. "Either of you. I'm fucking serious right now."

"Hey," Five says, sighing like we're keeping him awake. "Let's just all calm down and take my advice. Both of you shut the fuck up," he says, opening his eyes briefly before closing them again. "We'll sort it out in San Diego. I'm fucking tired and you do not want to piss me off when I'm tired."

Mysterious takes his attention to the view out his window and West puts a protective arm around me.

I look at Five again. Who is this guy? Should I be afraid? Is he like... mafia?

He doesn't look like mafia. He looks exactly the way West described him all those years ago. Privileged asshole. I can totally see it.

We are all silent for the rest of the ride to the airport. And even though Five was the one who said he was tired, it's Mysterious who grabs some z's. Five has to punch him in the arm several times to make him stop snoring.

I am just happy to get out of that car when we pull up on the tarmac. And I'm even happier when I see Jerry standing at the bottom of the jet.

As soon as the driver opens my door, I scramble out of the car and walk briskly towards him, smiling big.

"Miss Arias!" he says, giving me air-kisses to each cheek. "How have you been?" He holds me at arm's length for a few moments, like he's scrutinizing me after a long absence.

Which he is.

I laugh. "Jesus, Jerry. You never age! You look exactly the same as the last time I saw you."

"Ditto, you sweet flower. Now, you come with me and I will set you up in the master bedroom for old times' sake." He shoots a wink over his shoulder, presumably to Weston, and then we trek up the air stairs together.

When we are back in the private master bedroom at the rear of the jet, Jerry closes the door and looks at me.

"What?" I ask.

"What's going on? They are furious with Mr. Conrad."

"What?" I scowl. "What do you mean? Define furious. Because I get that they are upset about something—"

"It's beyond upset, Miss Arias. When Mr. Shrike called to schedule the jet last night he was yelling. At me!" Jerry says, pointing to himself with surprise. "I know he's not mad at me. But he's never been a man to treat people badly. He was beyond angry. What is going on?"

"I don't really know. We were—"

A loud, hard knock on the door stops me mid-sentence. The door opens without waiting for an invitation. Weston is looming in the door, looking pissed off and very tall. Has he always been this big? Why does he look so angry?

"Thanks, Jerry. I'll take it from here. We're still beat, so we're gonna grab some sleep. I think Pax and Five are gonna do the same, so you might as well go see if they need anything."

Jerry smiles and leaves. West closes the door behind him. "How you holding up?" he asks. Like nothing is happening here.

"Good, I guess. Except for all the secret glances and code words flying around. What's happening, West? Why is everyone so tense?"

"I don't know yet. But I'm still tired. You still tired?"

"Is that code for more sex?" I laugh.

"No," he says, dead serious.

"Oh. OK. Yeah. I didn't get much sleep. It's like five in the morning. And you and your friends are dead set on keeping secrets until we get to California, so I might as well pass the time in your arms in this bed." I smile, narrowing my eyes. "Remember all the good times we've had in this bed, West?"

259

"Burned in my memory, baby," he says. And in that moment the real West—the one I know, and have known, for ten years—is here and the one I don't know has been ordered back to wherever it is he hides.

I'm not sure what to think about this. The only thing I know is that if the Misters are taking over, and that Five guy is here, something big is happening.

CHAPTER THIRTY- EIGHT

WESTON

I spend the next fifteen minutes waiting for the questions. So far she's been unusually silent about what she has to know is a pretty big deal between me and Mysterious. He's an asshole, I've said it plenty of times over the years to Tori, but she's never seen us actually interact. She's only heard things second-hand.

He's dead fucking set on making her suspicious. And I know what that means.

He's going to use her against me in San Diego.

But for whatever reason, Tori isn't taking his bait. She's calm, controlled, and exceptionally congenial.

How long will that last?

I look over at her. She's snuggled up to me when we got back in bed. Not naked. Not this time. I guess my rude dismissal of her sex offer was taken seriously. I didn't mean it to come out that way. It's just... fuck.

Maybe Mysterious does know something? I mean, more than I know he probably knows. I get that that he's good at what he does. He digs up dirt on people. He fixes shit, or something. Movie stars get into trouble. Someone dies at their drug party. Or they get their seventh DUI. Or they are being blackmailed by the baby mama of their illegitimate children. And Paxton Vance is the man they call to sweep it all under the rug.

He does that with blackmail, or payoffs, or who the

fuck knows? Kills them, maybe? I don't know what he does.

I do know Pax has some serious resources. But only four people know my real story. One of them is dead and the other three have just as much to lose as I do if this ever gets out. So if Pax does know, then how did he get that information?

It's definitely not the other people in my little dirty past. I know that shit for sure. Two of them will never talk. Ever. And the last one... well, I have more on him than he can possibly have on me. I've had to renegotiate this deal before so I have triggers in place to make sure that shit gets out if anything ever happens to me.

He knows I have those triggers.

If he fucking went back on his word... well, I will fucking take him down with me.

Don't freak out now, Corporate. You're at the goddamned finish line. You just talked to him about it last week. Nothing was suspicious. Nothing was out of order. Everything is still cool.

Mysterious probably knows something, though. I just wish he'd let on to what it is.

I'm sure he knows about school. That's the only paper trail there is. That's it. He can't know anything else. He can't.

If he does... then who the fuck told him? No one knows what happened *that* night except me. No one.

They have to be bluffing.

I don't know if I sleep during that six-hour flight. Maybe I do, fitfully and in spurts. But I do know that when that knock comes to the cabin door, I'm awake.

And ready.

Tori won't take their side over mine. She won't. She belongs to me. I'm so close to sealing that deal, I can taste her in my mouth.

So let's go, Mr. Match. Let's get this show on the road, Mr. Mysterious. I'm a player. I'm a risk-taker. I'm a winner. And I'm not gonna let these assholes take me down. Not after the hell I went through to get this far. And I'm not gonna let them screw things up with Victoria and me. We are on our way to a full-on second chance.

So no fucking way. This isn't gonna go down the way they expect.

I'm ready. I've been preparing for this moment for fifteen years.

I'm all in, motherfuckers.

Let's do this shit.

CHAPTER THIRTY-NINE

VICTORIA

West has been different ever since Mr. Mysterious showed up, but right now, as we drive in the car that will take us to wherever Mr. Match is waiting, he's silent and withdrawn. Last night he was silent and attentive, so silent and withdrawn is yet another change that tells me something big is about to happen.

I look over at him, but he doesn't even notice. He's staring out the window.

I look across from me, at Mr. Mysterious, and he doesn't notice either. He's looking out the window.

I look at Five.

He shrugs and shakes his head, as if to say, *Don't bother.*

All of a sudden Weston sits up straight. "Where the fuck are we going?"

I look out my window as we pull up to a gated community not far from the beach. It's so close, I can smell the salt and feel the way the sea air changes things as soon as the driver opens his window to talk to the guard.

"Nolan Delaney is expecting Mr. Vance and Mr. Conrad," the driver says to the guard.

"I thought you said Nolan wasn't a part of this?" West asks as the guard opens the gate and waves us through.

"He's not," Mysterious answers. "But Oliver and I use this house for business."

"Do you now? Somehow I have a hard time seeing Nolan saying yes to that little arrangement."

"I guess that's why we don't tell him." He says it with a straight face too. Like this is no big deal. He uses houses that don't belong to him all the time. "Besides," he continues. "Nolan has enough houses for everyone. He doesn't come here. He's down in San Diego or out in the desert. What he doesn't know can't hurt him, now can it?"

"You know what I don't get," West says. "Why the fuck you think that what's ours is yours all the time."

Mysterious shrugs. "That's just how I roll, Corporate. Anyway," he says, suddenly looking over at West with a very serious glare. "You and him are alike, right? Silver spoons and all."

"Says the guy who grew up taking pony rides on horses worth two million dollars."

Mysterious doesn't even shrug it off. Just replies, "Maybe you and Nolan really don't have anything in common? Isn't that what you always said back in the day? You're so different."

I look at Five and he's pretending this conversation isn't happening.

"What's that supposed to mean?" West asks.

And this time Mysterious directs his reply to me. "You're about to find out, Mr. Corporate. And so's your little girlfriend. So if I were you, I'd enjoy this reality for a few more minutes. Because it's all about to come crashing down."

I reach over and take West's hand. Give it a squeeze. "It's OK, West. Whatever is happening, it won't change us."

"You better not make promises you can't keep, Miss Arias," Five suddenly says. He's been quiet in front of me almost this entire trip and now is the time he chooses to speak up?

"Well, Mr. *Five*," I say, sneering his fake name. "I'm just letting my boyfriend know that I'm on his side. Especially since the two of you are so dead set on ganging up on him. We're a team, and nothing you have to tell me can change that."

"You don't know anything, Victoria Arias," Five says back. "Nothing about what's happening here. So I'm gonna give you a small piece of advice. Wait until you hear the facts before you make any more declarations."

"Fuck you. You know what? We're out of here." West drops my hand and pulls out his phone, his fingers running through his contacts.

"Put it away," Five says. And when West doesn't listen he says, "Does the name Stewart Manchester mean anything to you, Weston?"

It must, because someone is talking on the other end of West's phone and West ignores the voice next to his ear to stare at both Mysterious and Five. He ends the call and puts his phone away.

What the fuck was that about?

I look over at West but he won't meet my gaze.

"Don't worry," Mysterious says. And when I look at him, I realize he's talking to me. "This is his big moment,

267

Victoria. Twenty-five years of lies are gonna come pouring out in just a few minutes."

I take West's hand back, squeezing it again, only this time harder. "Don't listen, West. I'm not going anywhere. It's us, remember? Us against the world."

West looks at me with a frown. "Maybe he's right. You should probably stop making promises, Tori. You might regret it in a few minutes."

"What?"

But there's no time to get any more information out of him. Because we pull up to a massive house and when I look out the window I see the last person in this little gang-up. Mr. Match is standing in front of a glass-front double door. He opens it at the same time Mysterious opens the door closest to us, and walks towards the car.

I get out, then Five and West.

Mr. Match greets me with an extended hand. I just look at him, refusing his gesture. He looks over at his friends and shrugs. "What's up, man? How was the trip?"

"Went as planned. As you can see." Mysterious points to me and West, who has come up next to me. West does not take my hand.

"Oliver," West says.

"We missed you at the last meeting back at Perfect's house."

"I work. I can't be taking off every time there's a problem with one of you guys."

"Well," Match says, "I think that's about to change."

"Is that right?" West asks.

But Match just waves his hand towards the house.

"Are we staying?" I ask West. "We don't have to stay, Weston. Let's just go."

"Sorry," West says. "But we do."

"We've got a lot to talk about," Match says. "So please, come in and make yourself at home while we hash it all out."

CHAPTER FORTY

WESTON

Pax is arranging furniture. Or, I should say, *re*arranging furniture. I've been to this house of Nolan's before. Not a lot, but we were only a couple hours apart before he took on that project in the desert, so I came down every once in a while. Del Mar is not halfway between my house and his, not at all. But when you're driving down the 5 freeway in bumper-to-bumper traffic on a Friday night, you're grateful you don't have to make that last trek into downtown.

So we met here.

This house is like a tribute to sleek modern design. And I know that Pax used to own it, that he sold it to Nolan, and then asked him not to sell it without asking him first—he's always had that entitlement mentality—and Pax made him pay cash.

I know this because Pax came to me the same day the house finally closed and he got his money. He came to me because he needed more.

I gave him that five million, plus another million a few days later. He caught me when I was flush with money and feeling magnanimous.

"What are you doing?" I ask Pax as I look at Five and Oliver having a quiet conversation out on the terrace. Pax ignores me.

Five. Yesterday on the boat he looked like a guy who's

271

just about done riding waves and just about to realize he's got nothing to show for all those years he spent on the sand but an old float plane.

Today he looks like a secret agent.

All four of us are wearing dark suits. It's like a uniform. We are all wearing black ties. I wasn't given a choice. My suit was provided for me. But Five is different than us Misters. He's got black sunglasses on as he gazes out over the terrace to the ocean. The horses aren't running at the moment, so there is no one down on the Del Mar Racetrack, which this mini-mansion overlooks.

It's not the sunglasses though. Or the dark suit. Or the way he went from frumpy to manscaped in less than twenty-four hours. It's *everything* about him. The way he talks—or doesn't talk, I should say. The way he listens, I guess. That detached expression he's always wearing. It's the confidence he has. Like he knows things. It's the money, too. Obviously, he's got plenty of it.

But we've all got money. And even though Pax has been borrowing like crazy over the years, I know he's good for it because I know he's fucking loaded up to the neck in real estate.

"What's their deal?" I ask Pax, nodding my head out to Oliver and Five on the terrace.

"We're gonna find out soon," Pax says, pushing a chair into position. Then he smiles, looking down at his arrangement like his job here is complete, and puts two fingers on his tongue and whistles sharply to get everyone's attention.

I look over at Tori to see how she's taking this.

She looks bored. So I shoot her a smile and she smiles back.

"OK," Pax says, rubbing his hands together when Oliver and Five come back inside. "This is what I call the Jesus Circle. Miss Arias," he says, stopping to stare at her across the room. She's sitting at the bar, sipping some water that she helped herself to. "Join us."

Tori glances at me. I shrug. She gets up, bringing her water with her, and stands by my side.

We are a team, that positioning says.

If Pax, and Oliver, and Five are a team, well, we can be a team too.

There are two sides in this room.

Us and them.

"The Come-to-Jesus Circle, actually," Pax clarifies. "And," he says, looking at all of us and then the furniture, "there are assigned seats, I'm afraid. But don't worry, Miss Arias." He gives Tori a wink. "I have you next to your BFF." He points to the first chair on his left. "Five," he says, "you sit here."

Five walks over to a big plush chair and sits down, casually kicking back, one ankle placed easily on the opposite knee like he's settling in for something long and boring.

"Then you, Corporate. And you, Miss Arias."

We are sentenced to sit on the couch, to Five's left.

"And you, Match. Right there." He sits in the chair directly opposite Five.

"I'm taking this one," Pax says, turning a dining room chair around so he can cop a squat on it, facing backwards, and prop his hands on the seat back.

"You want to tell us what the fuck is going on?" I ask, unperturbed.

"Don't be so antsy, Corporate. These things take time."

"You've got ten minutes. Then we're leaving."

Pax nods at me, a gesture that someone less familiar with him might mistake as backing down. But I know better.

"OK," he says. "I'll get this show on the road. I'm the one who set you two up with that whole Wallace Arlington job."

"There's no job?" Tori asks, her words a combination of annoyance and regret. "So you wasted our time and almost got us killed? For what reason?"

"Miss Arias," Pax says, slowly turning his head to look at her. "I'm in the hot seat right now. That means I talk and you listen."

"Fuck you," she says. Doesn't yell it or even say it with contempt. She states it. *Fuck him.*

I raise my eyebrows and smile at Pax when he looks back to me. "As I was saying before I was interrupted. My come-to-Jesus moment with you, Corporate, is that I set you up to be on that island." He smiles, then adds, "To get you killed."

"Excuse me?"

"Tori," I say, looking down at her. I take her hand and give it a squeeze. "Let him finish."

"But," Pax says, ignoring Tori's outburst, "you're not an easy guy to kill, are you, Corporate?"

"What would be the fun in that?" I ask, looking at Oliver. "You're in this too? You guys set me up?"

"Take your own advice," Oliver says. "And let him finish."

Tori's leg starts bouncing, like she's getting pissed off.

"Go ahead," I say, looking back to Pax. "Finish then."

"I got a call about a month ago. Just before all that shit with Romantic happened. It was your friend Liam Henry."

"Go on," I say.

"He said you were becoming a problem for him. He said Perfect's little altercation with Allen was also a problem. He said there better not be any more problems."

"You work for him?" I ask.

"Have. In the past. Strictly free agent stuff, you know. Contracts and shit. His son had a run-in with an ex-girlfriend a few years ago and I took care of it for him. Couple other small things. But when Romantic had that issue, well, Liam got nervous."

"Why?" I ask, trying to fit the pieces together.

"He never said. But I can read between the lines, West. And I've been putting the pieces together for a while now."

"So tell us," Tori snaps.

I place my hand on her leg and say, "Quiet." She has no idea what's happening. But I'm starting to understand. "Go on."

"I think I'm gonna hand the talking stick over to Five now. And we'll just let it all sort itself out in the circle."

I let out a deep breath and look at Five.

He says, "I'm gonna pass for now. I think I'll go last."

275

I look at Pax again and he smiles, "So you're up, Corporate. And start from the beginning."

"Maybe I'll pass too," I say, buying a few seconds to collect my thoughts.

"Sorry," Pax says. "No can do. But I'll help you out, if you need it. When you were seven years old your drunken asshole of a father found something interesting, didn't he?"

I look over at Tori, then catch myself and look back to Pax. I lied to her about this. I told her I was fourteen.

"Don't look at her, Corporate. She's not gonna help you out with this one. And you're not gonna send her out of the room to save face. So man up, asshole. It's time to man up."

"I already know," Tori says. "He told me the other night while we were on the island."

"Tori—" I say.

"Did he now?" Pax interrupts. "Somehow I doubt that. Oh"—Pax laughs—"I'm sure he told you *something*, Miss Arias. But whatever it was, it was a lie." Pax looks me dead in the eyes and says, "Everything he's ever told us has been a lie. Isn't that right, West?"

"West?" Tori asks. "What's going on?"

I stay silent, but Oliver is there to fill the space. "We know, West. So just come clean. We know what you did."

They cannot possibly know. They can't. I've never told anyone.

"We have our ways of finding things out," Oliver says. And when I glance over at him, he's nodding to Five.

I look over at Five too. He shrugs and says, "That's

why I passed. I already know everything about you, Mr. Conrad. And we just need you to come clean so we can clear the air and fix this shit."

"Fix it?" I ask. "Fix what?"

"The reason why people are coming after us is you, West." Pax says it. "We know it's you."

"Wait," Tori says. "Just... wait. I have something to say too. Before this goes any further."

But Oliver puts up a hand and says, "You'll get your turn next, Miss Arias. But his story has to come first."

I thought about it. I thought about all the ways I could be caught and this was never even up in the top hundred. Cornered by my own friends. My girlfriend in the room, listening to all of it. All the lies, all the plots, all the planning, all the betrayals.

But I feel a huge sense of relief too. It's time, I think. These guys are right. I've been running since that night I met Victoria out in front of the administration building.

I was on the verge of getting busted.

And then I wasn't.

I thought it was weird then and I think it's weird now. But they're wrong if they think this is my fault. I didn't start this shit. I had nothing to do with that girl who accused us of rape. I didn't even know her.

So fuck Mysterious, and Match, and their friend, Five.

Just fuck them.

I'm tired of running anyway. I'm tired of feeling guilty for putting myself first.

I'm tired of all this shit.

Fuck them.

277

I open my mouth and start talking.

****

When I was six things were bad. My father was a drunk, my mother was sick, the house we lived in was nothing but a shack. The school I went to was small but everyone knew who I was.

The poor kid.

But also the smart kid. The tough kid. The fighter, the troublemaker, the liar, the cheat, the thief.

My father was also a gambler. And even though the house we lived in was worthless, the land wasn't. We were land-rich. And every time a real estate developer came knocking because they wanted to buy the land around us and put up more luxury mansions, he'd ask for some outrageous number.

Fifty million. Hundred million. Prices just so astronomical, the developers took it as a joke.

He *wasn't* joking. He knew what we had. Five hundred acres of prime, undeveloped land on an island that has very definite boundaries. These developers saw dollar signs. Lots and lots of dollar signs.

But undeveloped, it was nowhere near worth the price my father was asking. "They'll give in eventually," he used to say. "They'll have to. Only one place on earth that looks like this, West," he'd say. "And I own it."

His grand plan started to fall apart during a Saturday night poker game about a year and a half later.

We were on a yacht, we were in international waters,

and he was drunk as I've ever seen him.

I realized later that it was a setup. But I was only seven back then, so how could I know? I was clever, but not wise. It went right over my head.

By this time my mother was already dead. And my father really *was* thinking of selling the land. And I had just finished my first season of illegal lobster trapping, which is how I knew about the cave.

My father lost our land in that game. But just as the rowdy group started to celebrate his loss and their gain, I spoke up.

"I have something worth a lot more than that land," I said.

No one heard me. No one paid me any attention. No one stopped drinking, or laughing, or celebrating.

My father had walked out, minutes before, calling for me to follow him or he'd leave me here with the bastards who'd just cheated me out of my inheritance.

I didn't really know what that meant. I just knew that the land was mine too. And I had just lost it.

My father did leave me behind. He never called for me again. Just had the crew shuttle him over to his boat and drop him off.

By the time I thought to go looking, the boat was gone.

But I didn't need him by then, anyway.

I had struck a new deal.

******

"You found that treasure?" Tori asks.

279

I look over at Pax and wait for the laugh.

But he doesn't laugh. Which means he really might know what comes next.

"I found the underwater cave while I was setting lobster traps that summer. And I found the first gold coin about two weeks into my little business adventure. I kept one in my pocket. I never showed it to anyone, I was smarter than that. But I kept it in there. No one was going to rob a dirty little kid. But that night on the boat I flicked it on the table while the men played. And I said, 'Give me back my land and I'll show you where you can find the rest.'"

"Did they?" Oliver asks. "Give you the land back?"

"Not quite," I say. "But I got a promise from Liam."

"*Liam*," Tori says, with equal parts sadness and disgust.

"What kind of promise?" Pax asks.

"I show them where the rest of the coins were and Liam would hook me up with a better family than the one I drew in the genetics lottery."

"Better *family*?" Tori asks.

I nod, unable to look at her.

"They killed my dad as soon as the land transfer went through. And I got sold to the Conrads. Liam kept my land. Oh, it was developed a long time ago. It's gone for good. Like it never even existed. Like my childhood never happened. But I have something they still want. Very badly."

"You never told them where the coins were," Five says.

I look at him and nod. "Hell the fuck no, I didn't. I took those crooks to another underwater cave. Similar to the one I found. The entrance was too small for a grown man, so I had to be their diver.

"It was not an easy dive to the cave where the treasure was. It was small, and cramped, and there was no air chamber once you were in there. It wasn't a scene from Goonies, you know?"

Pax and Oliver both shoot me a smile. I was obsessed with that movie as a kid. It felt like a movie about me. My life. I watched it a lot in the frat house. They watched too.

"It was dangerous and I only did it twice. Once, I took a single coin, just to look at it once I got back to the surface. It was fucking..." I stop talking for a moment, reliving that memory. My heart was beating so fast I thought I was dying. My hands were shaking with excitement then fear. My head was spinning, trying to wrap my thoughts around what was happening. "It was fucking gold, man." I laugh, and when I look over at both Pax and Oliver, they're smiling. Like they can feel what I'm feeling as I go back in time. "It wasn't crusted with crap, like you see on copper coins. It was fucking gold."

God, even if I wasn't a little kid with a big dream, I'd still feel the same way if I found it years later.

"I didn't go back down again for a few weeks. My dad was constantly drunk and pissed off. He was gambling like crazy. And losing. So I needed to work so I could eat."

I glance over at Tori and she's got a deep, deep frown on her face. I want to say, *See, I told you I knew what it was like.*

But I don't.

"And part of me thought... it can't be real, you know?

281

I'm not the kind of kid who gets a lucky break. But my dad had been talking about that big poker game all week. The one with Liam. He was a regular on Nantucket. He had a huge mansion and a big yacht. He invited my father out to play. And I know now that Liam was planning that game all along. To take our land. So every day my father was going on and on and on about getting rich off Liam Henry in the next poker game. But my gut knew better. I knew something was wrong. And I imagined things going down a hundred ways, and each one of them ended up with me hungry and homeless."

"So you went and got more," Tori says.

I nod. "I dove down again, only this time I didn't dare bring them up to the surface. I knew of another cave nearby. I got lobsters out of it often. It was small too. Not big enough for a man to fit. So I took about a few dozen coins and stashed them there, just in case I needed them quick."

"A few *dozen* coins?" Oliver asks, stunned. "How many were there?"

"Hundreds," I say. "Hundreds, you guys."

"Go on," Five prods.

"I took them to the second cave. I came back up with the stashed coins and I handed them over. That was the end of the treasure as far as I was concerned."

"Did Liam believe you?" Oliver asks.

"No." I laugh. "No, not even a little bit. They beat the fuck out of me for two weeks. But it was my first taste of power, you know? My first glimpse at what information gives you. And there was no fucking way I was gonna tell them anything. The Conrads intervened. They just wanted to adopt me. I was handed over with my eyes swollen shut, two broken fingers, and three cracked ribs. They took care of me, nursed me back to health. We left the island and all the memories behind and settled into a place in upstate New York. I stayed there for a few years, studying for the entrance exams that would get me into the right schools, and, well, you know the rest. I owe the Conrads everything. They're not bad people."

"They *bought* you," Tori snarls.

"They took care of me. Sent me to good schools. Bought me cars and shit. I can't complain about that transaction. And they saved my life back then. They believed me. And Liam owed them a favor. So they won. They got me out. They saved my ass."

"Liam owed them what *kind* of favor?" Pax asks.

I shrug. "Who knows. Something big enough to steal a smart kid from a poor family and not get caught."

Mysterious looks at me hard for a few seconds. "You're lying."

"I'm *not* fucking lying. Everything I just told you is true."

"Then how the fuck does Stewart Manchester fit in?" Oliver asks.

"Oh," I say.

"Yeah. Oh," Pax says, mocking me. "Let's keep this shit real, Corporate. We know about Stewart."

"How?" I ask. "I'll tell you, fine. Fuck it. But I want to know how the fuck you found out. Because if I need to cover my tracks—"

"Liam," Pax says. "He knew about that, West."

"Fuck," I say.

"Yeah, fuck," Pax echoes. "So continue, motherfucker."

I glance over at Tori and let out an exhausted sigh. She squeezes my hand in encouragement. "I'm not leaving, West. Don't worry. Whatever it is, I'm not leaving."

I look down and start talking at the same time. "Stewart Manchester was a summer kid on Nantucket. He knew me before the Conrads. I didn't come back to the island for years. It's like my parents wanted to forget I wasn't theirs, so we never came back. But I was in my senior year at boarding school and all my friends were going to Nantucket for summer break. So I went. I figured no one would remember me."

"I'm guessing you didn't count on Stewart's long memory?" Pax says.

"He knew, man. He knew I was adopted. He said I had my father killed."

"What did you do?" Tori asks.

"I fucking denied it," I say. "What the hell was I gonna say? Yeah, all true?" I laugh. "But then he says, 'I know about the coins too.'"

"Shit," Five says out of nowhere. We all turn to look at him.

"Shit," I say, agreeing.

"Did you kill him?" Pax asks.

I shrug. "He wanted the coins. I can't even fit *inside* that fucking cave anymore. And I wasn't going to just hand them over, anyway. So I made a deal. I'll go get them, we split them, and then we go our separate ways."

"So how did he end up dead?" Oliver asks.

"He and I met in international waters. He was alone on his boat. I was alone on my father's boat. And... it got ugly."

"You *killed* him?" Tori asks in disbelief.

"I didn't... *technically* kill him. We fought, he went over the side of his boat. He never came back up. I left. I never got the coins. They're still fucking down there in that cave for all I know."

"And that's it?" Five asks.

"That's not enough?" I ask back.

"It just doesn't explain what's happening now."

I stare at Five. "I don't know what's happening now."

"You're leaving something out," Pax says.

I'm leaving a lot out. But he can't really know that. He can't, unless Liam told him what our second deal was, and he didn't. I know he didn't. He can't afford to let people like Mysterious—people who treat secrets as a commodity—in on something like that.

"I told you the truth," I say, adamant enough to make it sound final.

The room is silent as we all think this over.

"And now?" Pax asks. "Where's this all stand now?"

I throw up my hands and sigh. "Here, I guess. With Liam double-crossing me and you guys looking for a scapegoat."

"That's not what this is," Oliver says quickly.

"No?" I ask. "Then what is this?"

"What's going on with your banks accounts?" Five

285

asks. "That's the last piece of your puzzle."

"What the fuck are you talking about?"

"Your money, Corporate. What the fuck are you doing with your *money*?"

"What I do with my money is none of your business, asshole."

"It is when millions of dollars in assets in your name are liquidated overnight."

"What? I didn't liquidate anything. I've got most of it stashed off-shore."

"You *did*, you mean," Pax says.

"What the fuck is that supposed to mean?" I ask back.

"If you didn't move it, then they stole it, Weston," Oliver says. "They stole all your money while you were stuck on that island. You've been cleaned out."

"And that leads us to little Miss Arias. Right on cue," Pax says. "She was part of that, West. You should know that up front. She was part of it."

CHAPTER FORTY-ONE

VICTORIA

"That's not true!" I say. "How dare you accuse me! I was stuck on that island with him, you jerks. I have nothing to do with any of this."

"You're wrong," Oliver says. "You're the whole reason we got set up in the first place."

"What the hell are you talking about?" I look at West, who stays silent. "West?" I ask. "You cannot believe them! I am not a part of this."

"OK," Five says calmly. "Let's just take a deep breath and start from the beginning with you, Miss Arias."

"No," I say, stomping my foot down on the tiled floor. "No. My past is none of your business. I'm not rehashing this with complete strangers." I look at Weston. "Please, West! Don't let them do this. I told you. That was hard for me. You have to understand that. It was hard for me. I'm not sharing these very personal things with your friends. No."

I feel the panic rising in me. I can't talk about this to them. No. My heart is racing, and my legs are trembling. I hold my hand out in front of my face and find it shaking so bad, it scares me.

"Tori," West says, pulling me into him. "Just take it easy. I think there's a connection here, babe. And I think we need to know everything in order to put all the pieces back together."

"I didn't steal your money. It's not my fault. I just answered the phone, that's all!"

"What's that mean, Victoria?" Pax asks.

But West hold up his hand and says, "Just hold up for a minute. OK? Just hold up." He stands, taking my hand and pulling me with him. "We're going upstairs—"

"Fuck that," Pax says, standing up and pushing West back with a flat palm to his chest. "Fuck that. Do you have any idea how fucking serious this shit is, Corporate?"

"If what you guys are saying is true, then I just lost everything I've been working for the past ten years, Mysterious," West says, eerily calm. "So yes, I'm pretty fucking sure I know how serious this is. I'm taking Tori upstairs to talk and we're going to figure it out together. And after we do, I'll let you know."

I can't look anyone in the face as West leads me upstairs. *It wasn't me. It wasn't me. It wasn't me.* I keep chanting it over and over, willing it to be true. *It wasn't me.*

It can't have been me.

The stairs lead to a catwalk lined with wire cables instead of a railing. And the catwalk overlooks the living room, so I don't have to move my head at all to see three sets of eyes staring at me from down below.

West leads me past them and into another part of the house. He goes by a few bedrooms and bathrooms, and stops in front of a set of double doors that open into an office.

He closes the door behind us, then twists the lock.

I meet his eyes. "What are we doing?"

"I just need a minute, OK? And I didn't want to leave

288

you down there with those assholes, so just let me have a fucking drink and we can decide what to do next." He walks over to a large cupboard, opens the doors, and pulls out a sliding tray set for drinks. "Want one?"

"Yes," I say. "Make mine a double."

West takes the ice bucket and opens another cabinet, where a small freezer is hidden. He fills the bucket as I look around the office and try to breathe.

"Nolan and I used to meet up here every now and then. After a while I just came for the ambiance, you know?" West looks at me as he picks up the small ice cubes with the silver tongs and places them carefully in our glasses. He lets out a small laugh. "When I was a kid I used to watch Conrad take meetings at home. This is how he had it set up too. I can only assume Delaney senior had something similar at his place. Powerful men all have decanters of Scotch in their office. Ice buckets, and tongs, and crystal glasses are a requirement for staying sane."

"Are you going to get me drunk?" I ask. "To make me talk?"

"I'm going to have a drink with you, yes," West says, still concentrating on the drinks. "And I'm sure we'll do some talking. But I didn't bring you up here for a lecture, Tori. I just need to get the fuck away from them for a minute. OK? I just need a drink, and a beautiful woman, and a nice view, and an office that probably cost more than my car to furnish. Because if they're not lying and I just lost everything, it's gonna be a hell of a long time before I ever get to do this again."

He turns to face me with two glasses in his hands. He

holds one out to me, I take it, and then he touches his to mine, making the ice clink and the crystal sing. "To better days," he says, and takes a drink without waiting for me.

"I didn't do it," I say again. How can he be so calm? How can he be so together? Why isn't he angry?

West grimaces as the Scotch burns its way down his throat, then lets out a breath and heads back to the decanter and pours the dark liquid back over his rocks.

He's smiling when he faces me the second time. "I don't care, Tori. I don't care what you did. I don't even want to talk about it right now. OK? I just want you to have a drink with me."

I look at my glass, scowling.

West gulps down his second and heads back for more.

I sigh, decide I probably need this drink more than he does if what happened over the weekend was my fault, and let the entire thing slide down my throat.

It burns like fuck. My throat is fire, my stomach is warm, and when I exhale, I feel better.

West is smiling.

I smile back. "It's good."

"Have another one," he says, taking my glass, refilling it, and giving it back.

"You're trying to get me drunk. You're hoping whatever it is I know will come pouring out with that bottle."

"I wouldn't mind it, Tori, but I just told you why I'm doing this. If I lost it all, I want one last chance at enjoying it."

"To better days," I say, touching my glass to his.

"We could probably both use some of those."

We drink together this time.

All the way down. One long gulp of confidence and sympathy in the form of a drink. And then I set the empty glass down on the desk and look at the man I love so much, it hurts. My chest is constricting and my heart is fluttering. And I might die if I find out I hurt this man by mistake.

West waves me over to the long leather couch on the other side of the room. I sit and he sits next to me. I cross my legs and his hand slips into place along my thigh.

"I can rebuild, you know. So fuck it. If he got my money and my assets, then fuck him. I can always make more."

"Who?" I ask. "Who would take it?"

"Liam, I guess. He was never happy about how I got away with what he wanted."

"The stupid coins?" I laugh. "This is really about those stupid coins?"

"They're worth two billion dollars today."

"They are not!" I laugh.

"But there's a problem." West smiles as he turns his head to look at me. "They don't belong to me any more than they belonged to the people who lost them in that wreck."

"What do you mean?"

"They belong to the Spanish government. So if I get them—and that's a big if, Tori—if I get those coins, then I have to turn them over to the Spanish government. It's their historical wealth. Liam knows this, but he's got people in the private market who will buy. I don't. I can't ever sell those coins."

"You had a lot of money saved, West? They took a lot?"

"Almost fifty million dollars."

I can't even comprehend fifty million dollars. "But... you were acting like you needed this contract so bad. Why? Why did you fight me so hard about it? Why not just let me have it?

He smiles, then looks at me and smiles bigger. "It wasn't the cash, I needed Victoria. It was the *job*."

"That makes no sense."

He just shrugs. "It doesn't matter anymore. It's over and the money is gone."

"I didn't take it," I say again.

"I know, Tori. I don't think you did."

I swallow hard and close my eyes. My heart thumps in my chest and I realize my breathing is coming in short, staccato gasps.

"Hey," West says, placing his palms flat on my flushed cheeks. They are cool and strong. He looks me in the eyes and shakes his head. "Don't," he says. "Don't do that. Not over this, Tori. Not over money. I don't need that money. It's probably a good thing it got stolen because it was turning me into someone I said I'd never be. All I want is you. We can make more money. All I want is you."

We're silent after that. Everything that has happened these past few days is rolling around in my head so much, I feel dizzy.

Now what? What do I do? I'm gonna lose him, I can

feel it. He's saying this stuff now, but once he finds out what I did...

I'm going to lose him.

And if I lose him, and my business, and screw up my father's legacy... what's left for me?

I feel like I should fight against this fate. I feel like I need to come out swinging. I feel like this is my last chance to keep something—the only thing I *can* keep—of this very fucked up life I've been given.

West.

He's the last thing I have left.

So now it's my turn to talk.

"I got a phone call, West. That's how I knew about Wallace Arlington and Liam's contract. I got a phone call from some guy who refused to give a name and he told me to contact Liam and tell him not to hire you yet, because I could get Wallace on board and you couldn't."

"I don't care," West says, kissing my lips. It's such a soft, gentle touch. He was always gentle with me, even though I was wild and rough with him. "And I don't even need to know the rest."

"I need to tell you the rest. I think your friends are right. I think we're connected in more ways than we know. He told me that if I got you out of town for a while, he'd pay off all my debt. My mortgage, my credit cards. All of it."

West is silent for a few seconds. I'm sure he's going to get up, walk out the door, go tell his friends, and never speak to me again.

But he doesn't.

He says, "I don't understand how you got into so much debt. You had what, seven million dollars from that Fullerton contract? How, Tori? How did that happen?"

"It was such a stupid mistake, Weston. You're going to be so mad at me."

"No," he says, kissing my lips again. "I won't, I promise. We all make mistakes."

"But it's so dumb. I bought that building for ten million back when the housing crash happened. It was worth at least twelve just a few years before. So I had some instant equity with my down payment. It was a good investment. But I went to make the first mortgage payment and I entered the numbers wrong. Instead of fifty thousand, I entered five million. And I didn't even notice. So then I had all seven million tied up in this building. I couldn't even pay my taxes the next year. I had to take out an equity loan. And it just all spiraled out of control. I lost all control."

"Fuck. How the hell do you write a check for five million instead of fifty thousand, Tori?"

"Online bill pay?" I laugh. I have to laugh. It's so fucking sad I have to laugh. "I just don't know how it happened."

"Do you think…" He stops, shakes his head a little. "It's stupid, but… do you think someone fucked up your payment on purpose?"

"Who would do that?"

"I dunno," West says. "Maybe a jealous mob boyfriend?"

"He wasn't my boyfriend," I snap.

"Sorry, I know that. I just don't have another label for him."

"Abuser," I say. "You can call him my ex-abuser."

"OK," West says. "*Him*. Do you think it was him?"

I want to say no. I want to say he's been out of my life for too many years to care what I'm doing. I want to say I got away and the past is in the past.

But I can't.

So I say, "Yes," instead. "I have always thought it was him. And I think he was the one who set me up with the Liam contract too. I think all of this goes back to me, Weston. Not you. The rape, the island, everything. It's all my fault."

CHAPTER FORTY-TWO

WESTON

We hold hands on the way back down to the living room where Five, Oliver, and Pax are sitting at the bar, drinking as they watch televised horse racing on the flatscreen TV.

They all stop talking and look at us when we come towards them.

"I think we have a problem," I say. Tori squeezes my hand and I squeeze hers back. Her squeeze says, *No, please, don't tell them.* My squeeze says, *Trust me.*

She stands still by my side, for once in her life taking my promise at face value.

I want to kiss her right now. I want to kiss her long, and deep, and softly. So softly, she will melt into my arms and we will float into some other life where shit is not hitting the fan and people are not trying to kill us.

But that has to wait.

So we tell her story again. Together.

Five stops us at the phone call at her work, asking, "Who was it? Did you recognize the voice?"

"No," Tori answers. "But he sounded young. Our age. I think it was one of Lucio's men."

Five walks over to a briefcase, pulls out a laptop, opens it up on the bar, and starts typing.

"What are you doing?" I ask.

"Checking her phone records for that day."

"Go on," Pax says, unable to keep the impatience out of his voice.

"He said he'd give me a fair chance at that contract to rebuild my business and he'd pay my debt off. All I had to do was keep West busy for a couple days."

"So they could rob him," Oliver says.

She shrugs.

"It's not your fault, Tori," I say. "The part you guys need to know, the part I never told you because Five insisted we not share stories, is what's important here."

"What's that?" Oliver asks. "What the fuck are you talking about?"

"I saw her," Tori says. "I was there that night she said she was raped, you guys. I was standing in the trees in the back of the house. It was dark that night, remember? So no one could see me. I was freaked out because my… rapist…" She stops talking and shakes her head, drawing in a breath like oxygen contains the courage she needs. "So I was hiding. Just waiting for West to come outside so I could see him."

It takes a lot of courage for Tori to use that word in front of my friends. So much fucking courage. I pull her in tighter and give her a hug.

"Lucio was looking for me. He attacked me the night before you guys were accused. And I have a feeling he is the one who set you up. I know Weston never touched that girl. She was drunk by that time, but I saw the entire interaction. West was with some buddies out back. They were drinking and laughing. Then they went inside and I was just about to make myself known when she came stumbling up. She had her hands all over West, but he pushed her away and asked her if she needed a cab home. She took a swing at him, missed, and fell down. That's when I came out of the shadows, and we went up to his room."

"You knew this?" Pax asks, looking at me.

"This was my story. I always had a witness. I was never worried about it. But Five told us to shut the fuck up, so I shut the fuck up."

Everyone looks over at Five, who is still typing away. "Keep going," he says, without taking his eyes off his screen. "I'm listening."

"It was him," Tori says. "It was Lucio Gori Junior who set you guys up. It was Lucio Gori Junior who raped me, over and over as a child. And if I had to guess, I'd say it was Lucio Gori's friend who called me and offered me that contract."

"Bingo," Five says, spinning his laptop around. "That call came from a bar owned by Lucio Gori Senior."

"That motherfucker set us up," Pax says. "I'm gonna kill him. I'm gonna fucking kill that asshole."

"No," Five says. "No, we're not killing him. The last thing we need is the mob on our asses. And we don't have any evidence, other than Tori's story, that any of them were involved in the rape accusations."

"Then we need to get that evidence," Pax says, walking towards us. "I want my fucking name cleared, do you understand me?"

He's looking at Tori like this is all her fault.

"Hey," I say, putting my hand up in front of Pax's face.

"She didn't smear your name. That Lucio asshole did."

"It doesn't matter. She's the one who can get the evidence we need. She's the one who can get close to him. Not us," Pax says.

"She's not doing anything, Pax, so back the fuck off. And don't give me this 'I'm innocent' bullshit again. We all know you're not innocent."

"Fuck you," he roars. "You don't know shit."

"I know you're one twisted dude."

"Fuck—"

"Hey," Oliver says, coming between us. "Knock it off, Pax. Just calm the fuck down and let us figure this out."

"What we need," Five says, head buried in his computer again, "is some incriminating evidence. Something to tie him to the whole rape thing ten years ago. Something concrete. Something irrefutable. Something that would stand up in court."

"Something like... a confession?" Tori asks.

We all turn to look at her.

"Yeah," Oliver says. "Something like that."

She bites her lip, like she wants to say more, and when I look at Pax and Oliver's faces, I realize what they're considering.

"Fuck you both," I say. "She's not gonna be the bait."

"How would you get a confession?" Five asks, walking away from his computer and towards us. "It was ten years ago."

"She's not gonna get anything," I say again, only louder. "Tori, you're not doing this."

"I think he's just arrogant enough to tell me the truth,"

Tori says.

"Stop it, Victoria." I look over at Pax and Oliver. "She's not participating in this con, you assholes."

"What if I go home to Brooklyn, let him know I'm there? Keep him in some public place. And then start telling him all these things about you guys that might lead him on. Make him talk?"

"Why the fuck are you ignoring me?" I grab Tori by her arm and make her face me. "Stop it. You're not going near that guy ever again. I don't care what kind of confession he might give up."

Tori looks me in the eyes, then turns away and resumes talking to Five, Oliver, and Pax. "What if I get him to admit what he did? And get it on tape. Then you have me first-hand witnessing that girl coming on to Weston ten years ago, and Lucio's confession. That's more than enough to charge him with *whatever*." She looks up at me, like she's just remembering I'm here. "What kind of charges could we get him on, Weston? If he planned all that ten years ago?"

"We're not doing this," I say, trying to remain calm. "You're not doing this. It wasn't even Lucio—" I stop before I say too much. Everyone is talking at the same time, putting in their opinions, Tori arguing that she knows that neighborhood, and him. Pax yelling about his stupid reputation. So my blunder goes unnoticed.

"Felony obstruction," Five says, answering Tori's question once things calm down. "Conspiracy, maybe blackmail. If we find more people involved."

"Tori, please. Listen to me. I'm not going to let you do

this."

Tory stays quiet for a few moments. I look at Pax, and Oliver, who are both refusing to meet my gaze. Then she turns to me and says, "You don't get to make this decision, West. I love you, and I want to be with you. But we have these *things*," she says, "hanging over our heads. And I can't live my life waiting for him to come back and hurt me. And you can't live your life waiting for someone to pop back up and try to nail this rape thing on you again. And before you say, *Who cares, I didn't do it*—it doesn't matter. If you're a team," she says, waving her hand at my friends, "then you stay a team." She turns back to the guys and says, "It has to be done. And I'm the only one who can do it. It just has to be done."

"He's never going to confess, Victoria. Never. He's not stupid. He's the son of a major mob boss. You won't be hunting him. He'll be hunting *you*."

"Well," she says, turning away from me and towards my friends, "then I guess I better get some pointers from Mr. Mysterious here." She looks me dead in the eyes for her final words. "Because I'm tired of being afraid. I'm tired of letting the memory of what he did haunt me. I'm tired of running, Weston Conrad. And you of all people should understand how that feels."

"I do," I say. "I fucking do. But we don't even know how this fits into the plot with Liam. Maybe it's nothing. Did it ever occur to you that Liam was the one who set us up?"

"Corporate's right," Five says. "It could be Liam."

"But wait." Oliver turns to look at Five. "We have to

follow the trail from the origin. And the only origin we have right now is Lucio Gori. We should go with Victoria's plan. And we should do it now."

"Fuck you," I spit at Oliver. "Just fuck you. The origin is Liam, asshole. Liam is the one everyone is connected to. And how much you wanna bet Liam and the Gori family are old friends. You're not calling the shots here, Oliver. We should go after Liam first. We all agreed to listen to Five ten years ago, so let's agree to that now."

"You're only saying that because he doesn't like her plan," Pax says.

"So? He's the fucking genius, right? We should listen to Five."

"What the hell is wrong with you?" Tori snaps, yanking her arm out of my grip. "How many times do I have to make this clear, Corporate? I'm not your property. You don't dictate my actions. You're not allowed to discount my opinions." She lifts her chin up in defiance. "You're not calling my shots, Corporate. I'm calling my shots. I'm doing this for me. Not your friends, *me*. I want Lucio gone and I want to be the person who puts him away. This is my fight, so stay the fuck out of it."

She turns and walks towards the front door.

I wince as the glass doors slam shut and then look over at Five. "It's your call. You let me know. But I'll make this very clear right now. If you say yes, and she gets hurt, I will fuck you up."

CHAPTER FORTY-THREE

VICTORIA

Why does he have to assume I'm going to get hurt? I am at least as dangerous as he claims to be. He knows this. I can handle myself. I can protect myself. I've worked my ass off for fifteen years to get to this point and if you ask me, this is like God telling me it's my turn. It's finally my turn to show Lucio Gori that he's not in charge of me. That I'm not afraid of him and his threats. That he has no power over me anymore. That I will fight back and I will kick his ass.

"Kick his ass," I say out loud to nobody.

"I'm sure you could."

I whirl around to find Weston standing just outside the front doors. "You say that, Weston Conrad, but you don't mean it."

"Victoria." He comes up to me and places both hands on my shoulders, gives them a little squeeze. He leans down into my neck. "It's just…" he says, his warm words tickling my ear. "Something like this can't be predicted. You're a fighter. I know that. You're tough, and strong, and probably very deadly. But you cannot predict him or his reaction. And a few advanced jujitsu moves will never change the fact that he will probably have a gun. That he could shoot you dead. And if that happens, I will die too, Tori. I will die getting revenge on him. Because now that I have you back I'm not letting you go. I won't let you do

305

this. I will tie you up and go take care of him myself if you try."

I whirl around, so angry. So pissed off that he can't see whose fight this is. "You have no idea the fear I had of him all growing up. You have no idea how many nights I still lie awake at night, wondering if he's forgotten me or if he's coming back. I need him to be *gone*, West."

"Let me do it, Tori. Please, just let me do it."

"And if you get hurt?" I ask, shaking my head. "If you get hurt doing what I should've done a long time ago? No. No, I can't live with that either."

"Then let the guys take care of it. We'll sit this out and let Mysterious work his magic. Let Five do his thing. You don't have to be the one who ends it to make it end."

The door opens and we both look up to see Five standing in the doorway.

"Choose carefully," West says. "I'm not fucking kidding, man. Do not make this choice lightly."

Five stares at West for a moment, then shifts his gaze to me. How I ever thought of him as Vlad the pilot is beyond me. He's one hell of an actor, because that persona is so far away from this serious man in black standing before me, it's scary.

"I think we should take a night to sleep on it, Weston."

I exhale, ready to blurt out all the reasons why I am the right person for this job. But West squeezes my shoulders again and says, "I'm taking her to my house in LA. We need to have a night alone. With no hurricane, or mercenaries, or any of this fucked-up shit hanging over us. So meet us there in the morning and we'll decide."

I expect a fight from Five, but he just nods his head, reaches into his pocket, and throws West some keys. "You can take my car. Mysterious can drive us up. But be ready at dawn. I'll have Match set up the jet to pick us up from Burbank near your house. It doesn't matter who we go after. The Gori guy or Liam. Both of them are on the East Coast, so that's where we need to be. And we need to move fast. Before they're on to us. Before they realize we're on to them."

We stand silent as Five retreats, and then I turn to West and slide my arms into his suit coat. The muscles of his waist are rock hard and his shirt is super-soft. I grab hold of the fabric and place my cheek on his shoulder.

"One night, Tori. In my house. With nothing between us. No lies, no secrets, no court cases, no hate. Just us, just the truth, just the love I know we feel for each other. I need that right now." He sighs. "I just really need that right now."

"OK," I say. I don't know how we can just put all this drama aside, but I agree. I need to decompress. I need to feel safe and loved. So I say it again. "OK. Let's go. Let's get the fuck out of here and just forget for a night."

We drive all evening. West talks about anything and everything except what really needs to be discussed. But I give in about halfway through the trip and just settle. I listen, and we laugh about things. And talk about things. And I think it hits both of us, somewhere near Disneyland, that we've missed so many moments over the years because we've been too busy fighting. Too busy looking for what we want and not being grateful for what we have.

He talks about business and his grand plan to expand globally. How he wants to set up shop in all kinds of places I've never been to, like Russia, and Japan, and France. Places he's already seen. He's familiar with. Places I haven't even had time to dream about, let alone visit.

And I talk about the kids at the house. And when I tell him about one boy I've taken a liking to—Ethan, a boy I've been thinking about adopting as my own—he goes silent. Just like I did when he told me about his travels.

He wants a family and I'm about to get one without him.

"You don't really need me, do you?"

"What?" I ask, as the darkness overtakes us and the city lights turn all this ugly traffic and urban decay into something beautiful.

"You don't need me."

"Why do you say that? I mean, I love you, Weston. I have always loved you. Before I even knew you were handsome. I met you in the dark when you were crashing. I didn't know you had money, or good looks, or grand aspirations. But I knew, that night when we were sitting under those trees, that I was going to love you. That you would be my best friend forever. And when it started falling apart I used to cry, you know. Just cry about how lonely I would be when you finally moved on. When you got tired of me."

"Tori," he says, reaching for my hand. "I just want to give you a better life. That's all. I don't want to capture your heart, I want you to hand it over."

"But you never asked what a better version of my life was. You never asked me anything back then. You wanted a family. OK, I do too. But I have a different vision of what family means, West."

"I know that," he says. "I mean, I guess I didn't then. But I realize it now. I'm just so tired of hearing you say no to my help. Why can't you just accept it with grace? Just say, 'Thank you, West. I needed that right now.' And let it go? Not have my help be an assault on your independence?"

"I don't want to stay home with kids, West."

"How can you say that? Your dream, from what I can tell, is nothing *but* staying home with kids. Just not *your* kids. So where's the logic in that? Tell me. Please. I'm dying to know, Tori. Because it makes no sense. It makes absolutely no sense that you want to have this home for neglected kids and you don't want to have a home for your own kids. If you don't want kids, OK. I'm not happy about that. But OK. I can deal. I can deal with adoption if that's your path and you can't stray from it. But don't tell me no just because you think I'm some kind of woman-hating asshole. I don't hate women. I don't hate you, for fuck's sake. I just want to provide for you, that's all. I want to give you the life my father never gave my mother. I want you to have the family I never did."

"Don't you see the irony in that? You were adopted. It was illegal, and I'll never look at your parents the same again. But you were adopted."

"I'm all for adoption," he says, sounding exasperated. "I am. But if that's your only option, then say so. If you don't want to have my children, say so and we can start from there."

I let out a heavy, tired sigh. "I don't want to fight with you."

"I don't want to fight with you either. I want to take you home, carry you up the stairs, lay you down on my bed, and make love to you all damn night. Every night, Tori. Every night for the rest of our lives. Why is that forbidden?"

"I just want you to ask—"

"Ask?" he says, his voice rising. "I've asked you to marry me six fucking times. I've gotten down on my knee six times. I've asked over dinner. I've baked the fucking ring in a cake. I've done it on Valentine's Day and Christmas Eve. I did it over a romantic weekend away and I've done it while we were cooking ramen noodles in that crappy-ass apartment in New York. How many other ways can I do it?"

"No." I laugh.

"It's not funny, Victoria. Do you have any idea how much it hurts to have the woman you love turn you down for marriage six times?"

"I'm not laughing. I swear." He's hurt. I can tell. He's hurt and he has every right to be.

"I mean, I guess I get it now. You had Lucio Gori hanging over your head. You were looking over your shoulder. But we're going to take care of him, Tori. *We*," he stresses, "will take care of him. Me and Match, and Mysterious, and Five. Us. Not you, dammit. Not *you*."

I fall silent. Trying to put it into words.

"Say something," he says, so, so, so ready for me to give in. "Anything."

"I'm just trying to figure out why I said no, that's all."

"Do you have an answer? Was it him?"

"No," I say, then correct myself quickly. "No, not really him. Or… not *just* him. It's… hard to explain. When you asked it felt like it comes with so many expectations. Mostly changes. And I'm just being honest when I say I wasn't sure if I was on board with those changes."

"So you don't want to get married?"

"I… might."

"Might?" he says, looking over at me with a scowl.

"West, when you were asking, it never *felt* like you were asking. It felt like it was expected. My yes answer was expected."

"Fuck." He laughs as he gets off the freeway and heads up towards some hills. "It never felt expected to me. Unless you count all the ways I imagined you saying no and then I went ahead and asked anyway."

"I'm sorry," I say. And I am. "I never wanted to hurt you. I just needed to feel like we were entering this new relationship as partners. Not as husband and wife."

"What else can I call it then?" he asks. "Huh? If you don't like husband and wife, just pick two more titles and

311

I'm on board. We can be cat and dog if you want. I don't give a fuck what you call us."

"That's not what I meant."

"Then explain. Please. Because from my end, Tori, it looks like you're saying no just to be on the safe side. You think I might mow you down. OK, I get it. But I promise, I don't want that. And after that last time I came to the conclusion you just like to hear yourself say no. No is your safe word, Victoria Arias. No, no, no, no, no. If you say no, you're safe. Isn't that right?"

I want to dismiss him immediately and say no. But... that's stupid. Because he might have a point. "I say yes a lot too, you know."

"Yeah," he says, sadness creeping into his voice as he pulls up to a guard house in front of a gated community. "You say yes a lot when it comes to sex. But I don't only want your body, Victoria. I want your heart. And I just can't seem to capture it. It's something very elusive and I just don't have the right equipment, or lure, or whatever it is you want." He lets out a long, tired breath of air.

Before I can answer he tabs the window and it slides down, where a serious-looking man in a dark blue uniform is peering inside.

"Oh, hey, West. Haven't seen you in a while. Got a new car, huh?"

"Nah, it's my friend's car. Just got in from the Bahamas. Really tired, so sorry I can't stay and chat."

The security guy gives him a little salute and says, "No problem," as he talks into the radio attached to his shoulder. The gate opens and he waves us forwards.

312

West calls out, "Thanks," as he slides the window up again.

"That's some serious security you've got here," I say.

"Yeah, well. If we had kids, I wanted them to be safe in this city. I wanted all of us to feel safe in this city, Tori. That's all. And I had the money, so why not? Although what will happen to this house if they really did steal it all away is a thought for another day."

I pout a little at all that. He's been planning our future this whole time? "Kids with me?" I ask, just to be clear.

"Who else, Victoria? It's not like I date much. And believe me, I'll never ask another woman to marry me. Ever. It's you or I'm gonna be alone for the rest of my life. I can't fake it. Not after I found the real thing and lost."

We are silent as he navigates his way through the community, the only sound an occasional jet taking off from the nearby airport. That must be Burbank. And with that thought everything that happened earlier comes rushing back.

We are going to New York tomorrow on the Mister jet. And one way or another, Lucio Gori will be confronted. Should I let West have his way? Just once? Would it kill me to just let him call the shots?

He pulls into a driveway where a white Tudor-style house is elegantly lit up. The spotlights highlight the tall two-story front windows and the perfectly placed palm trees. There's a shimmer on the side of the house that tells me an equally perfect swimming pool is waiting in back. And when West gets out and comes around to my side to open my door, I have a sick feeling of regret in the pit of my stomach.

Was I wrong to say no?

No. That's not what I'm asking myself at all.

I'm asking myself if this relationship can be saved. Somehow, some way. Can we salvage something and find a future together?

I *was* wrong to say no.

He is, and has always been, the perfect man for me.

CHAPTER FORTY-FOUR

WESTON

I'm nervous as I open the front door and wave her forward. Why? *Why?* So many reasons why. Everything in here is about Victoria Arias. Everything.

"Wow," Tori says, her fingertips lingering on the white linen fabric upholstery of the straight-backed chairs that welcome her to my home. "This is beautiful."

"Thanks," I say, dropping my keys into a porcelain dish on the small table that sits between the chairs. "I wanted a mudroom, but this house doesn't really lend itself to one in the traditional sense. So this is it. Just a place to stop and check your hair before a date."

"Oh," Tori says, looking in the mirror above the table and wincing. "Jesus. I shouldn't have looked."

"Stop," I chide her. This woman can't look anything but beautiful to my eyes. I don't care if her hair is a wild mess. I like it that way. It reminds me of better days. Days when I had her all to myself. When I knew every night I'd fall asleep to the rhythm of her breathing and wake up craving the moans of her arousal.

"So…" she says, turning away from the mirror to face me. "Do you check your hair there often?"

I smile. "It's not for me, silly. It's for you."

"Well." She chuckles. "Sorry, I don't get a lot of chances to use it."

"Hopefully that will change now. Come in, please.

315

Want the tour?"

"Yeah," she says with a sigh as she takes in the room.

It's the effect I was looking for when I furnished this place.

"It's so… not really you, Corporate. I was expecting something like your friend's house back in Del Mar. Something modern and over the top. But this place is… anything but that. Hey," she says, walking forward quickly towards the center of the room. "Is this is the coffee table we bought at that antique mart in Albany?"

"Yeah," I say. "The one and only."

"Oh, my God. You still have that trunk too!" She laughs with excitement as she walks over to it, and again, her fingertips touch it like it's something that needs to be felt. "Remember how much I wanted to use this for that practice honeymoon we took? Ha! Those people on that island would've laughed their heads off at me."

"I wanted you to take it."

"I know. I can't trust you. That would've been a mistake." She sighs again. "Well, I'm glad you still have some of our old stuff. Glad it didn't all go in the trash."

"Trash?" I ask. "*Trash*? Please. I saved everything, Tori. I have everything we bought together over the years. And if you look at my life close enough, you'll find it's all still here."

"What? Are you serious? Jesus, I thought for sure you'd throw it all away after that last break-up."

It was an epic break-up, that's for sure. Dishes flew like crazy. Stiletto heels dented the walls in that old apartment we were renting. She was so angry with me. I was so

316

furious with her.

It wasn't pretty.

"I felt a little sad when you left it all behind, to be honest."

Tori has picked up a pillow off the couch, another one of our shared treasures, and she's pressing it to her cheek to feel the soft fabric when my words come out. She lowers the pillow and looks at me. "Why? I figured it was best to forget, you know? I didn't want to be reminded of all the ways we fucked it up."

"I guess we're different in yet another way as well," I say, some sadness creeping into my voice. "Because I never wanted to forget. I only wanted to remember. Even if we had a lot of bad times, we had a lot of good ones too. Moments worth making are moments worth remembering. That's why I kept everything."

She sets the pillow back down on the couch and wanders into the dining room. "I bet this house is a fabulous place for a party. The rooms are all open. You can cook and talk to guests at the same time. Never missing out on the fun and conversation."

"Or watch children when you prepare grilled cheese and tomato soup for lunch."

She smiles, her shoulders hiking up in a shrug. "Or that."

"I haven't had any parties here, Tori. I haven't had anyone here. Not even a date. No one has checked their hair in that foyer mirror except you."

She continues into the kitchen, which flows naturally from the great room. I watch her, standing still where I'm at. I watch her take in the white cabinets and the dark soapstone counter tops. That's what she always wanted. She touches the stone with that same reverence as the trunk and the pillow.

She continues on, glancing at the white dishes in the glass-front cabinets. "Those are—"

"From the wedding registry we did that one time you thought we were playing around."

"West," she says, turning to face me. "Is this…"

"All for you," I say, shrugging. "What do you want me to say? I'm sorry if it's creepy. But I never stopped hoping, Victoria. I couldn't even imagine a life where you were not here. Enjoying our home with me. And I didn't bring you here to pressure you, or make you feel bad, or fill you with regret. I just need you to know that… I love *us*. And if you think we even have the slightest chance at making this work, then please, just give in to me. I promise to be careful with you. I promise to go slow. I promise everything. I promise to be patient, and I promise to listen to you. I will do anything—whatever it takes—to make you mine forever. And no piece of paper or rehearsed wedding vow is necessary. I don't care about that. At all. I swear, I don't care. Just think about it. Think about the happiness we can create and then tell me what you need me to do to make it happen. I will do it, Victoria. I promise, I will do it. Because I love you. I love you so much."

It comes out like a whisper. Like I'm afraid to say it. And I am. I'm afraid that she will take one look at this place, call it a sick shrine, and tell me to get on with my life as she walks out.

It could happen. It could happen and she could say it right now.

But before she gets a chance, I say, "I just need you to know that I am here. Waiting. For as long as it takes for you to be ready. And I'm sorry I never said it that way before. I have so many regrets for the way we ended our relationship. I should've been able to articulate it before. But I guess… I just never understood what you wanted. Why you didn't want what *I* wanted. It was just bad timing, you know?"

She walks on, her fingertips tracing the back of the antique whitewashed barstools, unable to stop herself from holding a blue and white striped dishtowel hanging off the oven handle on the wall next to her. She looks up, all the way up, to the windows in the cathedral ceiling, then turns to the French doors that open to the backyard.

One thing you get living in this gated community in Burbank Hills is a nice-sized back yard. She always wanted one of those. And a pool. An in-ground pool.

It's fantastically lit up right now, the subtle movement of the water reflecting the light across her face in a way that makes her look surreal. My fantasy. That's what she looks like. She is my fantasy. And I cannot believe I have her standing in this kitchen right now.

How many times have I imagined it?

But then I forced the thoughts out of my mind.

I guess I never really admitted to myself that I was building this home for her. That every piece I bought to furnish it was with her in mind. But it's very clear to me

319

now.

What would Tori want?

What does Tori like?

What would Tori say?

And later, after I had already given up that this would ever become a reality, *What would Tori want me to do?*

"I love it," she says, turning to face me. "God, I love it so much."

"I could lose it, you know. If they are stealing my life away. I could lose this house, but I wouldn't care, Tori. Not if you wanted to start over with me. They can take whatever they want, as long as they don't take you. The only thing I care about is a second chance at what we know we have. So please. *Please,* when we get on that plane tomorrow morning, don't keep insisting that you take part in whatever Oliver, Pax, and Five are planning. Just leave it to us. Because if something happened to you I would die too, Tori. I would not want to live."

She has a sad, sad smile on her face. But she walks over to me, slips her hands around my waist and presses her face into my chest.

I breathe in her scent. I touch her long wild hair, and when she lifts her head up and meets my gaze, her eyes are a swirl of violet. The storm we left behind is gone and instead I see nothing but the purple flowers she reminds me of.

A whole garden of flowers. Something we had, and lost, but now have again.

"Take me upstairs," she whispers. "I want to see my bedroom now."

I reach underneath her, lift her in my arms, and walk us upstairs. There are four bedrooms, but the only one that matters is the one at the end of the hall.

I place her gently on top of the king-sized bed without turning the light on. There is a spotlight aimed at a palm tree just to the left of the large picture window outside. More than enough light for what I'm about to do. She is nested in the thick down comforter; her hair is splayed out on one of the many pillows I have waiting for her weary head. Her knees come up out of instinct, wanting to cover her bare legs as the short sundress settles by her hips.

But I gently grab her ankles and drag them down the cool cotton duvet and spread her legs at the knees.

I catch a sharp intake of breath, and maybe she's nervous. I'm nervous. Even though I've had sex with her several times in the past few days, I'm nervous because this is the one that counts. This is the one that says, *You are mine. I am yours. And you are never getting away because we're in this together now.*

I reach under the light fabric and find the elastic of her panties, pulling them down her thighs as she lifts her hips and closes her knees to help me slide them all the way to her ankles. My touch is so light, she shivers, sending a chill of bumps up her legs for a moment before she sighs, relaxes, and opens her legs back up without any help from me.

"Victoria," I whisper as I kiss my way up her body. I linger in so many places. I stop at her ankle, then her knee. She arches her back and sighs, her fingers threading into my hair. I continue, switching to the soft skin on the inside

321

of her thigh. "Victoria," I say again.

"What?" she breathes out. "What?"

"Be here," I say, reaching under her ass to lift her hips, bring her pussy in line with my mouth.

"I am here," she replies, her grip on my hair loosening, her hips moving, positioning.

"Stay here," I say, easing my tongue into the soft folds. I lick and she draws in a long breath. "Just stay here with me and I swear, it will be good."

"Weston Conrad," she says. "I've always been yours. You should know that. I have never belonged, will never belong, to anyone but you. Even when we're apart, I am yours and only yours. Forever."

I lick her pussy until she is writhing. I squeeze her breasts until she whimpers. I kiss her mouth like I'm hungry and the only thing that can nourish me is her. Her taste, her lips, her tongue.

And then I ease into her, slowly. Just the way she likes it. There are plenty of ways to have sex with her. Hard and rough, the way I sometimes prefer. We can talk dirty, or not. We can go fast or not. We can do it standing, in the shower, against the wall, or outside in the pool. We can fuck so many ways.

But tonight I make love to her. Love. Soft and sweet, just the way she likes it. I know her heart and it is soft. I know her soul and it is sweet. I know her, and I want her to know me too. *This* me. The one who cares so deeply, he's willing to give up everything for the only woman he will ever love.

It's not a night of multiple orgasms. It's not a night of

screaming my name, or me shoving my dick down her throat so I can feel her muscles contract as I come. It's not even about coming, together or otherwise.

It's just about being there. In the moment when we decide, yes. We will stop all the nos and just say yes to each other.

Yes.

Yes.

Yes.

I say it as I move inside her. She says it as she digs her nails into my back and bites my shoulder. We say it together, just once. But once is all we need. Once is more than nothing. Once is enough.

I fall asleep, exhausted, spent, and happier than I have ever been in my life.

Victoria Arias, the love of my life, falls asleep, cradled in my arms, her head resting on my chest. Our breathing is matched and perfect. Our love is complete, because no matter what happens, we have this night. This one perfect night with her in the bed I made for her. With her in the house I want to give her. Next to me, Weston Conrad, her soulmate.

But when I wake up, ready to face the challenge ahead of us, it all feels like a dream.

Because she is gone.

CHAPTER FORTY-FIVE
VICTORIA

My leg is bouncing as the pilot tells me we're about to land in New Jersey. I calculate the route back into Brooklyn from the private airport and debate whether or not I should call someone and announce that I'm coming back home.

No. Let Lucio be surprised. Let him see me sitting there, in his bar, his disbelieving eyes wide and his mind racing with all the possible reasons I might have come back.

Fuck him. *Fuck him.* That's all I've been thinking since last night. West was so sweet and genuine. So perfect. God, how did I ever let this shit go so far? Why didn't I know that Lucio was the one who set them up? Why didn't I look into it at least?

Fear.

I hate myself right now. Hate myself for letting Lucio control me—even after I got out of that situation, he controlled me in so many ways.

The fear of being alone in the daylight. Fuck the night, I was afraid of the light.

It pisses me off so bad.

West's phone vibrated last night, just after we fell asleep, and I checked it. It was Jerry, saying the jet was all fueled and the flight plan filed for New Jersey at seven AM. I got up, waiting to see if West would notice. And when he didn't, I slipped my clothes back on and crept out of the house, snatching his keys from the foyer on my way. Burbank Airport was only a few miles away. It was like… meant to be. Like fate was telling me this was my problem and I needed to solve it myself.

"Um, Tori?" Jerry is worried, I can tell. I don't think West has noticed I'm gone yet, so I still have time to get there and not have anyone stop me. But he's gonna know soon. "Are you sure you don't want me to have the pilot radio someone?"

"No, Jerry. Please. I just need to get home. ASAP." I lied to him. Told him West and I got in a huge fight, the Mister flight was canceled, and I just needed to leave. And he bought it. God knows, I've used the same excuse before, while we were dating. Only all those times it was true and this time it's not.

"I'm sorry things didn't work out."

My face crumples. Because everything is working out. And how is that fair? To anyone? Especially West. How could I possibly let him and his friends fight this last battle for me when I was the reason their lives were ruined? Still am, apparently.

"You two are so right for each other," Jerry says, noticing my pained expression. "I know you can work it out if you just try. Maybe talk things through? See where you can't come together? And find some kind of compromise?"

But we did that. Mr. Corporate was straight with me last night. Everything I've been waiting to hear from him came pouring out. And now, the only thing left in our way is this one last loose end. My loose end.

"I know," I tell Jerry. He's always been so good to me. Always been so understanding. And this is not the first time I've hijacked the Mister jet for my own personal escape. Only this time I'm not running away, I'm going home to finish what I started.

I'm coming, Lucio Gori. I'm coming for you. I'm gonna settle this once and for all.

CHAPTER FORTY-SIX

WESTON

"You have no control, do you?" Mysterious is sitting across from me in Five's private jet as we try to race Victoria back to the East Coast. He's drinking a mint julep, complete with a few sprigs of mint leaf sticking out of it, and something about that is so wrong. I get he's from Kentucky, but who the fuck drinks mint juleps?

I decide to ignore him.

"I mean, this chick, Corporate. She's got you by the balls, man. She's got us all by the balls. And I'll tell you what, I don't care for it. I'm the master in my relationships. My woman would—"

"Would you shut the fuck up?" Five says, from across the plane. He's got the *Wall Street Journal* spread out in front of him, scanning the financial page like this is just another day.

"What?" Mysterious says. "Don't get pissy with me, Rutherford. This chick is gonna ruin everything."

"Use my real name again, motherfucker," Five says, looking up, expressionless, "and I'll throw you out of this jet from thirty thousand feet."

I have to hide my smile. Not many people talk to Paxton Vance that way. But Pax just shrugs it off and says, "Don't wet your panties, *Five*. Corporate's one of us. So what if he knows your real name? And I'm just fucking with him, anyway. You're so fucking serious."

329

"Yeah," Oliver says. He's also been doing his best to ignore the fact that shit is going wrong in just about every way at the moment. "Which means we cut him slack when he needs it, Pax. And he needs it, OK? I know Victoria better than you do. So I know there's no stopping her once she's got an idea in her head. And it's partly our fault for encouraging her last night. So shut the fuck up and chill out. We're gonna land less than an hour behind her, so we've got time. Five's got the addresses of all the Gori businesses and we've narrowed them down to two or three possible places where she might confront him. Until we're on the ground, just drop it."

I have to hand it to Oliver Shrike. He's always been in control of his shit. Maybe it is weird that he never has a girlfriend, but whatever. He's good people. He must have a valid reason for that. He's not excitable. In fact, Oliver and Five have a lot in common and it occurs to me, maybe they've known each other for a long time. Maybe they are related or something?

"We've all got a lot at stake here, so I get it," Five says, folding his paper and pushing it aside to reach for his coffee. "You're worried. And you're next, right?"

"What the fuck is that supposed to mean?" Pax asks.

"Well, we know more than we told Tori," Five says. "She thinks this is the end game. She really thinks Lucio Gori is the one who set us up."

Five looks at me and I have no escape, so I just shrug. I'm not telling him shit unless I have to. And I don't have to *yet*. I'm not convinced this is all tied back to what I suspect. Best to keep that secret under the hood a little longer.

"But it's not the end game. None of this Lucio shit adds up, does it Corporate?"

I shrug again. Keep fishing asshole. I'm not gonna bite.

"So you're next, Mysterious," Five says. "Then Oliver, probably. Lucio cannot be our final target; it can't be that easy. So you better step your shit up, son. And pull yourself together."

"Maybe we're wrong?" Pax says, taking a seat across from me. "Maybe it's not who we think."

But he doesn't ask it like a question. He doesn't ask it because he knows his theory is weak. I know this is tied back to Liam. They know this is tied back to Liam. But what they don't know is how Liam got involved.

I don't know that either. So I keep my mouth shut and think about all the moving parts in this machine.

We each have a theory. Even Nolan and Mac have one, but we've thrown those out. I don't think Nolan's sister, Claudette, is the mastermind behind all this. Besides, she wasn't around back when we were accused of raping that girl. She was off causing trouble somewhere else. And Allen, the reappearing thorn in Mac's side, *was* there. But he's just not smart enough to pull off a con like this. Besides, he could've gone down with us.

Should've gone down with us, I correct myself.

"We're not wrong," Oliver says. "It's definitely Liam calling these shots. He's pissed off that West stole that treasure. And you know what? I can't believe I'm saying that with a straight face. Who the fuck gets caught up in some kind of buried treasure scheme?"

He's looking at me with an accusatory glare. "Hey," I say, throwing up my hands. "I was seven years old. I didn't ask to find that shit."

"But you played along," Five says, our temporary alliance gone.

"I was *seven*. What kind of seven-year-old doesn't wish he'd find buried treasure?"

"Your life is some kind of *Goonies* movie sequel, Corporate," Pax says, smiling.

I smile back, because whatever. We're all in this together now, like it or not. We're a team.

"I'm waiting for the cool shit to start. Maybe we'll get to play the bones with sexual torture devices?"

Pax, Oliver, and I all laugh. Fucking *Goonies* was a favorite in the frat house when we were partying.

"Laugh it up, you assholes," Five says, opening up his laptop. "And you won't have to wait long for your shit to hit the fan, Mysterious." Five takes a sip of his coffee. "Like I said, you're next."

"We'll see," Pax mutters, finding a loose thread on his suit coat to pick.

I shrug. "Maybe you're right," I tell Pax. "Maybe it's not Liam and this Lucio fuck will get what's coming and everything will go back to normal."

"Normal?" Oliver says, swiveling in his chair like a kid. "I don't think the lives we were living before all this started back up were anything I'd call normal."

"Mr. Five," the flight attendant says in a soft, apologetic voice. "We just got word that the Mister jet has landed. Miss Arias took a cab from the airport. They've got a tail on her. We're a little ahead of schedule, so we'll be landing in about thirty minutes."

"Good," Five says. "Make sure the helicopter is ready. Mysterious, I hope you can land that thing in Brooklyn. Because if not, Corporate can kiss his girlfriend goodbye. My associate just sent me a slew of reports about Mr. Lucio Gori's suspected offenses." Five stops talking and looks straight at me. "Do you want to know? Or not?"

"Tell me," I say, my heart beating faster than ever. "I want to know just who this fuck is. I want to know all of it so when I kill that motherfucker, there's not a drop of remorse in my blood."

"Sex trafficking being the most serious on this list. Of course, he was never charged, or even brought under suspicion. His father had deep pockets and connections that go back more than fifty years. Alonzo Gori, Lucio Gori Senior's maternal grandfather, started a trucking company in Brooklyn in the early sixties and since then their territory has grown steadily. Gori Senior was made boss in 2001, after he killed his own father in an argument regarding online gambling."

He pauses there, waiting to see if I say anything.

But I don't. I know when to keep my mouth shut.

"Since then, most of the online sites have been shuttered, and business moved away from drugs and towards the sex slave business due to increased demand in other burgeoning crime families, especially the Russians."

He stops again, but I stay silent.

"OK," Five says. "You can keep your own confidence if you want, Corporate. But this shit will all come out in the end."

"What's that supposed to mean?" Pax says. Apparently this is news to him, which should make me feel smug. Five is clearly his source. Apparently Mr. Mysterious isn't omnipotent.

"We can wait," Five says. "No one's life is on the line or anything, right?"

"Just get on with it, will you?" I snap. "If I had more info you needed, I'd fill you in."

"Right," Five says, looking back down at his computer. "An unnamed girl got away about fifteen years ago"— Five glances at me to make sure I picked up on the timeline, and I have—"and a sting operation was put in place based on her private testimony to a judge."

"I guess we can safely assume that was Victoria?" Oliver says.

I ignore him as Five continues. "She disappeared before the trial and nothing ever came of it, aside from rescuing about half a dozen girls from a slave house in Brooklyn. So looks like Lucio has been biding his time. But now that Victoria is on her way back to confront him, all bets are off as to how he plans on paying her back. So there you go, Corporate. You keep your secrets. But if something happens to your girlfriend, don't blame us."

I swallow hard as the seriousness of what we're doing hits me again. Like a fucking brick to the chest.

"Don't worry," Pax says, leaning over to clap me on the shoulder. "She's gonna be OK. We got your back, bro. No matter what, we got your back."

I believe him, of course. Pax doesn't say shit he doesn't mean.

But there's so much more going on than they know.

I do have more secrets.

CHAPTER FORTY-SEVEN
VICTORIA

The main hub for the Gori crime family is Flats Trucking, a large warehouse with a small five-truck fleet that has no purpose whatsoever other than the obvious cover they need for their illegal money laundering. I can remember cops being there all the time when I was a kid. I used to think, *Finally. They will go to jail and I will never have to see any of them again. Lucio will be locked away and I will be safe.*

But they were never arrested. They never went to jail. I was never safe. My adopted father was the only who cared back then, and he wasn't even in the area. He made some kind of deal with Lucio and took me far enough away to let people forget.

"He's reasonable," my father said that day. "He understands when he can't win."

I used to believe that.

No. Wait, I never really believed it. I wanted to think my father is all-powerful. That he was the strongest man alive. That he could save me from anything because he talked Lucio Gori into letting me go fifteen years ago.

But it was a deal with the devil, as they say.

So no. No one is clean in this. Not the Gori crime family. Not my father. Not me.

I get dropped off about three blocks away from the trucking company. They don't hang out there anyway, it's just a front. No, I get dropped off at ground zero for the Gori family.

Hederman's Bar.

There are three or four bars where Lucio always worked and hung out. But Hederman's was always his first choice.

So it's my first choice now.

I don't even know what I'm doing here. I just feel the need. Some kind of internal need to confront him. The only recording device I have is a cheap pay-as-you-go phone I bought, along with a fake leather purse, at the airport. I doubt the sound quality will be great inside my purse, but I switch on the voice recorder as I approach my destination.

There are no windows to look in from the outside, but there are plenty of ways for them to see out and it starts with the CCTV camera mounted at the corner of the front door.

The bar is always locked. You knock, you wait, they come, or they don't. You go in by invitation only.

I don't need to knock. It opens just as my knuckles are grazing the old, weather-beaten wood.

A man appears on the other side, someone I have never seen before. Young, muscular, frightening.

He doesn't ask who I am or what I want. That's not his job. His job is to open the damn door, so that's all he does.

I step into the hazy darkness. It smells like cigar smoke and stale whiskey. There are four men playing pool in the back, three couples having lunch in the dark red booths along the perimeter, and no sign of Lucio Junior.

I stare at the bartender, who is doing his best to ignore me, but failing. When he notices me noticing him, he ducks his head and begins wiping down the bar.

Lucio does that to people.

Scares them.

"Violeta," the smooth voice says from the far side of the bar.

The way he says that name makes my stomach clench in fear. I hate that name, I hate that name, I hate that name. *Keep calm*, I tell myself. *Just keep calm.*

He knows I hate that name.

I look to find Lucio Gori standing near the back, holding open a red velvet curtain that leads to his private work area.

"Victoria," I say, with as much defiance as I can muster. "My name is Victoria."

"Sure," he muses, like I'm nothing but a joke. "You will always be Violeta to me. But come in the back, Victoria. I can adapt to a new name. Let's catch up, eh? It's been a long time."

I lift my head and walk slowly towards the back, eyeing all the men in this small bar. Thinking about all the ways they can hurt me. How quick they will be to grab me with one word from their boss.

"They know better, my sweet. Don't even look at them. They are not worth your attention. Besides, I have someone you know back here. And he is very eager to see you again. I hear you've had some trouble this past week?"

My heart sinks, thinking of who he has in that back room. It can't be West. It can't be him. There is no way he

339

got here before me.

"Hurry now," Lucio says. "He's uncomfortable."

Jesus Christ. Why did I come here?

"I knew you'd come back of your own free will, Violeta," Lucio says once I'm within arm's reach. He brushes the back of his hand down my cheek as I stand in front of the half-drawn curtain, hesitating. "Oh, now is not the time to be afraid, Violeta. There is plenty of time for that."

I swallow hard and look him in the eyes. Those dark eyes. Almost black, just like his soul. "I'm not afraid," I say. "I'm not afraid of you, Lucio."

"You should be." And then he draws the curtain all the back so I can see who is waiting for me in the back room.

My father is tied to a chair, his face so bloody, I barely recognize him. "Pops!" I rush over to him, my hand on his shoulder, shaking him. He doesn't move. "Pops," I say again, softer this time. "Please. Answer me." But he doesn't. He is out cold, maybe even dead. I can't tell. I whirl around to face Lucio. "What did you do?"

Everything I came here to do flies out the window. There will be no confession, I understand that now. Weston was right. Lucio knows how to hunt. But West doesn't have to worry, I'm not the bait. My father is.

"He came to me, *Tori.*" Lucio snarls the nickname West uses like it's a filthy word. "He came to me asking where you were. Threatened me, Victoria. And I admit, I had my doubts when I waited so patiently these past few days and you never came looking for him. I started imagining all the ways your little revenge scheme might play out. I even sent people to track you down, but you disappeared in Miami. With *him*."

I don't need to guess who he's talking about. "That was you on that island, wasn't it? You were the one who came and tried to kill us."

Lucio laughs loud and long. "Island? No, my sweet Violeta. That was not me. But I would have," he says, turning his head so he can give me a sidelong glare. "I would've come to kill Mr. Corporate if I had known where the two of you were. Instead I took it out on your dear Pops. He took it well, I have to admit. Like the tough guy he used to be. But, well, everyone has a time and a place. He won't be able to walk out of here, I'm afraid. His knees are broken. But if you give me what I want, I'll let him live."

And then, just to illustrate his point, Lucio pulls a knife from his boot and cuts my father free from the chair. He slumps forward, teeters to the side, and just... slides... down, down, down until he is bent in some unnatural position on the floor.

I have to swallow down the bile that rises in my throat. Lucio Gori *tortured* my father. Killed him. The only man who ever took care of me. The only man I ever *let* take care of me.

"I was going to bargain with you, you know. At first. I figured I'd rough him up a bit and summon you. And when you came I'd bargain for his life. You for him. I'd keep you, the way it was always meant to be. And he'd walk away. But..." Lucio laughs and *tsks* his tongue loudly. "We're way past that now. You kept me waiting."

"I never got a summons," I say, my voice weak with terror. Terror I haven't experienced in ten years.

"How could you?" he growls. "You were out of town. Fucking that Mr. Corporate. Well, he's not going to be around much longer either, Violeta. You will end up with me in the end. Ruined and broken just the way I like you. But it's too bad so many people will die because of your poor choices."

I take a deep, deep breath and try to gather myself. He's playing with me. My father starts gasping for air—he's still alive!—when Lucio kicks him in the chest and makes him groan. It's the half-hearted groan of an unconscious man.

"Let's go on a date, Violeta. Huh? Just you and me?"

I double over trying to stop the sick from spewing out of my mouth.

Lucio is there, taking my hand, placing another one on my back as he says in a soft voice, "Come on now, you always liked our dates, remember? Remember how I forced my cock in your mouth? How I took your breath away?" He laughs so loud, it makes me jump.

He fists my hair and yanks my head back so hard, I hear a snap in the muscles that run along my shoulder. The pain shoots up into my head, right behind my eye. And even though I know I shouldn't, I react. Years of training and practice have instilled instincts in me.

My hand reaches around his leg, right behind his ankle, and I squeeze. It's not as effective as it could be if he didn't have boots on. But it takes him by surprise, stuns him, just for a moment, and he is off balance. I grab his foot and yank it, making him fall. I fall on top of him, and then he's yelling. The sound of thumping boots echoes in my head and I know I have only one chance to make it out of here alive right now.

I grab for the gun I know he keeps in the back of his pants and take it out, frantically searching for the safety—finding none—and pulling the trigger before I even think twice.

It's an automatic, so three shots go off before I even realize what's happening. People are shouting, Lucio is struggling, trying to wrench the gun from my hands. Plaster is falling from the ceiling from the wild gunshots.

"You bitch," Lucio says, bringing his fist down on the back of my head. I see stars and things begin to go black, but I shake my head, the shooting pain behind my eyes even more acute. More piercing. He is trying to get the gun from my grip, but I know—I know—if he gets this gun, I am never leaving this bar. My father, regardless of how bad he's hurt, will never recover.

I will lose. Lucio will kill me, or torture me, or take me as his little sex slave again.

"No," I yell, just as more shooting comes from the other side of the curtain.

"Oh, yes," Lucio purrs in my ear. He's almost overpowered me, and every stupid little jujitsu move I've ever learned flies right out of my head. I am weak. I am not safe. I am nothing but Lucio Gori's prize.

I elbow him in the kidney, making him back away, just enough for me to keep the gun from his hand, and I have no choice, I drop it, kick it away so he can't get to it.

There is even more shooting out in the front of the bar

343

now. Bullets come blasting through the thin walls of the back room. A bullet hits the chandelier and it comes crashing down, not more than a few feet from where Lucio and I still struggle.

People are screaming—no, I am screaming—but more people too. Women, those women who were having lunch. Men, the ones playing pool, maybe even the bartender. Everyone is screaming.

And then I hear a voice.

Oh, God, no!

"Victoria!" West calls. "Can you hear me?"

"I've got her," Lucio says. And he does. Our brief struggle ends when he throws me face down on the hard concrete floor and steps on my neck.

And then everything happens at once. West appears, throwing the curtain aside. Lucio has another gun, not the one I kicked away, and he shoots. West disappears again. Lucio presses on the tender vertebrae between my shoulders and I know, just a little more pressure and my neck will snap. I will die like this. I will die his victim.

No!

I twist my body when Lucio pulls the trigger and break free. I grab his ankle again, and use all the remaining strength I have to pull…

Lucio goes down, West is there, Mysterious and Match are there. Everyone has a gun but me.

Everyone is going to get their chance to kill this asshole *but me*.

I roll away, kicking Lucio in the face, making his lip bleed, making his nose gush hot, sticky, scarlet.

And I reach for the gun I threw away, my fingers feeling for it. Praying for it. Don't let them have this moment. Don't let anyone take this away from me. I want to kill Lucio Gori myself. I want a taste of that rage he has always felt. I want to harness all the hate I have and be the last thing he sees when I take his life.

I find the cold, hard steel of the gun and then…

And then…

I feel warm fingers grasping my hand. I turn to look and find my father, lying on the dirty floor, covered in caked blood and bruised almost beyond recognition. He has managed to crawl over to us and there's a sick trail of crimson behind him.

He says, eyes closed shut from all the swelling and his voice low and weak, "Let me. It's the only thing I want. Just… let… me…"

In the moment I take to pause and feel sadness, and loss, and regret, and all the other things that come to mind when your father is about to die…

He squeezes my hand. The hand that is holding the gun. And pulls the trigger.

I watch helplessly as Lucio Gori's head explodes.

CHAPTER FORTY-EIGHT
WESTON

Perfect, Romantic, me, Mysterious, and Match all in the same room with Five.

It's not a good feeling.

Not at all.

The last time this happened we were being charged with rape.

After Pops killed Lucio, the whole place just went crazy. We got the fuck out of there. It's mob territory and no cops coming, were coming to help. Mysterious led us through the back door. I picked Tori up and threw her over my shoulder. She was screaming. Calling her father's name. But Match picked him up, all broken and bloody, and took him with us to the helicopter waiting on a roof a few blocks away.

Dozens of people saw us.

No one tried to stop us.

"At least we know more than we did," Perfect says. Then he shrugs, because really, we don't. Add in the fact that we don't know what Allen was doing when he started fucking with Perfect's girlfriend, or whether or not Romantic's psycho sibling was in on anything back then, not to mention I've still got a secret or two I'm not ready to talk about and… yeah.

Nothing is settled at all.

We might even be worse off than we were.

"How's Tori?" Mysterious asks. He's been weird since that night. He's beating himself up because he didn't get us there just a few minutes earlier. Just a few minutes earlier and we'd have left Tori out of everything and taken care of business. But he's getting better now. Calming down. I've come to the conclusion I prefer calm, asshole Paxton Vance than agitated, manic Paxton Vance. He's got one of those mint juleps in his hand. He's sucked down like six of them since we got here.

"Good, I think. Relieved. Sad about her father. But I for one am glad he's the one who pulled the trigger and not her." He died in a Colorado hospital about two days after that whole thing went down. Five arranged the hospital.

Fucking Five.

And no one came looking for us about Lucio Gori Junior.

Fucking Five again, I think.

Tori was a mess. But I'm just grateful—blessed, happy, pleased, thankful... whatever you want to call it—that it was him and not her. I am all of those things. It's horrible to think that way, but I don't care. "Or any of *us*," I add, looking around the room.

Romantic nods and takes a deep breath.

"So?" Match says. "What's next?"

"Me?" Mysterious says, making himself a new drink. "I guess. I'm the next target, right? They had my evidence in Nolan's house. No one saw it but me and Romantic, but how long do you think we have to wait until we figure out for sure that Lucio Gori was not the one who really set us up? I mean, will we have to live with this hanging over us for the rest of our lives?"

"I think," Five says, leaning up against my kitchen counter, "I think we give it some time, see how things shake out after a few weeks. Maybe whoever it is will be happy with what they got?" He looks at me, waiting to see if I'll add anything to my story.

But I don't.

Won't.

That shit needs to stay where I left it. Buried in the past.

Lucio Gori's family did steal my money, that's what Five was referring to. And it's gone. For good. But I meant what I told Tori. I don't care. We can start over. Once a self-made man, always a self-made man. That's one thing I learned from my good-for-nothing real father.

Besides, Mysterious has already transferred the money he owed me into a new set of accounts. I'm good. No man should complain that he only has several million in the bank. So I won't.

The last time we had a Mister meeting was after all that shit went down with Romantic. And it's starting to become a pattern. They fuck with us, we win, we settle down, they come back and try again.

I guess we won't be able to settle down.

"A few weeks, huh?" Perfect asks Five.

Five shrugs. "Give or take. If it was Lucio, then we should be fine. The threat has been neutralized. We should just stay the fuck off the East Coast for a while."

Despite the seriousness of that warning, we all chuckle. Fucking mobsters. They can have New York. We're all out west now, anyway.

"It wasn't Lucio," Mysterious says. "I think we all know it wasn't Lucio who set us up."

Well, I think I'm the only one here who knows for sure who it was. I didn't before all this happened. Not really. I've had my suspicions over the years. But after that island bullshit. That whole Wallace Arlington contract—which turned out to be fake. I called him up after the shit settled down and he had no clue what I was talking about—Yeah. It wasn't Lucio. I'm glad he's dead. But it wasn't him who set us up back in school. Nothing about that makes sense.

"You ever gonna get a girlfriend, Match?" I ask, trying to change the subject. Get them thinking about something else. "I mean, for fuck's sake. What kind of man runs an online dating site and doesn't even use his own service?"

"If you headhunt me a girl, Corporate, I swear to God..." But we're all laughing.

It's good to laugh about it.

What else can you do? Let it change you? Let it control you? Let it eat you away from the inside out?

"Well," Perfect says. "Match and I are leaving for Colorado in about an hour."

"Have fun," Romantic says. "I gotta get back to the resort, anyway. Big chef's class coming up this weekend. What about you, Five?"

"No personal details, friends. It's better you don't know."

"Right," Mysterious says, downing his drink as he gets up from my dining room table. "All secrets all the time with you. I've got no one at home for me, but hey, there's always work. So that's where I'm headed. New case came in today. Gonna take it, I think. Just to get my groove back."

He's not as cocky as he was a few weeks ago, that's for sure. And I hope they leave us alone. I hope he doesn't have to deal with the bullshit Perfect, Romantic, and I have gone through.

But it's wishful thinking.

There's more coming.

We're not done yet.

"Hey," Match says, looking at Mysterious. "What's with you and these girly fucking drinks, anyway? The last time I saw you, it was straight bourbon all the time.

"My hot new assistant has me hooked on them," Mysterious laughs. "She's a fucking wild little trip, man. And goddammit, she's good in bed."

"Well, that fucking mint julep reminds me of my damn sister."

"Ariel?" Mysterious laughs. "I cannot picture Ariel drinking mint juleps."

We all laugh at that. Fucking Ariel is one tough chick. She's not a girly-drink kind of girl.

"Not Ariel, you dumbass," Match says. "Cinderella."

Mysterious spits out the alcohol he was just about to swallow and it goes all over Five, who narrows his eyes and brushes off his suit. "What did you just say?" Mysterious asks. "You do not have a sister named Cinderella."

"Cindy, you freak. You've never met her. She's the black sheep. Took off when she turned eighteen and became some kind of wanderer."

"I gotta go," Mysterious says. He grabs a pack sitting by the door and two seconds later, it's like he was never here.

"What the fuck was that about?" I ask.

"Who knows with him," Romantic says. "He's probably banging a girl named Cinderella and now he thinks it's your sister."

Everyone but Match thinks that's hilarious.

VICTORIA

Weston Conrad, AKA Mr. Corporate, asked me to marry him for the seventh time on my thirtieth birthday.

I said no.

He didn't care, he just pulled that ring out, shouting and screaming, "You're mine and goddammit, you're gonna wear this ring!"

I let him do that. I even frowned, and then said, "OK, I'll wear the ring," like I didn't want to, just to keep up with my wild side.

And he said, "OK? You'll wear the ring?"

I said, "Yeah. Didn't you ever notice that our initials go together?" He gave me this puzzled look until I made a V with my two pointer fingers. Then I moved them apart a little and made a W with my pointer fingers and my thumbs. "V is one half of W. I'm only complete when I'm with you."

He couldn't put that ring on my finger fast enough. He even got down on one knee to do it.

I have a feeling West and I might never get married. I think I might just wear his ring forever. I think I might even have his children and cook dinner, and have it waiting on the table when he gets home from work.

I can act like his wife without being his wife. Right?

When I told him that, he agreed and hugged me tight for several seconds, then dragged me upstairs and wanted to fuck me against the wall.

He can own me if he wants.

I don't seem to mind it these days.

Everything seems different since my last trip to Brooklyn. I feel free. Like the past just drifted away and left me behind.

I lost the building in Manhattan, and the charity. It was inevitable. And ironic, I think. That once West knew, and was willing to help me keep it, and I was willing to accept his help, it was all taken away because they wiped out his bank accounts. The East Coast, and everything back there, is history. I left it all behind when I came to California. But we worked our asses off to place all the kids in the best possible foster homes.

All except Ethan. He's mine.

No.

He's ours.

And watching West with Ethan is eye-opening. They play baseball in the back yard. West is teaching him how to swim. Ethan is finally settling in and he even called me mom once last week.

This is the reason I might let West knock me up. It's the reason I might let him make me stay home while he earns the money. It's the reason I do everything these days.

Weston Conrad might've gotten the short end of the stick as fathers go, but he's not going to be the asshole who perpetuates the cycle.

When he's in, he's all in.

We started a new charity, too. West paid off our house

with the money Mysterious owed him. West said we needed that security. So all three of us know that house is ours and no one can ever take it away. Then we started Corporate House. A safe place for kids in Hollywood. We're open twenty-four seven. They can come eat, or sleep, or play games. Whatever it is that's missing in their lives, we're there. Open arms, ready and waiting, for any kid who needs us.

Maybe someday every kid will have loving parents and a happy home. But until that happens, they've got us to look out for them.

Mr. and Mrs. Corporate.

It's just business, Mister style.

End of Book Shit

Welcome to the End of Book Shit - or as we call it around here, the EOBS. I write these at the end of every book to kind of give readers a little insight to the story they just read. They aren't edited, so don't mind my typos.

Some of them are epic. I think the last one for Mr. Romantic was pretty good. Some of them, especially the early ones, are just *meh*. It really depends on the story and how it affected me as I wrote it. Some are hard to write, some are very easy. Some are controversial, some not so much. And sometimes I just want to talk.

Mr. Corporate is funny because I started this series with Mr. Perfect being so damn perfect and then jumped right into the controversial subject of rape fantasy with Mr. Romantic. I am not afraid to write about anything. I mean, if that's how the story says it's going, I'm like – *OK. Let's do this shit.* And even though I knew the overall series arc for the Misters, I don't plot the books out separately too far in advance. I pretty much plot the next book during the time I'm writing the last 25% of the current book.

So I was plotting Mr. Corporate while all that rape fantasy stuff was going down in Mr. Romantic. I knew that the book was going to push some buttons. I didn't care, mind you. But I knew. And I knew Romantic was over the top, and Perfect was so damn perfect. So I wanted West and Tori to be more "normal" but is a completely different way.

I wanted West to very traditional. He wants very traditional things. A wife to stay home with the kids, the house, the corporate job, and dinner on the table when he gets home.

I think this is kind of a big trigger, not just in romance books, but in society in general. Men aren't allowed to want these things today. They are sexist if they want their wives to be… well, *wives.* I'm talking as a career choice. I think "wife" can be a career choice. It doesn't have to be, but it can, just like "mother" can be a career choice.

No, you don't get paid, per se. But you enjoy the rewards of the partnership by working together.

And even though West had a mother and father while he was young, and after he was adopted, he never had anything close to traditional. I didn't explore West's feelings about his new family (I will, later), so you don't get much from him about that. But I did know that he missed out on something he felt other kids got. A "normal" loving family life. So this was his motivation in his romance with Tori. He loves her. She's wild and crazy and hot-tempered. And he can't get enough.

But he needs to tame her ass down if he's ever going to fulfill his desire for a "normal" family.

And Tori had her background to run away from. She was forced into things as a young girl/woman and so all she can do is resist this trap West is setting. He stifles her with his expectations.

She and he are not on the same page.

So what does it take to change someone's world-view?

That's a hard thing to do, right? Especially as you get older.

How does one make a wild woman like Tori understand that giving in to a traditional role in a relationship is not giving up her identity as independent?

In the "romance world" there are so many ways to write a relationship. But mostly the women are supposed to be strong, but nice. And the men are supposed to be alpha, but not demeaning.

Well, in Julie's world, that's not really the case. In fact, I think every expectation except for the two golden rules of no cheating and the mandatory happily ever after, should be thrown out whenever possible.

I kind of like traditional. And I especially like writing about women who choose to be mothers instead of career women. I don't know why, really. I was a single mom for half my kid's childhood. And I have always worked. Not always out of the house though. I found ways to work from home. But I never wanted to change my choice, so writing women who choose a traditional role isn't based off some regret I have. I just think it's a great job and so many women see it as a trap.

So I loved writing Victoria coming to terms with Weston's "demands" that she be his "wife". And I loved her reasons why she was refusing. I liked that she made him work hard to understand her point of view. She kept him at arm's length until he understood her issues with it. And I think they probably have a good, healthy attitude about who wears the pants in the family now that they're at the end of their story.

Oh, hold up. We didn't have a wedding, did we? In fact, we're missing quite a few weddings in this series. Hmmm... what might that mean? ;)

I also loved that Victoria always knew West was innocent. It was such a breath of fresh air after Nolan's complete weirdo fucking meltdown of a life over that whole rape thing, you know? He took it to one extreme and Corporate took it to the other.

Everyone thought Nolan was guilty. Hell, even Nolan thought he was guilty. Maybe people thought Corporate was guilty too, but who cares? He had a witness. His life after those rape charges was almost no different than before. He had his girlfriend, who also knew he was one hundred percent innocent. So what if he didn't finish college? I don't think it mattered to him the way it did Nolan. Nolan came from a family filled with great expectations. Weston had zero expectations to live up to. I think he was probably more surprised things were working out so well, more than anything. So when he was asked to leave school because of the controversy, he just took it all in stride and moved on. He's definitely a roll-with-the-punches kind of guy.

I also love Corporate's backstory. That was another surprise. I knew going in I needed to make him fit into the over-all series story. And I was hesitant to keep adding in more and more people to the mix because I have to tie it all together in the last book, right? No pressure there.

So I was aiming for super simple. I was aiming at Claudette, if I'm honest. I was going to put her in this story somehow. But you know, I really hated her. I didn't feel like giving her so much power or page time. And I liked the thought of West being from Nantucket. I had done all that research for Ivy and Nolan in New England and I really wanted Corporate to be from "that kind" of family.

Old money.

But with a twist. Because old money can be boring too, you know. Besides, Romantic was from super-old money. And I didn't really get into Perfect's money genealogy, but it was several generations. Mysterious is half old money, half new. And Match is Spencer Shrike money. ;)

So Corporate was my only real chance to come up with some cool new-money story. I don't remember why I was watching the Goonies recently but I was. God, the Goonies, right? That is so my generation. It was a great new-money story and every kid I knew wanted to be part of that team.

Which leads me to another thing I like to do in my books. Contradictions.

I love contradictions. Sexy fucking Ford Aston and his sexy fucking brain. Jesus Christ. He is the perfect contradiction. Spencer Shrike and his fun, easy-going attitude combined with his obsession with guns. Ron the Bombshell Vaughn with her giant tits, blonde hair, and job as a tattoo artist who ends up having six kids. Rook and her wide doe-eyes isn't exactly innocent by the time you get to Panic. And Mateo and his star tattoos and astronomy job. This is the stuff of great characters.

My aim in Corporate's story was to present this ridiculous contradiction between a boat-rat kid who finds a treasure and the super-successful self-made man. The more ridiculous the better I like it. It's a challenge and I'm a hell of a character developer. So I'm OK with just about any scenario.

The contradiction with Tori was her desire to save kids, yet refusing to have any of her own or be part of the expected "nuclear family" because it feels like a trap.

It's irony, right?

I first got the idea that Corporate was some kind of con-artist when I saw a movie recently called This Boy's Life. Leonardo DiCaprio plays a kid back in the Fifties who is trying to get as far away from his small-town life and abusive father as he can by applying to elite private boarding schools. So he gets his nerdy friend to fake some transcripts for him and works hard to pass the entrance exams, even gets himself a scholarship.

I thought to myself, yeah. This is Mr. Corporate's background right here. But I needed more, and I knew I wanted him to be from Nantucket (contradictions, right? He lives in a shack on land worth millions of dollars). So I put him on that lobster boat and started asking myself what could possibly happen next.

I am constantly being asked by other authors how I flesh out my characters. Do I map it out? Do I have a time line? Do I keep one of those story bibles with every little detail outlined?

I don't do any of that. I just come up with a childhood and shape my character from that. You know, just like Mother Nature does it in real life. You are this blank canvas when you're born. And pretty soon you're back packing the Appalachian Trail as a four-year-old with your dad. Or visiting the physics lab with you mother at six. Or learning how to ski, or golf, or surf because your parents are ski, golf, surf bums.

It shapes you, ya know?

But the really fun part about shaping characters is the contradiction. If I'm going to write a stripper he's not going to be just any stripper. If I'm going to write a rock star he's not going to be just any rock star.

And if I'm going to write a five-book series based on the "office romance" trope, well, don't expect the sex to happen on a desk in every single book. I just don't roll that way. But if you look closely, every one of these books are absolutely an office romance. That was the very first unifying premise of the whole series. Even before I had the whole rape accusation I had the "office romance".

So I hope you're enjoying my take on that trope. Personally, I find office romances among some of the most boring stories ever told. (I'm just being honest here) But Perfect was perfect for the trope and the longer I thought about each Mister in this context, the more I liked the idea.

Mac and Ellie are boss and subordinate, pretty clear cut with very few contradictions. Super seductive, Nolan, is interviewing little inexperienced, naïve, Ivy. West and Victoria are competitors after the same contract, dragging a whole lot of baggage behind them.

Which brings us to Mr. Mysterious. Jesus Christ, I'm not gonna spell it out for you, but I hope you got that little hint at the end of West's last chapter. I'm so fucking excited about this next book. And then Match and Five and holy fuck, I cannot wait.

Anyway, I hope the Misters were fun reads so far. That's what I'm aiming for. I have a lot of dark erotica coming up starting in January, but I like to do fun stories for summer. And maybe Romantic wasn't as fun as Perfect, but I promise to make it up to you with Mysterious. He should be dark, right? Right? Let me just say – expect the unexpected. It's what I do best.

If you'd like to hang out with me on Facebook I have a private fan group called Shrike Bikes. Just ask to join and someone will approve you as soon as they see it. I am in that group chatting with the fans every single day and we have a lot of giveaways and fun stuff going all the time. Especially around release days. I usually do a takeover and give away all kinds of stuff related to the new release, so come on by and say hi.

If you enjoyed this book please consider leaving me a review where you purchased it. I'm still indie. And the success of each and every book I put out depends on readers like you leaving their thoughts and opinions about the story in a review.

Thank you for reading, thank you for reviewing, and I'll see you in the next book.

Julie
JA Huss

About the Author

JA Huss is the New York Times and USA Today bestselling author of more than twenty romances. She likes stories about family, loyalty, and extraordinary characters who struggle with basic human emotions while dealing with bigger than life problems. JA loves writing heroes who make you swoon, heroines who makes you jealous, and the perfect Happily Ever After ending.

You can chat with her on Facebook, Twitter, and her kick-ass romance blog, New Adult Addiction. If you're interested in getting your hands on an advanced release copy of her upcoming books, sneak peek teasers, or information on her upcoming personal appearances, you can join her newsletter list and get those details delivered right to your inbox.

JA Huss lives on a dirt road in Colorado thirty minutes from the nearest post office. So if she owes you a package from a giveaway, expect it to take forever. She has a small farm with two donkeys named Paris & Nicole, a ringneck parakeet named Bird, and a pack of dogs. She also has two grown children who have never read any of her books and do not plan on ever doing so. They do, however, plan on using her credit cards forever.

JA collects guns and likes to read science fiction and books that make her think. JA Huss used to write homeschool science textbooks under the name Simple Schooling and after publishing more than 200 of those, she ran out of shit to say. She started writing the I Am Just Junco science fiction series in 2012, but has since found the meaning of life writing erotic stories about antihero men that readers love to love.

JA has an undergraduate degree in equine science and fully planned on becoming a veterinarian until she heard what kind of hours they keep, so she decided to go to grad school and got a master's degree in Forensic Toxicology. Before she was a full-time writer she was smelling hog farms for the state of Colorado.

Even though JA is known to be testy and somewhat of a bitch, she loves her #fans dearly and if you want to talk to her, join her Facebook fan group where she posts daily bullshit about bullshit.

If you think she's kidding about this crazy autobiography, you don't know her very well.

You can find all her books on Amazon, Barnes & Noble, iTunes, and KOBO.

Made in the USA
Monee, IL
12 February 2021

60317991R00218